EXPOSED AT THE BACK

ARILD STAVRUM

Translated by Guy Puzey

**FREIGHT
BOOKS**

First published in the UK, September 2014

Freight Books
49-53 Virginia Street
Glasgow, G1 1TS
www.freightbooks.co.uk

A CIP catalogue reference for this book is available from the British Library

ISBN: 978-1-908754-66-0
eISBN: 978-1-908754-67-7

This translation has been published with the financial support of NORLA.

Typeset by Freight in Plantin
Printed and bound in Poland

the publisher acknowledges investment from
Creative Scotland toward the publication of this book

Part 1

25 July

Football was so straightforward. It was 11 against 11, and whichever team put the ball into their opponents' goal the most times won the match. Many people had tried to glorify the game as if it were something more, emphasising the symbolic significance it could have for a town or area, or even how closely a club or national team could be connected to the very development of a country. But at the end of the day football was straightforward to the point of banality.

Arild Golden had been a football agent for over 20 years, and he knew the process inside out. On the agenda that day was the sale of Vålerenga's captain and top midfielder Per Diesen to Everton, the highest-profile transfer of the year in Norwegian football.

Also present were four representatives from Everton and Golden's two lawyers. The location was the Wimborne Room at The Ritz. English football executives loved luxury. Golden went for The Ritz because it was in London, far away from Everton's home town of Liverpool, where the local press would be on the look-out. He got up.

'Gentlemen, please excuse me,' he said. 'I need a break.'

He walked out into the reception area, looked at the rug covered in pink, flowery patterns, the huge centrepiece of fresh white roses. He stared at his reflection in the large mirror behind the desk.

His face had a Mediterranean complexion, the skin under his chin taut. His hair had a few grey streaks but, as long as he combed it straight back, that only made him more distinguished. He let out a quick sigh and rubbed at his brow. Then he walked out of the hotel, round the corner and into Green Park.

He went along the path, tarmac cracked in places, past the deck chairs and further into the park. There weren't many people around, and the traffic noise was just enough to be soothing. A squirrel ran towards him.

Golden sat down on a wooden bench, pulled out one of his mobiles and phoned Vålerenga's director of football.

'I'm afraid it's going slowly here. What's the absolute lowest offer you can accept?'

'We can't let Per go for anything less than 20 million kroner,' came the reply.

Football executives. Imagine them giving an agent carte blanche to negotiate over the only thing they had of value: their players. Per Diesen was the biggest name in Norwegian football and his club hadn't even sent their own people.

'20 million might be tough, but I'll try,' said Golden. Everton had already offered 4 million pounds. The current exchange rate was 9.2 kroner to the pound. Golden did a bit of mental arithmetic and came to 36,800,000 kroner.

Half an hour of further negotiations and the deal for Per Diesen's transfer from Vålerenga to one of England's biggest clubs was sealed with a handshake. Golden had pushed the transfer fee up to 46 million kroner.

Golden had been representing Diesen for several seasons. He was special and deserved a million-kroner bonus. Another 4.6 million kroner ended up in the 'sundry' column when it came to the accounts. Vålerenga would of course get its 20 million share, except they would have to pay Golden a 20 per cent negotiation fee, so 4 million came back to him. All in all this transfer meant that Golden Boys was left with considerably more money than Vålerenga, the transfer netting his company 24 million kroner, plus small change. 400,000 in small change.

Murder on Sports Review

'I know that bloody corpses are usually something for the main news, but don't forget Arild Golden was the most powerful man in Norwegian football,' said Benedikte, getting up from her chair and planting her hands on the table.

Benedikte Blystad was 26 years old, a blonde city girl from Oslo, but her job as TV2's sports anchor had made her tougher than her age or appearance would suggest. Still, she'd never seen Kåre Jan Vasshaug as worked up as he was now, as they argued in the channel's cramped meeting room in Bergen's Nøstet district.

'You can't seriously think that the year's number one national news story should be put in *Sports Review*!' said Vasshaug, loosening his tie and throwing off his suit jacket.

Benedikte listened, just like the rest of Norway did when the respected news anchor spoke, but she gripped the edge of the table, her knuckles turning white as Vasshaug's voice bounced off the walls. Vasshaug's Sunnmøre accent gave him the authority he needed to report on 300 people dying in a plane crash or a flood in Bangladesh, or to underscore the unlikely idiocy of his top story ending up in *Sports Review*.

Benedikte rubbed her cheek as she held Vasshaug's gaze.

'I was just speaking to the editing team,' she said. 'They won't be able to get the report finished until 20 past. That'll be too late for the main news.'

'Rubbish. I can talk our way through it.'

'The story needs pictures. We'll have to wait.'

'Now listen,' Vasshaug began before being interrupted by the controller of TV2, on a live link from his home in Oslo.

'Sit down,' he said. 'We need a decision. What do you think, Bertil? Has Benedikte got the gravitas to present such a tough story?'

'Benedikte will be great,' said Bertil Olsen, chief editor of TV2 *Sports Review*. 'I understand Kåre Jan's objections, but the story has an obvious sports interest too. A football agent's been killed three days before the transfer window opens. But the most important thing is that the editing team's running late. We don't know whether it'll make the main news.'

'Sports interest!' said Vasshaug, spreading out his arms. 'Golden was also the agent of that teenage idol pop star, Sabrina.'

Benedikte had her iPhone hidden beneath the edge of the table. She texted the head of the editing team: 'OK, you get one dinner.'

Seconds later the head of the editing team popped his head round the door and said: 'Sorry folks, I'll need more time.'

'That decides it,' came the voice from the TV monitor. 'Kåre Jan, you won't say anything, and Benedikte, you prepare a teaser. Say as much as you can without mentioning Golden's name, but make sure you get people hooked, I want record ratings for this broadcast. Now let's get moving with a quick auction by our biggest sponsors. They will have to bleed if they want airtime between the main news and *Sports Review*. Benedikte, get yourself ready.'

Benedikte gave Bertil a quick nod before running off to her work station. Her hands were shaking as she sat down at her computer to write the text for the autocue. She was feeling nervous for the first time since her on-screen debut. The words for the camera were more important than ever. They weren't about Vålerenga players out on the town, line-dancing border collies, cheese rolling festivals or some other crap meant to calm down the viewers after the main news. Today it was serious.

She got up and hurried down the corridor. Past computers and messy desks where tobacco tins, Coke bottles and empty pizza boxes fought for space with tatty old tabloid papers and editions of *Rothmans Football Yearbook*. She went round the corner and ran into a cameraman on his way to the lift, but she just kept moving. She swung open the door and threw herself into the make-up chair.

'I haven't got much time, Karianne,' she said.

The make-up artist opened her powder palette and pulled out her brushes in a single movement. The brushes sped over Benedikte's cheeks, forehead and neck, spreading the make-up so that she looked exactly like she always did on TV.

'He was such a handsome man,' said Karianne, concentrating on

Benedikte's face.

'Who?' asked Benedikte.

'Arild Golden. I heard that he's been killed. It's awful.'

'Did you ever meet him?'

'He sat in this chair a few times and he was always so considerate, completely different from the impression you get through the media.' Karianne started with the airbrush. She sprayed a little extra make-up on the small birthmark under Benedikte's left ear. Benedikte couldn't stand the airbrush. They said it was make-up for HD when they introduced it, but she got fed up having it sprayed up inside her nose. Now she just agreed to that little final touch.

She left the make-up room and took the lift down to the studio, jumping over strewn cables and more pizza boxes from Dolly Dimple's. She sat down in the chair next to Kåre Jan, who'd done up his tie and put his jacket back on.

Benedikte looked down, like she always did in the last few seconds before going on air. A black jacket with a purple silk top. The first time she was due to present she'd worn a polka dot shirt. 'That won't do,' Bertil said, making her get changed. Dotted or chequed shirts or anything with intricate patterns interfered with the TV picture. Now she had to check every time: no patterns, and not too much blue.

Silence. They were live. Vasshaug turned to her and said: 'And now over to you, Benedikte, with a most serious story from the world of football.'

'That's right, Kåre Jan. As we all know, Norwegian football has been in a downwards spiral for the past few years. The national team has been losing and our clubs plummeting out of European competitions. We've brought you reports on doping, match-fixing and widespread financial corruption, but tonight's story is the most serious yet. You'll hear about it right here, in a TV2 exclusive, straight after the break.'

The main news faded out, and the transmission went to an unusually long break. Then the screen showed vibrating red and blue outlines, numbers and letters flying across into a kind of net. Benedikte looked down at her clothes, then at the autocue. She paused for a second longer than usual and didn't smile.

'Good evening. Arild Golden, the long-standing football agent and well-known TV commentator, was found dead this evening in his office at Ullevaal Stadium in Oslo. The police are regarding the death as suspicious and have begun investigations. TV2 understands that there have been no arrests in connection with the case. TV2 *Sports Review* will follow this story over the coming days. Visit our website at www. tv2.no/sport to read the latest news on Mr Golden's death.'

Quitting Lasts Forever

Steinar Brunsvik heard the sound of breathing behind him as he passed the big block of flats in Grefsenkollveien. He looked over his shoulder. There were two men in their twenties on racing bikes. He couldn't just let them overtake him. Sweat was dripping from his forehead down his cheeks and into his mouth. It tasted of salt. He spat and wiped his face.

It was high summer, the last day of July, and would soon be 6 o' clock in the evening but it was still 30 degrees.

'Bloody heavy bastard mountain bike,' Steinar said. He fixed his gaze on the rough tarmac and kept on pedalling. It helped to hear the other two on his tail, their breathing more and more laboured.

'1 km,' read the white paint on the tarmac. *Less than a kilometre to go*, he thought while passing.

10 metres further on he would hit a steep hill. Steinar turned to see the young men behind. When he moved his hand towards the gear shift he saw the relief on their faces. The ruse worked. They thought he was about to move down a gear.

Just as the younger men changed gear, Steinar responded with a tougher gear. The men changed into the wrong gear again. Steinar gained a few metres, then a few more. Soon he was 50 metres ahead, putting on as much of a spurt as he could. 500 metres to the top. He was nearing his maximum heart rate. Had he wrong-footed them too soon?

His thighs and calves were on fire, and the saltiness in his mouth was replaced by the tang of battery acid. Steinar concentrated all his force onto the pedals. Down into the next push. 'What the hell am I doing?' he thought, gritting his teeth and pedalling even harder.

They were approaching the final bends. First a gradual one to the left, then a tighter one to the right. 100 metres to go.

He caught a glimpse of the black wooden building on the left, but his gaze was fixed on the road. One of the younger cyclists was right behind him now. 50 metres to go. 20 metres. The other guy's front wheel was right next to Steinar's. 10 metres. 5 metres. 2 metres from the top the young guy slipped past, winning by a just a few centimetres. Steinar collapsed on the handlebars.

'Bloody hell, you're crazy. On a mountain bike,' said the younger man.

Steinar managed to give him a high five as the other man came up the last few metres. He wheeled the bike over to a bench outside the café at the front of the wooden building, and lay down. He had an uncontrollable spasm in his left calf, and his head was swimming.

A few minutes later he sat up and pinched the root of his nose hard between his thumb and forefinger as he closed his eyes. He let out a deep breath before opening his eyes again.

The view took away what little breath he had left. It always did. He held both his hands like a visor above his sunglasses, which weren't giving him enough protection in the late afternoon sun. He let his eyes drift from the top of Ekebergåsen to the centre of Oslo and the port, across the harbour to Bygdøy and all the way over to Bærum. Everywhere looked warm and deserted. Oslo was at its best in July, when half the inhabitants left the city. Why didn't more of them stay in Oslo and go on their holidays in freezing, foggy November instead?

For the second day in a row the Golden case was on the front page of the papers. The tabloid *VG* had the headline 'BRUTALLY MURDERED' and a picture of Golden framed by what was supposed to resemble a blood spatter. The headline was taken from a brief police statement, which also said that the culprit was unknown and that no apparent motive had been found yet. The amount of money Golden kept in his office led journalists to speculate that Golden had interrupted a burglary in progress. Steinar thought about the possible motive. It wasn't strange that somebody would kill a football agent. The strangest thing was that it hadn't happened before.

Steinar didn't normally read the sports pages anymore, but now football was everywhere. It was even creeping into the comment pages, and he could barely open his web browser without encountering photo galleries of Golden meeting football executives at home and abroad.

Steinar took note of one person in particular in the background of one of the photos. A man whose name the journalists hadn't found out, described only as Golden's business partner, but who Steinar recognised well. Business partner? Steinar had no idea that Golden had anything to do with that bastard. He got back on his bike and gripped the handlebars. They creaked.

Steinar took a long sip of his special blend of coffee, Red Bull and cranberry juice. It washed away the last remaining taste of blood and acid. He put the bottle back in its holder, turned the bike round, started his stopwatch and began rolling downhill. He sped up as the view vanished, then he turned the bike into the woods, down along the steep gravel track.

His cycling computer showed 55 km per hour. With little shifts of his weight he managed to avoid the biggest stones, but he hit a large bump and the bike took off, so high and far that he had time to think in mid-air. He made a perfect landing then threw himself into a sharp bend. As he rounded the corner a man was standing 10 metres in front of him with his back turned, waiting for his dog to do its business.

'Out of the way!' Steinar shouted.

The man turned his head, eyes wide open, but stood stock still. Steinar swung onto the high bank above the ditch, cycling along it almost horizontally.

His muscles couldn't take the strain for more than another few tenths of a second. He used all his strength to force the bike back onto the track, scraping against a withered tree trunk. It would hurt tomorrow, when there was no more adrenaline to relieve the pain. He heard the man behind him shouting four-letter words.

The track flattened out. Steinar kept on pedalling until he came to a small car park in the woods at Akebakkeskogen. He stopped the clock.

His arm was bleeding from the scrape with the tree, but the cut looked clean. In the old days, Steinar had lost pieces of flesh on bone-dry astroturf and slid on muddy grass pitches with open wounds. This was nothing.

A couple of minutes later his heart rate was back to normal. He checked his watch. Four seconds off his personal record. So close it was irritating. Lance Armstrong's mantra came back to him as it always did in such situations: 'Pain is temporary, quitting lasts forever.'

Steinar had quit too soon once before. He got into the saddle and started back up the hill.

30 minutes later he was back in Akebakkeskogen. The same course, the same route, a new personal record. A feeling of calm descended.

He drank his lukewarm cocktail and wiped his hand over his drenched forehead. The blood on his arm had dried now, but it was probably best to wash it before going home.

He wheeled his bike between the houses until he came to the junction of Lofthusveien and Kjelsåsveien. A couple of pensioners were sitting on the terrace outside the little red newsagent's shop. One of them was holding up a lottery ticket. Ahead of Steinar was a low building with the big yellow and black sign of Skeid sports club. He walked towards the changing rooms. A man was sitting on the steps that led into the kit room. The man was in his fifties, wearing only a pair of blue Adidas shorts. Everything about him was sagging, the bags under his eyes, his flabby pecs, his arms and the length of ash from his cigarette almost touching the ground. It seemed highly unlikely that he would manage to lift it back up to his mouth.

'I'm just going to use your loo,' said Steinar.

The man didn't answer. He'd given in to the heat.

The changing rooms were decorated with the odd patch of faded red paint, and the benches had been given a bit of blue; otherwise the space was dominated by black mould, which made it look as if flames had licked up the once-white walls. Steinar went into the showers.

He cleaned his cuts and patted them with toilet paper. Then he went back out of the changing rooms, ready to walk up the gravel track and out of the area.

At the top of the climb he looked down at the gravel pitch, and at the red shelters over the substitutes' benches. Grass was growing through the gravel in a few places. Nothing in the world could match the beauty of an old gravel pitch. Then Steinar heard a whistle from the astroturf behind him, the referee blowing for a foul. A voice cut through the air: 'No!'

Steinar had dropped football altogether, but he recognised the sounds instinctively. And the smells. Of newly baked waffles, coffee and sweat. He had to watch, at least for a while.

10 years had passed, and Steinar thought he'd got over it, but the picture in the paper had reawakened the ghosts of the past.

How could the man who destroyed Steinar's life and career be Arild Golden's partner?

The Talent Factory

'No!'

Like the rest of the people in Nordre Åsen, Benedikte jumped when she heard the scream, which echoed halfway up the Grorud Valley. An over-excited supporter of the Oppsal Gutter 95 boys' team had seen enough of Stanley's dribbling skills.

And it was Stanley, Skeid's child prodigy, who Benedikte had come to see. Stanley was considered Norway's foremost footballing talent, and he would soon be 15, the age when agents could secure the rights to represent young players. According to a tip-off received by TV2, Arild Golden had reached a verbal agreement with the family, so the other agents in Norway had given up. But now that he was dead, Stanley was fair game. There would be a real fight to sign the Skeid player.

Every time Stanley got the ball it was as if the whole world stopped. For a brief moment, Benedikte was able to sympathise with the Oppsal defender who had his eyes nervously fixed on Stanley's red Nike boots. Then Stanley shimmied to the right. A hundred small pieces of black rubber were sent flying up from the artificial turf. The defender had sunk down on both heels, glued to the playing surface, his hands out to the sides, palms facing forward, his mouth wide open. He was like a cartoon character who had run straight into a pane of glass, trying to get his body to do as it was told, to follow the red shoes, but it was too late.

Benedikte looked over towards the chain-link fence next to the corner flag. Per Diesen had arrived. Diesen was wearing a plain, white V-neck T-shirt and blue tartan shorts partially held up by a gold-coloured belt. His hair was bleached white and stood on end here and there in a kind of organised chaos. A pair of scintillating blue eyes were hidden behind his black sunglasses. He bent one knee and leant against the fence, resting most of his weight on his elbows.

Stanley was unknown to most football fans but Per Diesen was a superstar. Diesen was 22, a playmaker with Oslo club Vålerenga and on the Norwegian national squad. For several months now he'd been linked to a number of major European clubs. But he'd started at Skeid. Like many other top Norwegian players, he played at youth level here in Oslo's East End talent factory.

His transfer to the team's big brother Vålerenga had been controversial. There was a media storm, like so many times before when a major talent had been 'stolen' from a smaller club. Skeid claimed it was swindled out of both his transfer fee and a percentage of any possible future transfers but, luckily for Diesen, all their anger was directed at his agent, Arild Golden. Here, on his home ground, everyone seemed genuinely pleased to see him.

Per Diesen's talent was unquestioned. His looks led to a host of sponsorship deals and he was usually chosen as the players' media spokesman, not to mention securing various modelling contracts. Arild Golden had promoted Diesen as a Norwegian David Beckham, his potential earnings much higher than his basic player's income of 2.5 million kroner.

Diesen was the first Norwegian football player from the top league, Tippeligaen, to live-tweet from the changing rooms at half-time. Arild Golden launched an online reality show, in co-operation with the tabloid paper *VG*, based on Diesen's life. The title was *Per Diesen TV*, or *PDTV* for short.

The series went through a tough start. Like most famous footballers who made money out of their appearance, Diesen was rumoured to be gay, which turned off large segments of the football audience. At away matches in Bergen or Lillestrøm he was bombarded by chants about how much he liked 'back passes' and 'banana shots'.

'Peeeeep!'

The referee, in his luminous yellow strip, had to blow his whistle especially hard since he had no desire whatsoever to move outside the centre circle. When he awarded a free kick, the whole neighbourhood knew about it. Benedikte looked over at Diesen again, who ran his left hand through his hair.

PDTV was intended to be a kind of football-meets-*Entourage* concept, with a handsome, young player working his way through Oslo's most attractive women. The only problem was that Diesen didn't have any of these female liaisons. If a single footballer went for more than a few weeks without pulling a girl, he had to be gay. Surely a man in his position had plenty of opportunities? But he hadn't been linked to any minor *Pop Idol* contestants or even to an extra from that interminable soap opera *Hotel Cæsar*.

Everything changed, though, when Golden introduced Diesen to the glamour model Sabrina. They fell in love and moved in together. The homophobic chants died down, and his playing became even better. Diesen was leading the fantasy football statistics in the papers, his self-confidence was back, and his web series had become Norway's most watched online programme. Per Diesen had a lot to thank Arild Golden for.

PDTV was also where Diesen's pop career was launched. Together with his best pal and teammate at Vålerenga, macho centre-back Marius Bjartmann, he'd recently released the single 'Bleed for the Team', which was currently at number one in the charts. It was true: a footballer could be more than just a footballer.

A ripple of expectation went through the crowd. Skeid had been given a throw-in and Stanley was getting ready. Throw-ins weren't usually exciting, but Stanley did somersault throw-ins. Benedikte had seen them before, but not from such a young boy. Stanley ran towards the touch-line, dropped the ball to the ground and spun in the air. He made a perfect landing on the touch-line and let the ball go just as it passed his head, but he threw it too far. The ball flew over all the players who'd gathered in front of the goal, and there would be a throw-in from the other side. Still, the boy's not even 15, thought Benedikte, before turning back to look at Diesen.

Diesen looked uncomfortable as Skeid supporters crowded around him. He signed autograph after autograph but also checked his watch several times. Eventually, he patted a young lad on the back, said something and walked towards the exit. The lads sang the well-known chorus from his song: 'Yeaaaah! Bleed for the teaaaam!'

The Small World of Football

'Kick him, for fuck's sake!'

Steinar turned towards the shouting. A man in his forties, wearing glasses and light-blue clothes, was gesturing at the pitch. He carried on screaming abuse at the Skeid players in their red strips, and at the referee, with the occasional bit of praise mixed in for the right-back on the team in white.

A few yards behind him stood two African men, over 6 feet tall and broad shouldered. One of them had to grab onto the other several times to hold him back.

The right-back miskicked a pass straight out of play. Undeterred, the man in glasses shouted, 'come on Oppsal!', his voice annoyingly high-pitched.

Skeid took a quick throw in, the ball ending up at Stanley's feet. The players on both teams were shouting his name continuously. Either, 'pass to Stanley' or, from the other side, 'mark Stanley' and then more and more often, 'get Stanley!'

Stanley was right in front of the man in glasses, showing off. He put his foot on top of the ball purposefully. Two players from Oppsal were blocking his way. He performed the slightest of feints, a minimal shift of weight from right to left. Steinar felt the same movement in his own legs, how many times had he done the same? Stanley took off and sprinted down the touchline.

Steinar didn't read the sports pages any more, but it was impossible not to pick up on the biggest stories. He knew that Spain had won the World Cup, Lionel Messi was a fantastic footballer, and Liverpool had gone from three goals down to victory against AC Milan, but he hadn't seen it himself. Still, it was so easy to recognise a dummy on the pitch.

'Shit,' said the man in glasses.

One player had reacted and was now approaching at full speed from the side. He was clearly fed up of Stanley laying waste to them. He closed his eyes and flung himself with both legs stretched out, one along the ground and the other high in case Stanley jumped. This tackle had to hit its target. Either the ball or the player, preferably both.

Stanley stopped and the Oppsal player went past him, onto the tarmac surrounding the astroturf, crashing into a large rubbish bin. By the time he opened his eyes Stanley was long gone.

In between the artificial grass pitch and the gravel pitch there was a small, grassy knoll, a natural grandstand usually reserved for the players' parents and friends. Today it seemed as if there were an unusually large number of people watching this match between two of Oslo's boys' teams.

Steinar looked along the crowd. A couple of them nodded at him, a few others trying unsuccessfully to put a name to his face. He moved, scanning for a free spot away from the others, then he saw her sitting there on the grass.

Above her light summer trousers she was wearing a blue sleeveless shirt, holding one slender hand over her sunglasses. The evening sun rippled down over the apartment blocks below the pitch. The lenses on her Ray Bans were darker nearer the top, and her blonde hair also went through different shades.

Steinar was afraid he'd been studying her too closely, so he looked over at a small step where he could stretch out his legs, which were stiff after the bike ride. Just as he started walking towards it he heard her shout: 'Steinar Brunsvik!'

You might hate hearing about rally speed tests, the national cross-country skiing championship and the Gundersen method in the Nordic combined; you might think Swix was a kind of chocolate bar, not ski wax, or that Offside was the name of some distant country, but you would still know who Benedikte Blystad was.

His legs steered him towards her, but he didn't answer. The ball was out of play, Benedikte was looking at him, and the whole neighbourhood had fallen silent. He had to say something.

'You know me?'

'Do you know *me*?'

'You work for TV2.'

'Why are you so surprised that I recognise you?'

'It's a long time since I was last in the sports news.'

'You're still a frequent discussion topic over lunch at TV2. A quiz question. "Name a man who made a legendary exit."'

Steinar felt his body itch. The blood was streaming from his lower legs, through his hips, up through his chest, on its way further up. He rubbed his hand on his forehead and tried to push the blood down through his face, down to his neck and away. He didn't want to blush now, couldn't blush now. He was 35, for Christ's sake.

'You talk about me at TV2?'

'Why so surprised?'

'No, I just didn't think, I thought, I don't know...'

'Straight from the Norwegian First Division to Ajax Amsterdam. Everyone was sure you'd come home with your tail between your legs but you ended up in the Dutch Team of the Season. You're one of the few footballers who've played on the Norwegian national side without having played in top-flight Norwegian football. But that's not the most interesting part of the Steinar Brunsvik puzzle.'

'What do you mean?' asked Steinar.

'Why did you stop playing? You were a standard fixture at Ajax, a regular on the national team, only 25 years old, just approaching the best age for footballers. Then, during half-time in an international match at Ullevaal, where you were the best player on the pitch, you just vanished. Never to be seen on a football field again. Why?'

Steinar was out of practice. All the sports journalists in the country had tried to solve the puzzle back then, but it had been a long time since anybody had shown interest, not least such a beautiful girl.

Steinar didn't generally watch sports programmes, but he'd seen Benedikte at least twice on TV2's Friday late-night talk show. There it had seemed as if she were playing some kind of role, although they probably all did. Her voice, in particular, was different now in real life. Softer, perhaps. And she appeared genuinely interested as she looked at him, asking why he'd stopped.

Luckily, they were interrupted by a plump young man in a suit. The man cocked his head and gave a crooked smile. He pulled a business card out of his pocket and gave it to Benedikte.

'My name's Ola Bugge, football agent. If you need a strong new voice on TV2, an expert commentator with charm, just give me a call.'

Bugge winked at Benedikte, holding his eye closed for several seconds before bowing his head, then lifting it back up and opening his eye again. He turned, carried on walking along the crowd, handing out cards to everyone whose eyes met his. Benedikte looked at him, then at Steinar, and puffed out her cheeks.

The interruption had given Steinar time to regain his composure.

'What are you doing here?' he asked.

Benedikte looked at Steinar through the darker part of her sunglasses.

'I'm a journalist. I want to find out who killed Arild Golden. This is my chance for a scoop, and the clues are to be found here, in the world of football.'

She nodded at the astroturf, where Stanley was performing a double step-over feint.

Part 2

24 July

Arild Golden stood at the busy junction of Oxford Street and Tottenham Court Road. Outside the Dominion Theatre was a gold-painted statue of Freddie Mercury with the promise: 'We will rock you.'

He walked a short distance up Tottenham Court Road and took a side road to the left. It was narrow and dark. At the end of the blind alley stood a tall, heavy-set man, dressed in black, who opened the unobtrusive door. Golden walked downstairs, and a smiling woman in a raspberry-red dress showed him the rest of the way.

The bar was at least 15 metres long. Shadows danced on the grey brick wall behind the eight barmen, and music by Massive Attack was playing. Golden loosened his tie just a little, undid the top button on his shirt and sat down on a bar stool. He didn't look at the cocktail list, ordered a drink he knew wasn't on it.

'An Old Fashioned, please.'

'With whisky?'

'Tequila. Jose Cuervo, Reserva de la Familia.'

'You know it'll take about 15 minutes?'

'I know.'

The barman took out two glasses. Into one he poured the tequila. In the other, a heavy on-the-rocks glass, he put some sugar, which he dampened with a few drops of Angostura bitters. He crushed the mixture with a long, twisted steel mixing spoon. Then he added a minimal amount of tequila and an ice cube. He stirred it for a couple of minutes before fishing out a small piece of orange peel, which he singed, then put in the glass, stirring some more.

Into the bar came the man who had so often ended up in the 'sundry' column of Golden's accounts. A number of the patrons glanced up. Everton manager Brian Fulton was a well-known face. Fulton wasn't bothered by people looking and made a beeline for Golden.

Fulton was wearing a dark grey suit with a white, partially open shirt. He was still slim, even though it was a few years since he'd stopped playing.

'For Christ's sake, Golden. Who the fuck is this fucking Per what's-his-fucking-name?'

Golden signalled to the barman and asked for a beer for his friend. The barman served up a bottle of Sapporo Black Label. Fulton brought it to his mouth and drank half the bottle in one go.

'And what's this fucking piece of Japanese shit?' he said, before going on to drink the rest.

Golden ordered another one, and Fulton took a swig of the Japanese beer that clearly wasn't so bad after all. Golden leant closer to Fulton.

'Per Diesen is Norway's best footballer,'he said. 'He'll fit in perfectly in the English league. Your team needs a playmaker, and Diesen will be a star for you. I've never let you down before.'

'We do need midfielders, but there are loads of them out there,' said Fulton, finishing his bottle and starting another. He was on auto-pilot now.

'7 per cent,' said Golden.

'15.'

'Are you mad? 8.'

'I'm taking a big risk with this transfer. 12.'

'There's a good tradition called meeting each other halfway. Let's say 10 per cent.'

Fulton downed his third beer in a single gulp, then put down the bottle, shook Golden by the hand and left the bar.

As if on cue, the barman put the Old Fashioned he'd finished mixing down on the bar. Golden closed his eyes and took a good sip. He controlled the two men from Everton he needed. Any other representatives would be like the damask rug in the Wimborne Room at The Ritz, unnecessary decoration.

He had a deal.

Pride

Steinar looked out the window and saw a man walking around on his property, a white van parked in the drive. Steinar went outside. The man was wearing a blue boiler suit, and he was scratching the part of his scalp not covered by his cap, which he wore backwards.

'How does it look?' asked Steinar.

'Looks like there's still a fair bit of activity, I'm afraid. Especially at the bottom of the house. It might be slugs eating the poison there, though.'

The man was from Rentokil. The company's mission was to fight vermin, and Steinar thought that it's name was almost perfect. Why hadn't they gone all the way, though, changing the middle vowel and calling themselves Rent-a-kill? Together with some of his neighbours, Steinar had called in the company after last year's neighbourhood barbecue was interrupted by a lethargic brown rat sauntering off with a Hungarian sausage.

Rats were unavoidable in a city like Oslo, in fact, they said there were twice as many rats as people there. But even though, statistically, Steinar should have to house two of them, neither he nor his neighbours were willing to accept that.

'Well, at least there'll be fewer slugs then,' said Steinar, who had just as little sympathy for the Spanish slug as he had for *Rattus norvegicus*.

'No, they just scoff the poison. They think it's tasty; it doesn't hurt them. They don't have any blood in their bodies.'

'They snack on rat poison?'

'That's what they do,' said the Rentokil man, putting on a cheerful face and standing stock still. After a few moments, he spoke again. 'Sorry, I was just thinking how cool it would be if my body had the same kind of tolerance for Coke and crisps. If none of it stuck. If it just passed straight through.'

He picked up a grey, metal box with yellow stickers on it and opened it with a special key. Inside was an empty, white plastic bowl.

'You see how the bowl's been practically licked clean? Typical slugs.'

He sprayed the bowl full of blue foam and locked the metal box with demonstrative thoroughness. The rat poison looked like toothpaste.

'Humans can't keep down enough of the stuff for it to be dangerous. It contains an emetic that rats don't react to, but that makes us throw up. It's an ingenious little product, this is, when you think about it,' said the man, taking off his plastic gloves. 'Turns out this is the last time I'll be here. I've got a new route. It's a shame, because there are so many nice people in this area.'

'Do you like your job?' asked Steinar.

'Yeah, I get to be out and about lots, meet new people all the time. I love it.'

'Good luck, then.'

Steinar thought the conversation was over, but there was something keeping the man here. He looked down, cleared his throat and said: 'I've got a nephew.'

Steinar looked at the man, who gave no sign of continuing. Steinar knew where he was heading, but he still waited for him to go on.

'He's football mad. He practises the whole time. Well, he's quite good at skiing too, but in the summer it's nothing but football.'

'Great.'

'I'm sorry to ask, but I'd really like to have your autograph. For my nephew, I mean.'

'That's no problem,' said Steinar, looking at the man. Now, according to the usual custom with autographs, the man would normally produce something to write on and something to write with. After a brief pause, the man started patting down his pockets. He'd clearly left his pen in the van. He apologised and went to get a biro and a piece of copy paper that he used for his reports. He asked Steinar to write on the back.

'Thank you so much. He'll be happy with this,' said the man, meticulously putting the top back on his biro. 'So what are you doing these days anyway?'

Instinctively, Steinar was about to answer 'I'm a footballer.' He'd worked so hard at it for so many years, it was still part of his system in a way. But he looked at the Rentokil man and told him what he did.

'I'm a lawyer.'

'Blimey.'

Steinar gave a lop-sided smile. The man held up the little scrap of paper in the air.

'Thanks. I'll make sure the next technician gets all the information.'

Technician, thought Steinar. So that's what they call themselves.

Ambitions

'The post-mortem report isn't ready yet. What I can give you is a short summary of the report from the first unit on the scene, but you can't tell anybody where you got it,' said Arnold Nesje, on the other end of the phone.

'Of course not,' said Benedikte.

As a sports journalist, Benedikte had some regular sources. She had a couple of players who could speak well for themselves, and whose clubs used them for everything from advertising jobs to entertainment programmes, as well as requests from journalists. She had a couple of coaches in clubs that were so uninteresting their boards had given them strict instructions not to hold anything back. She had directors of football who almost wept tears of joy when somebody called them, and fellow journalists with chronic verbal diarrhoea. For the Golden case, though, Benedikte needed to think beyond her normal sources, but it was a little harder to call Nesje than most other people, they'd had an on-off relationship for several years. Nesje was in the police, currently with the National Police Immigration Service.

'Golden's neck was broken,' he said. 'It's presumed that some kind of striking weapon was used, making several perforations in his neck, about a centimetre in depth. The impact killed him instantly. But there are also signs of a struggle before the fatal blow.'

Benedikte took a note of the information. A broken neck, a weapon, holes in his neck, a struggle. This was something brutal, but was it planned? Was it done in anger? Was hate behind it? Or was it money? Bearing in mind that a football agent was involved, it could be a combination of all these factors.

She had so many questions, but she knew that Nesje couldn't answer them yet, nobody could. She looked back down at her notepad.

'I need more help,' she said.

'What are you up to, anyway?'

'I'm trying to investigate the killing of Arild Golden.'

'I know that, but why?'

A couple of months previously, Benedikte had presented a story about a 29-year-old Norwegian sprinter who'd had to retire. She couldn't get the story out of her head. It reminded her of the more senior colleagues she'd seen vanish from the TV screen. Colleagues who hadn't managed to keep their positions after maternity leave. Colleagues who'd had to watch others being offered the job of presenting the *Gullruten* TV awards or *Idrettsgallaen*, the star-studded annual review of Norwegian sport. Her meeting with Steinar Brunsvik made her reflect on this too. He was younger than her when he stopped playing. If there was one thing sports personalities and female faces on commercial TV channels had in common, it was their early sell-by dates.

The Golden case was her big chance to be something more. Success depends to a large extent on luck, and journalists depend on other people's achievements or failures. Where would Woodward and Bernstein have been without Nixon? Things like that didn't happen in football. People in football barely knew who Nixon was, let alone Woodward or Bernstein. The biggest news stories would always deal with somebody getting mixed up with a prostitute, and that somebody would almost without exception be a player in the English Premier League. So for her as a sports journalist, a homicide at the epicentre of Norwegian football could only be described as one thing: a stroke of luck.

'I want to go deeper,' said Benedikte.

'Give me the names and I'll check them out.'

She was still young, but the experience of how easily life could change was burnt into her. How easily a life could be destroyed. It was so long ago, but those tough years still haunted her.

A Team Sport

Steinar needed to study something serious when he came back to Norway and ended up choosing law. Law was a marathon, a 50 km ski race, it was certainly nothing like the explosive nature of football.

The lecturers and his fellow students soon realised that Steinar wasn't interested in talking football. The law faculty was well insulated from the Norwegian sports press, so Steinar was able to study in peace. Not long after his last exam, he started as a trainee in Tangen's law firm.

One day Steinar assisted in an industrial dispute negotiation meeting. His company was representing a business carrying out massive changes to its employees' contracts without really needing to, coming up against quite legitimate opposition from union representatives in the process.

The battle was ended by senior partner Edvin Tangen throwing the statute book on the table and saying: 'Tell me where it says in here that employees on temporary contracts have the right to stay in their positions.' The employees' lawyer, who was terrified of Tangen – known for taking well over 3,000 kroner an hour – capitulated on the spot. At the same time, Steinar felt the appeal of working for the company vanish. He handed in his resignation the same day and rented a small office of his own at Sandaker, in the north of Oslo.

He had to air out the office for two weeks, painting every square inch of the yellowed walls. He replaced the wall-to-wall carpet with light parquet flooring and bought a large, semi-circular desk. To finish with, he ordered business cards and a sign for the door, showing the name Sandaker Criminal Law. Even now, he was wary of revealing his name. Nonetheless, he was still asked fairly frequently: 'But aren't you…?'

Maybe a bit of extra PR wouldn't go amiss, though. Steinar had taken on both criminal cases and civil cases; he had sufficient practice as a trainee lawyer and had taken the required exam. He could now dispense with the word 'trainee' in his title and rightfully call himself a lawyer, but he was still not getting enough cases. They weren't covering the company's running expenses.

The years spent studying law, his investments in his own company and life in general had eaten into the savings from his football career. If the current situation continued, Steinar would soon have to swallow his pride and beg Tangen to give him back his job. If nothing else, that would at least make the work Christmas party a bit more interesting than it was in his one-man firm.

The quiet days gave Steinar time to think, bringing back how much he missed football. He started to think of the man who'd ruined everything, Golden's partner. Steinar had even given the man a name. He called him Vlad Vidić.

There was something intense about the man, something harsh, something bottled up that made Steinar think of the Balkans. Perhaps he'd unconsciously named him after Manchester United's tough centre-back, Nemanja Vidić, a footballer he'd noticed even though he was trying to close himself off from the game.

Steinar checked that his phone wasn't on silent. No missed calls. Then he sent a text message: 'I'm on my way.' Then he started thinking of Vidić again.

Nemanja was too sweet as a first name. When Steinar played football, he always used to focus on his opponents' weak points. If a goalkeeper often let in low shots on the left, then Steinar would send the ball blazing towards that corner at the earliest opportunity. If a player was a little apprehensive when challenged, Steinar wouldn't be adverse to tackling him over the touchline. And if he'd been up against Nemanja Vidić in a match, then he would've just thought about what a sweet, innocent name Nemanja was, merely to get the psychological upper hand.

Was that why he'd given Golden's partner a more bloodthirsty first name or had the name Vlad Vidić come from somewhere else?

Steinar got up and watched the tram going past. There were two questions he couldn't quite answer, nor get out of his mind. How had Vlad Vidić managed to stay anonymous all these years? And had Arild Golden himself had a hand in what happened to Steinar?

Soccer School

Benedikte sat in one of the large substitutes' shelters next to the astroturf ground at Valle. Vålerenga's training session was officially over, but some of the players had stayed on for a bit of extra practice.

Per Diesen fired the ball on target. From 20 yards he bent it up in the air, over an imaginary wall, past an imaginary keeper, in off the post and into the empty goalmouth. He put down another ball and sent it curving almost as high into the corner. Per Diesen was the best free kick taker in Norway.

Benedikte liked to see how carefully he prepared the ball. How he paced it out and how he exhaled before every shot. How high and hard he kicked the ball. Journalists don't spend enough time studying what footballers actually do, she thought.

A short distance away, Marius Bjartmann was doing sit-ups. He'd taken off his T-shirt and was using it to lie on. The sweat glistened on his sculpted abs.

Kalid Jambo was still there too, running a series of 17–13 intervals. He shot along the length of the pitch, turned and went back a good distance in the 17 seconds he was running. Then he walked for 13 seconds to recover, throwing the odd remark over at the players fetching the balls.

Picking them up were Otto Cana and a couple of the other young lads. It was traditional in most football clubs to give that job to the youngest players. And it was also traditional in most football clubs for the youngest players to moan about it.

Bang, Diesen hit the crossbar, which rattled.

He shot off another three free kicks, and Bjartmann finished his strength training. They left together, walking by the Vallhall Arena, the large sports hall next to the pitch, Kalid Jambo tagging along. After a couple of minutes' vaguely focused searching, the young lads found the last ball, then they too headed off towards the arena, where the changing rooms were to be found.

The structure of the grey and blue arena, with its curved roof, was becoming worn. Pieces kept falling off. When this happened on the wall facing the car park it looked like a large, beached whale with tooth decay. That day, the team had probably done their training outdoors on the astroturf because their next league match was away at Aalesund's Color Line Stadion, with its artificial pitch. But why, in winter, did Vålerenga's first-team players prefer to train outdoors in the slush and freezing temperatures, and right next to one of the busiest roads in Norway, rather than inside the warm arena?

Vålerenga's development coach, Andrei Sennikov, went over to Benedikte when they'd finished training, as agreed. The development coaches were responsible for the most talented young footballers, with the responsibility of nurturing them into first-team players. The idea was that they would take four to six players in each club under their wing, teach them about nutrition and training, and make sure they went to school and did their homework. A large part of the development coach's day consisted of making home visits.

This social care dimension was important, but the development coaches had ever-expanding job descriptions. The less money the clubs had at their disposal, the more they tried to squeeze into these positions, Benedikte thought. Nothing changed for the managers. Goalkeeper coaches went on shooting straight instep drives at their apprentices at the start of training sessions, while the development coaches became increasingly worn out. Hardly anyone stayed in the role past the age of 50.

The development coaches possessed enormous knowledge. They were the ones who knew the most about what was going on in Oslo's football world, and if there was anybody who could fill in the gaps in Benedikte's knowledge of football agents it was Vålerenga's development coach.

Sennikov led Benedikte up the wide metal steps and into the long, narrow corridor where the Vålerenga offices were.

'These offices are reserved for the marketing department. Those of us who work on actual football, we have to fight over these meeting rooms.'

Andrei spoke without so much as a trace of accent. Although he was of Russian ancestry, Benedikte knew that he'd lived his whole life in the East End of Oslo, but she still found herself listening out for a foreign twang.

'Sorry, but with everybody complaining to me the whole time, I have to speak my mind now and then.'

'What do they complain about?'

'Either it's the smaller clubs saying we're stealing their best talent, or it's people on the board or even you lot from the media saying we're not bringing enough good players up through the system. It's all wrong anyway.'

'How do the transfers from smaller clubs take place? Via an agent?' Benedikte didn't have the patience to listen to his complaints.

'There are normally agents involved. It's not unusual for 13-year-olds and their parents to have advisers.'

'Isn't there a lower age limit of 15?'

'To get a written contract you have to be 15. Many of them come along to meetings for "support", or they come up with some other excuse. But you're right, the players have to be 15 to have a legally binding contract. Anyway, these agents are just getting worse and worse.'

'What do you mean?' asked Benedikte.

'We've seen some agents going through matches on video with the players.'

'Is that so bad?'

'We're the ones who are supposed to go through matches with them. We're supposed to say what they've done well or what they can improve on, based on Vålerenga's playing style. What do you think is at the forefront of an agent's mind?' asked Sennikov. For the sake of his forefinger and of the meeting room table, Benedikte hoped that he wouldn't use the word 'we' much more today.

'That the players should make themselves marketable,' she answered.

'Exactly, so the agents, who often lack any technical background in football whatsoever, tell the players that they shouldn't pass, but that they should shoot from every possible range; that it's their own performance that counts, not that of the team.'

'Who are the most active agents?' asked Benedikte.

'Arild Golden practically had a monopoly on the biggest talent. Things are a lot less clear now that he's dead. But don't despair, if there's one thing you can count on, it's that other vultures will turn up.

Would you like some coffee, by the way?'

Benedikte shook her head. Sennikov pushed down a few times on the top of a large pump-action coffee pot, which squirted out smaller and smaller doses. A gurgling sound filled the meeting room, and eventually Sennikov sat back down. He looked into his cup, which was far from full, and groaned.

'Back to Golden. Have you thought how insane it was that he had his own soccer school? A travelling soccer school. With the pretext of bringing money to smaller clubs, his Golden Boys system allowed him to appraise and make contact with the best 14-year-olds in the country.'

'Pretext? What do you mean?' asked Benedikte. She'd heard about Golden's soccer schools, but had thought of them as a charity gesture on his part, as if he'd sucked so much money out of football that he'd decided to organise them on a not-for-profit basis almost to redeem himself.

'Golden let the smaller clubs arrange a camp every year, and the clubs made a couple of hundred thousand kroner out of it, but that wasn't the main idea behind the camps. The best 14-year-olds took part in the camps with the football association's blessing. Camps that were off-limits to other agents. Think how ludicrous that is. The Association sent talented players to a camp closed to other agents that they themselves had licensed. They gave Golden a monopoly. Golden filtered out the best talent in Norway and got to know the boys and their families. That's how he got control of Stanley.'

Benedikte nodded as she thought about it. It seemed incredible that the NFF, Norway's largest single-sport association, could allow itself to be so manipulated by a single agent, and that they let one agent take control of the country's best 14-year-olds. 14-year-olds who would soon be 16 and would go on to international academies with Golden Boys owning their rights.

'You just said now that the state of the market has become a lot less clear since Golden's death. Why? Did Golden have partners?' asked Benedikte.

'He might have done, but the contracts are tied to each agent individually, not to companies, so many of Norway's most attractive players are unrepresented now. There's a power vacuum, and the transfer market opened yesterday.'

Benedikte thought about Stanley. He was a potential international star. Norway's Zlatan. Almost 15, which was a golden age, foreign clubs couldn't sign players then, but agents could. And surely Golden Boys wouldn't just want to let him go? They had a verbal agreement with his family, after all. Or did they? It struck Benedikte that Golden had been such a visible front man for his agency that she didn't know whether he had any other employees. Benedikte's thoughts were interrupted by Sennikov.

'Football's not like it used to be,' he said. 'Now we've got superstars at lower secondary school and first-team players who are reality stars. I don't know how they manage to keep focused.' He shook his head slowly while dipping his fingers into a box of *snus* tobacco, digging out an improbably large pinch and manoeuvring it into position under his lip in a masterly fashion.

'Has the club got involved in this?' asked Benedikte.

'It's hard to have an overall policy. It's so new for us to see our players broadcasting from their own flats. We have to deal with it on a case-by-case basis, but it's no secret that we had meetings with Golden to make sure that Per stayed focused on his football.'

'How did that go?'

'Golden made some good arguments, Per was performing better than ever, after all. Vålerenga wanted to maintain good relations with Golden too, so perhaps we weren't as critical as we should've been.'

'Didn't Golden have a point, though? Diesen is at the top of the fantasy football stats in most newspapers, and not just in *VG*, which is probably giving him high marks to promote their *PDTV* series anyway.'

'That's just it. The club let it lie, as long as he kept on playing well, but where should we draw the line? Reality TV's fine, but what about porn? Is that okay as long as they score on the pitch too?'

Benedikte started fidgeting with something in her pocket in the somewhat uncomfortable pause that followed. It was the business card she'd been given by that portly football agent she'd met at Nordre Åsen. She fired a shot in the dark.

'What about Ola Bugge? Do you know him?' she asked.

'Bugge, yes. He's different,' said Sennikov.

'In what way?'

'Golden had the ones with the very best talent, while the fairish ones were swept up by other agents. Bugge started something completely different, he signed Oslo's worst footballers.'

'That doesn't sound like much of a business plan,' said Benedikte.

'Players were queuing up. He had the ones who'd played on the second-best youth team at Kjelsås, the ones who'd turned 28 and still thought that Real Madrid had their eyes on them, the ones who were in their third year playing for Bjølsen and thought that they deserved a contract they could live on, or even that they could live well on. These were players who weren't paid by their clubs, in some cases players who didn't even have a club, who couldn't even get a Fifth Division side to go to the trouble of submitting a transfer form to the local association. Players who were perfect for Bugge's plan.'

'Perfect?' asked Benedikte.

'These people were so bad that nobody wanted them, while they themselves thought they were good enough for any top-flight Norwegian team. Then Bugge played on the fact that Golden and the other agents could easily demand 20–30 per cent of players' salary, which of course can be enormous in cases when players earn 20–30 million kroner. So, instead, Bugge asked for what he called a symbolic payment, in other words a flat payment of 1,000 kroner a month.'

'So Bugge's profits are based on his number of players?' asked Benedikte.

'That's right. If he could get enough players to pay 1,000 kroner a month, he could just lean back without doing anything at all and make a good wage for himself.'

'Genius,' said Benedikte.

'Just one problem. Judging talent is an art. Anybody can see that Stanley from Skeid is going to become a professional footballer, but often the next best players carve out careers for themselves too, not least out of real need or hunger, and it's a lot harder to gauge those ones. Two of Bugge's players turned out well: Kalid Jambo and Otto Cana.'

'I didn't know Bugge was their agent. I thought they were with Golden Boys too,' said Benedikte.

'They were with Bugge until they were selected for the national under-17 side. Golden became their agent immediately after that.'

'How did he get them away from Bugge?'

'I don't know. Who knows how Golden really operated? In any case, Bugge's now more involved with the better players. Actually I think he's dreaming of signing Stanley,' said Sennikov.

'Why haven't you taken him on? I thought Vålerenga could practically have any players they wanted in Oslo.'

'He's too good.'

'Too good?'

'He'd leave Norway before playing a single first-team match with us. The big international clubs are counting down to his sixteenth birthday next year, when he'll be able to go abroad. The only unknown about Stanley is who'll be his agent, and who'll end up hauling in the big catch.'

'What would you advise Stanley to do?'

'The same thing I advise all players. Listen to your coach and stay away from agents.'

Soul of Fire

'It doesn't look good,' said Dr Ramstad, putting his hand on Steinar's shoulder. Bjørnar Ramstad and Steinar were childhood friends, having grown up together in Lofthusveien, in the East End of Oslo. Practically every time they'd met as adults, they'd argued about which neighbourhood Lofthusveien was in, whether it was Grefsen or Årvoll, but not today. Steinar nodded ever so slightly before drawing his breath and opening the door to room 3206, on the second floor of the Cancer Centre at Ullevål Hospital.

Steinar's old coach, Ståle Jakobsen, was sleeping in bed. Jakobsen was a football coach of the most politically incorrect school. He wouldn't have given a damn about giving a seven-year-old a dressing down for a poorly executed tackle, and ideas such as squad rotation or prizes for everybody weren't part of Jakobsen's ideology. Nevertheless, warmth was the quality that Steinar associated with him most.

He turned back to Bjørnar and whispered: 'Bloody hell, he's fat!'

'Yes.'

'How did he get so fat?'

'How long has it been since you last saw him?'

'A few years.'

'Same here. So I made some enquiries. He's barely left the sports centre over the past few years. He stopped eating his dinners and was living almost exclusively on energy bars and XL-1 energy drinks.'

'He loved that indoor pitch. He was the one who got it built, after all. He even threatened to beat up people from the council's planning department, and they coughed up the money in the end. What he did was a political miracle here in Oslo, where it's only skiing that gets the real money.'

Steinar thought about the old sports centre just beyond Årvoll

School, towards Trondheimsveien, with its indoor synthetic grass pitch. The centre that had meant so much to him when he was growing up.

'Lung cancer,' said Bjørnar.

'You can't get lung cancer from being fat, can you?'

'No, but that's what he's got anyway, and it's at an advanced stage too. I've spoken with the doctor dealing with his treatment. It's not operable, I'm afraid.'

'But I can't remember ever seeing Jakobsen with a cigarette.'

'Smokers make up 80 per cent of cases. 20 per cent are down to other causes.'

'How did Jakobsen get it, then?'

'I've got a theory, but I need to investigate a bit more first. Can we meet up tonight? Seven o' clock at Magneten?'

'Okay.'

'Then I'll tell you what's killing him.'

Fair Play

Benedikte's white iPhone 4S rang. She looked at the display. It was Per Kristian Boltedal from the financial newspaper *Dagens Næringsliv* finally returning her call.

Boltedal was known as one of Norway's best investigative journalists. Corruption among business leaders was his speciality, but his greatest passion was football. Every other Sunday on the stands at Ullevaal Stadion he did the customary *jenka* party dance with the rest of Klanen, the Vålerenga supporters' club.

'Benny Bly! Long time no speak! How's it going?'

'Fine thanks, but I need some help.'

'And here was me thinking you just wanted a wee chat.'

'What can you tell me about Arild Golden?'

'He's dead.'

'You know what I mean.'

'I'm only pulling your leg, but Benedikte, you know you're a rival too, I…'

Benedikte interrupted him: 'I just need it for background information.'

'Alright. What do you want to know?'

'I'm especially interested in Golden Boys.'

'Golden Boys is Arild Golden's agency, easily the biggest in the Nordic market and one of the biggest in Europe. I've tried, but have barely been able to find out anything else at all about the company.'

'How can that be?'

'Golden Boys is registered in Guernsey and the board's made up of two English lawyers who refuse to comment.'

'What kind of structure do you think the company's got, then?'

'Its accounts and the details of its ownership aren't public. There are many ways to hide these, for example through an agreement with the lawyers, or with the shares being owned by a foundation in Liechtenstein or somewhere. And, if you're really paranoid, you can use bearer bonds.'

'What are they?'

'Whoever physically holds the bonds owns the company.'

'Could these have been kept in Golden's office?'

'Anywhere. It's probably most common to keep them in a safe-deposit box. The point is that if you want to keep details about ownership a secret, then they're impossible to find. Just imagine if Golden kept those bonds deposited in a Swiss bank and memorised the account number and the code needed to access them. Then we'll never find out anything about the company's structure or what happened to the money.'

'What about his address and phone number?'

'I've spoken to Golden on the phone several times, but I can't manage to trace any record of his number. As for his home, he spent so much time travelling outside Norway that he didn't have to be registered as a resident. I can't even find any documentation on his transfers. Just rumours.'

'I like rumours.'

'Per Diesen and Everton.'

'Is he going there?'

'Was going there. Everton were about to buy him this month, but now that Golden's dead it seems as if the planned transfer will suffer the same fate.'

'Why?'

'Golden sold players in turn. The last two had gone to West Ham and Aston Villa, and next on the list was Everton and Diesen. What's more, the Everton manager Brian Fulton suffers from a gambling addiction, and Golden knew how to exploit that.'

'What's that got to do with it?'

'Golden bribed Fulton, not to mention other football executives, both in England and in Norway. That's why there was never any correlation between which players the clubs needed and the ones they got.'

'But that's illegal, isn't it?'

'That's how football works. It's not how good you are that decides where you end up playing. It's how creative your agent is, how selective his morality, and how many contacts he's got. With Golden gone, so went the tasty morsel of a few extra tax-free million, and so there was no more space left at the end of Everton's subs' bench.'

'Why does nobody report these things?'

'Who'd want to do that? The agent sits on every side of the table, and it's not so hard to agree with yourself. We're talking about a business that's rotten to the core.'

'Do you know about anything else that might have led to his death?'

'I said that everybody was fine with it, but Africa is usually the exception. It's impossible to work down there as much as Golden did without making enemies.'

'Have you got any rumours about that, then?'

'Nothing about Golden himself, but I have heard of other agents taking young girls as payment.'

'What for?'

'They promise young lads a professional career in Europe in exchange for sex with their sisters. I've heard of a Belgian agent who set up a small harem in Africa while the girls' brothers were in transit, unable to get through the visa checks. We haven't managed to link anything like that to Golden but, as I mentioned, you can't operate in Africa for that long and stay legal. By the way, I think one of your colleagues from TV2 was working on an African angle to the story.'

'Do you know what it was about?'

'Something about a footballer from the Cameroonian under-17 national side who was kidnapped and forced to play for a team in Egypt. A totally normal transfer for African football.'

'Normal?'

'An incredible amount of these things are going on and nobody seems to care, but apparently, in this case, there might have been a trail back to the Golden Boys system. The company wanted to develop the player through the Egyptian team, which they pretty much controlled, and then sell him on in Europe. Maybe you'll find something in the TV2 archives?'

Benedikte thought that African football was all about children dribbling a ball on orange-coloured sand, and the players who were exported from African football were supposed to be like George Weah. He'd come from the slums of the Liberian capital Monrovia and was 22 years old when he was bought by Monaco. The FIFA rules state explicitly that it's illegal to transfer players under the age of 18 from one continent to another. In reality, Barcelona, the world's best club for player development, was tearing 11-year-olds away from their families in Cameroon.

Benedikte thanked Boltedal for the information and promised to return the favour.

A few hours later, she had her phone back in her hand. 'Get to the point, straight to the point,' she told herself, dialling the number.

'Hello, Steinar speaking.'

'This is Benedikte Blystad from TV2 here. Your name's come up in connection with the Golden case.'

'What?'

'Meet me at the TV2 offices in Karl Johans Gate tomorrow at 12 o' clock,' she said, hanging up.

I Know What's Killing Him

Steinar was waiting at Magneten, the pub in Torshov, which was almost like a little town of its own within Oslo, with a butcher, a theatre and a sports shop in three parts criss-crossing the busy Vogts Gate.

He couldn't remember ever having been in this pub before. When he was young, he'd shunned alcohol to become a good player, and after his career he'd had other things to do. Going to the pub with friends was a rare event. TV screens hung on the walls, one showing a repeat of Everton vs. Birmingham. There was also black and yellow Skeid memorabilia on the wall. 'The Real Pride of Oslo,' read one of the pennants.

Bjørnar Ramstad came down the stairs and across to Steinar. He chucked down the pink sports supplement from *VG* on the table, with Arild Golden on the front page. 'SEE WHO STANDS TO GAIN FROM GOLDEN'S DEATH,' read the headline. It was four days since he'd been killed. The police hadn't released any further information and the newspapers were speculating wildly.

'What a sick story!' said Bjørnar.

'Madness,' said Steinar, skimming through the article, which mentioned most people in Norway. It was almost as if it would be an insult not to be on the list.

'The first one's on me,' said Bjørnar, heading to the bar.

Steinar looked at Golden's face. The short conversation he'd had with Benedikte Blystad was playing on a loop in the back of his mind. What did she mean? He turned the sports paper upside down.

Bjørnar lanted a lager in front of Steinar. 'Tell me about that play-off,' he said. 'Don't forget I was a medical student in Sweden back then.'

'Up in that place Luleå or wherever? Call that studying?'

'Umeå. And it was hard.'

'Hehe, I'm only joking.'

'But that play-off, what happened? How did you do it?'

'It was 1999, and I don't think there have been many bigger sensations in Norwegian football history than when us lot from little Årvoll FK found ourselves in a play-off for the top division, for Tippeligaen,' said Steinar, enjoying a long sip of his lager. 'Clubs like Årvoll are usually stable fixtures in the Third Division, possibly making a rare appearance in the Second Division, but the indoor pitch changed everything. Everyone who was there in 1999 had started on that indoor pitch in 1984, aged seven. But you know that much; you were one of us too.'

'For a while, anyway,' said Bjørnar.

'We were the first team to have Ståle Jakobsen as our head coach, and we were going to be the best in Norway. Nobody was allowed to go on holiday or attend confirmations, funerals or weddings. And, in the end, nobody wanted to either. We were part of something bigger. When I think of it, you were the only one I remember who quit. Why did you?'

'Jakobsen said I was academically gifted and should focus on that path instead.'

'Was he keeping an eye on your marks at school, then?' asked Steinar, barely managing to hold back his laughter.

'I know school was an excuse to chuck me out. I wasn't good enough.'

'You got a pretty good job, though.'

'But not the same kind of experience as the rest of the guys did. I would gladly have swapped my education for one year as a pro.'

They'd all been marked by football in some way. Even Bjørnar, who was now a doctor, couldn't get over the fact that he never made it as the new Johan Cruyff.

'Jakobsen took us up from one age group to the next,' said Steinar, 'and we became like a single organism, with one movement automatically triggering another. I knew exactly what would happen if the ball was in defence or midfield. As a youth team, we won the final of the Norway Cup 4–0 against Bayelsa United from Nigeria.'

A man in stained denim who'd been sitting alone at the next table without a drink got up, walked over to the TV and switched off the Everton vs. Birmingham match. He grumbled something under his breath and sat back down. Bjørnar frowned before nodding at Steinar, who continued.

'Vålerenga, Stabæk, Lyn, Skeid, Lillestrøm. They were all interested in our players. Representatives from the top clubs were at our pitch on a daily basis. I remember one time Jakobsen chasing away a Lillestrøm executive, shouting: "Don't you fucking touch my lads!"'

'I can picture that.'

'He also chased away Årvoll's existing first-team players. In those days, Årvoll was an average Third Division team with a stock of players in their late twenties. They could still stay but, as Jakobsen told them in his typically subtle way, they wouldn't do any more training or play any matches. Everyone who got to play was 17 or 18, so bigger, heavier opponents wore us out physically for the first two seasons, but in our third season we were promoted, and we went through the Second Division unbeaten. It was us against the rest of the world. We had one mission: to win. We were a team of 11 practically insane footballers whether we were playing away against Levanger, at home against Bærum or travelling away to Strømmen Stadion. Even before the last league round, long after our promotion had been secured, Jakobsen stood there with his top off, pounding his chest, telling us: "Now it matters more than ever."'

'Which year was this again?' asked Bjørnar.

'We went up from the Second Division in 1998. Then came our legendary 1999 season in the First Division, on Linderud's astroturf. On the touchline we had a speaker with a megaphone and a portable cassette player with a tape of Prince's classic hit "1999", which we played during half-time. The start of the season was beyond all our expectations, and by halfway through we were top of the league. Then Ajax called.'

'Did they call you personally?'

'Yeah, I didn't have an agent. Ajax had been following me for two years, and it was my boyhood dream. The team that had won the Champions League four years earlier with almost exclusively home-grown players. There was no better club to join, but I was terrified of telling Jakobsen.'

'What did he say?'

'He started crying.'

Bjørnar looked at Steinar as if he were lying. Steinar started to smile, then tilted his head and nodded, confirming Bjørnar's suspicions.

'No, he told me that he knew he couldn't keep me forever, but it was a tough thing to take nonetheless. I stammered a few words to the effect that I hadn't made up my mind yet. Then Jakobsen looked at me harshly and said: "You're going!"'

'Why?'

'He couldn't compete. He didn't want to. Jakobsen came along to Amsterdam, negotiated my contract and got them to agree that I'd finish the season I was playing with Årvoll. It was a bizarre situation. An Årvoll player on his way to Ajax, and Jakobsen negotiating with them as if he'd never done anything else. Later that evening I lost him in the centre of Amsterdam, but that's another story altogether.'

Bjørnar laughed.

'We had a few injuries during the autumn and had to keep making changes to the team. We still ended up in third place and met Kongsvinger in a play-off match. We travelled to Gjemselunden, drawing 0–0, meaning we had one foot in the top division. For the second-leg match, 2,150 spectators came to Linderud, which was practically impossible, but they piled one on top of the other around the pitch. We were leading 1–0 until the 92nd minute, when Johan brought down Kongsvinger's striker, and I'm not lying when I say that it happened two yards outside the penalty box. The referee awarded a penalty. Of course we all protested wildly, all except Jakobsen, who stood absolutely still. The Kongsvinger player was seriously arrogant and took a two-step run-up. He managed to fool our keeper and chipped the ball straight into the goal. It happened as if in slow motion. We just managed to take the next kick-off before the referee blew his whistle. One ref's mistake away from the top division. I completely lost it and got a five-match ban for starting a fight. Ajax were about to cancel my contract.'

'I remember. It got a lot of space in the Swedish papers too. But what about Jakobsen? Didn't he snap? You said he just stood there calmly, watching.'

'After calming down, I took a long shower. I was the last one there as I left the dressing room. Jakobsen took me aside and said: "I'm glad."'

'What?!'

'He said that the team would fall apart the day one of us left, and then the top division would be too big for the club. That's why he was also going to quit as first-team manager. Since he thought it was better for the club that we hadn't made it, he couldn't carry on.'

Steinar shook his head, took a last sip of his lager and saw that Bjørnar's glass was empty too.

'Let me get you another. Same again?'

Bjørnar nodded. Steinar went to the bar and held up two fingers, even though the place was almost empty and the barman would quite easily have heard him. Steinar paid and went back to their table.

'As I mentioned before,' said Bjørnar, 'Jakobsen's going to die, and I think I know what's killing him. He put me down as his next of kin, so I've got more access than I would normally have. His condition made me read up on synthetic turf and its health risks. Have you heard of PAHs: Polycyclic Aromatic Hydrocarbons?'

Steinar shook his head.

'They're carcinogenic compounds that can be found in artificial turf. In the rubber. It's the rubber that's most dangerous, and the indoor pitch gets extremely dry with the enclosed air and poor ventilation. This makes these substances swirl around even more, and Jakobsen's been breathing them in for years. The indoor pitch, which he loves more than anything on earth, has slowly but surely been killing him.'

'What do you mean by rubber?'

'Chopped-up old car tyres.'

'Huh?'

'I see it's a while since you last trained on artificial turf. So they can control how much the ball bounces and reduce the pain from falling, they use rubber granules. The cheapest way to produce these is by grinding up discarded old tyres. An average pitch will have something like 100 tonnes of granules spread across it.'

'Why is it dangerous?'

'Because car tyres contain more than 60 different chemical substances, a number of which are linked to cancer risks or other health problems.'

'But aren't there guidelines on how you should dispose of tyres?'

'Sure, car tyres are supposed to go to approved tips. There are strict rules about it: they mustn't be dumped in the countryside or in the sea. The upshot is that it's a bit odd they can be used in synthetic grass pitches or as a soft surface in playgrounds or nursery schools,' said Bjørnar.

'Nursery schools too?'

'This stuff's being used all over the country. Children are playing on it, falling and bleeding on it. The youngest ones are even licking these surfaces with highly aromatic oils and PAHs leaking out of them, not to mention nonylphenol, zinc and all kinds of other crap.'

'Why hasn't the indoor pitch been closed?'

'Because all the research on the health risks of artificial turf is being hushed up, discredited. Some researchers at the University of Connecticut demonstrated a link between synthetic turf and a risk of cancer, only to find the outcome of their research toned down to avoid panic. Someone called Dr Daum from Chicago Children's Hospital found a link between artificial turf and MRSA. The *New England Journal of Medicine* has found the same too. And the thing with medicine is that when something's been proven, then there are thousands of other dangers that we can't prove.'

'Why has this been hushed up? With so many young people playing on synthetic pitches, you'd think people would look into the health risks.'

'Partly, but everyone's so happy with synthetic turf. Politicians gain in popularity when they open a new pitch. There are positive side effects in terms of combating child obesity and idleness. Everyone likes sport, and nobody wants to admit they've made a mistake. Still, I'm taken aback when I see statements like the one made by the Norwegian Institute of Public Health.'

'What did they say?'

'They said something about it not being dangerous and that people didn't have to replace the rubber now, but they still recommended not using tyres in future. That's like saying they haven't got a clue.'

'I still don't quite understand why this is just being ignored.'

'It's hard to prove it beyond all doubt. Even just diagnosing an illness is an uncertain business, while etiology, finding the cause of an illness, is harder still. We know that tyre rubber causes lung irritation and allergic reactions to the eyes and skin, we know it's led to cancer and impaired development, as well as liver and kidney damage. It's even been linked to autism. But it's harder to prove that an illness might originate from the ground rubber granules in synthetic turf. The number of MRSA patients might be rising in parallel with the number of artificial grass pitches, but can we prove the link? My opinion is that we need to use our heads. If there are so many chemicals that are proven dangerous present in artificial turf and in the granules they use to cover the pitches, then there's a risk. I'm convinced this is how Jakobsen got lung cancer. I can't prove it, but I'm convinced about it. And what's really ironic is that the other kind of astroturfing has a lot to do with it.'

'The other kind?'

'Astroturfing was an expression first used in the United States about fake grassroots movements, ordinary people coming forward to sing the praises of some product or another. Think about how many positive stories you've read about synthetic grass. Local council leaders cutting ribbons and happy children in the sunshine on a perfect green mat. The Language Council of Norway should really consider introducing "astroturfing" as a new word in Norwegian.'

'But what's the motivation behind hushing it up?'

'The similarities with the tobacco industry are frightening. For decades, smoking was made to look harmless. What for?'

'Money?'

'Exactly. The tobacco industry suppressed research, positive reports were bought, film stars went on smoking and critics were subjected to smear campaigns. Enormous sums of money were involved. The same goes for artificial grass. Have you thought about how much money's in it? Hundreds of pitches that need to be replaced every five years, on average. Hundreds of new ones every year. Indoor pitches. A couple of hundred seven-a-side pitches. Almost 2,000 multi-use games areas. All this is a breeding ground for a cynical new billion-kroner industry that doesn't want the research to get out. An industry with all the power invested in that man there,' said Bjørnar, grabbing the sports supplement from the table and pointing at the photo of Arild Golden. 'If I were the police, I'd look for the people who got their hands on Golden's rights to build artificial pitches.'

No Concrete Evidence

Benedikte stepped out of a silver-grey taxi and went up the stairs to the Ekeberg Restaurant's outdoor veranda. A waiter stopped long enough for her to grab a glass of Sancerre.

The brown and blue wooden chairs were all taken, and with the crush, two of the patrons trod in the fountain. The veranda was on the small side for all the people who'd chosen to come and bid farewell to Arild Golden, while maybe also saying hello at the same time to the agents, players and other people looking for power in the wake of Golden's exit. Benedikte couldn't spot anybody who really looked sad. Were people just looking for new opportunities after Golden's death? Was the killer here?

On the small, makeshift stage between the stairs and the long white bar where Benedikte stood, Sabrina was getting ready. Just behind the stage was a gigantic green plastic plant that made Sabrina look even smaller, if such a thing were possible. 'Tabletop tits' was what they called her in journalistic circles, and she couldn't be more than 5 feet tall at most. Perhaps she lied on her passport too, just like Benedikte, who liked to have her height listed as 5 feet 7 inches, even though it meant she always had to go through passport control on tiptoes.

Sabrina pulled herself up, making a face. She was dressed in a little black number that was just provocative enough to stir the male section of the audience without being disrespectful. All the men watched as she straightened her dress, reached up to the microphone and adjusted a screw to lower it by a few inches. Then she pulled her skirt down again, after her movement had pulled it up to quite an immodest height. Glamorous and grieving.

Benedikte hadn't been able to find much on Sabrina from before Golden had taken her under his wing. The closest thing she'd had to a breakthrough before then was as an audience member on the very edge of the TV screen in NRK1's musical game show *Beat for Beat*. Now she was the new star among glamour models.

Sabrina's real name was Ida Therese Hauge, but her almost Latin looks, as well as her frequent visits to the best plastic surgeons in town, made the name Sabrina much more practical. She'd borrowed her name from the 1980s Italian star who'd had a hit with *'Boys'*, along with several other songs that reached the top three in Finland.

There was a regular feature in *PDTV* in which Sabrina sat alone in the bedroom, revealing small secrets about herself, Per Diesen, their relationship and life in general. In one recent episode Sabrina revealed that *'Boys'* was her favourite song as a little girl.

As an agent, Golden had mainly stuck to representing footballers. Sabrina was an exception. Benedikte had spoken to several media editors, and Golden had promoted Sabrina on a grand scale. Golden himself had once been a model in a couple of advertising campaigns and knew people in every nook and cranny of the Norwegian media. The result was that Sabrina made appearances in four episodes of *Paradise Hotel* on TV3 and had two half-page spreads between the front and centre pages of lads' mags *Vi Menn* and *FHM*, before she was ready for her big breakthrough on the Norwegian edition of *Strictly Come Dancing*, TV2's *Skal Vi Danse?*

Sabrina fell in her paso doble and was the first participant to be sent home, but straight after her tearful post-show interview, Golden showed up and introduced Sabrina to Diesen, sending rumours flying as early as that same evening's transmission of the entertainment programme *God Kveld Norge*. *VG* printed some grainy pictures in its Sunday edition (and the very same ones on Monday). By Tuesday the glossy magazine *Se og Hør* was exclusively able to confirm that Diesen had comforted Sabrina at the Beach Club diner, then on Wednesday the violinist Gudmund Eide overstepped in training, so Sabrina was back ballroom dancing by Thursday.

At Christmas, Sabrina was in the final, up against the news anchor Kåre Jan Vasshaug. She was a frisky eye-catcher who couldn't dance, while he was a professional presenter who was TV-savvy enough to hold a microphone, but couldn't dance either. Vasshaug didn't stand a chance. The circus around Sabrina and Diesen had become so huge that she won with a massive 85 per cent of the vote. The camera managed to pick up the tiniest of tears from Diesen, which became the subject of an entire episode of *PDTV*, with the pair sitting together on the sofa watching a repeat of the tear, which, in turn, led to further tears. From both of them.

A towering African man stood at the bar, a short distance away from Benedikte. She recognised him from a couple of newspaper articles as Chukwudi, an agent Golden had worked with.

Benedikte had checked the archives after speaking to Boltedal from the *Dagens Næringsliv*. Before Golden's death, TV2 had been working on uncovering some dubious sides of his business dealings, with a particular focus on Africa. Golden had also begun pocketing training compensation, solidarity payments and future transfer rights, all things that represented real opportunities for the small clubs in the big world of football.

This was done by giving the African club, which was often a somewhat diffuse academy, a small sum in exchange for them waiving any rights to future payments. The sum might be between 1,500 and 8,000 dollars. A lot of money in some parts of Africa, but peanuts when transfer fees might be in the tens of millions, and when the academy or club was formally entitled to 5 per cent.

In some cases these contracts were signed by people who couldn't read. In other cases, the money vanished after direct threats were made, money that, by rights, should have gone back to Africa. At least, that was the idea when FIFA laid out the rules. Benedikte noticed the man looking at her as she shifted her weight from one leg to the other.

Under the chestnut tree by the entrance, with the best view of the stage, sat Per Diesen with his teammate and best friend, Marius Bjartmann, on a grey rattan sofa. Benedikte had heard the organiser asking if they'd like to perform their radio hit '*Bleed for the Team*'. The pair had turned down the offer.

Bjartmann had made his mark late as a footballer. He'd never played in a national youth side. Actually, to tell the truth, he'd never even been close to making his regional team. Bjartmann was one of those footballers who had to become a first-team player before managers saw their real worth. Bjartmann was no prolific dribbler; he was a defender. The kind of footballer who shouldn't get the ball at all. A footballer who was only good at getting in the way. 'Red Marius' was his nickname, playing on both the colour of his hair and all the times he'd been sent off over the years.

He was a perfect foil and partner for Diesen. They were very different, and the complexity of their partnership caught the public imagination. They appeared as guests on late-night talk shows *and* breakfast shows. They turned up at fashion shows, film premieres and restaurant openings. They were everywhere. When their single, written by that year's main *X Factor* judge, Jørn Engen, reached number one in the charts, the gossip reached fever-pitch among opposing teams' supporters. This dynamic duo was the gayest thing in football since Elton John became chairman at Watford. Golden wasn't so keen on that. There were no indications that big sports brands like Adidas or Nike were planning on using homosexuality in their advertising campaigns. It would be a good idea to get Diesen and Sabrina to hook up.

Diesen stood up and went to the bar, waving modestly to Benedikte, who noticed that he was unusually good-looking at close quarters. Diesen was about to order when Sabrina cleared her throat and spoke into the microphone.

'I want to dedicate this song to my good friend Arild Golden. I think it's fitting for this sad occasion.' Sabrina closed her eyes, having timed her introduction perfectly with the playback, and let the first lines of the Monroes' classic 'Cheerio' drift out over the assembled audience and down the hillside to the seemingly permanent building site at Bjørvika, while she mimed along with just the right amount of sensuality. 'Cheerio, cheerio, bye-bye, cheerio-o, it's too late to try.'

Benedikte just hoped that the line 'I will never know the reason why' was not the one that would stick.

After the song, Diesen ordered drinks from the bar. The bartender mixed them but refused to take any money. Diesen went back to his table. He put one of the glasses down in front of Bjartmann and held up the other as a kind of toast.

'What the hell are you doing, bringing us two cosmos? Holding the glasses by the stem?' said Bjartmann, far too loudly. He looked round at the neighbouring tables, realising that the scene he was making wasn't appropriate, and gave Diesen a sign to sit down. Bjartmann leant forward and carried on whispering as he gesticulated wildly.

Somebody tapped Benedikte on the shoulder. She turned around. It was a journalist, whose name she couldn't remember, from *Se og Hør*.

'Have you heard the latest rumours?'

'That they're gay?' asked Benedikte.

'No, that's a load of rubbish, of course they're not gay, but apparently they've fallen out. Arild Golden, Per Diesen and Marius Bjartmann were pals. At least until Golden started fooling around with Sabrina. Pretty ironic.'

'Why ironic?'

'Well, Golden added a clause in the contract for Diesen's online show that Diesen and Sabrina wouldn't have sex on camera, because that would harm Diesen's chances as a professional footballer abroad. And then Golden goes ploughing her instead.'

'But why did Bjartmann get so angry?'

'Don't know. Maybe he thinks it's pathetic of Diesen to let the girl sing here, in honour of the man who she slept with. Best friends tell each other these things, after all.'

'Are you going to write about this?'

'I've got no concrete evidence, just a colleague who saw Golden leaving Diesen and Sabrina's flat while Vålerenga were training. Not enough to write about when we're talking about dead people, but I know it happened. Golden was shagging Sabrina.'

Offside

Steinar realised that he was wearing the wrong clothes as soon as he entered the TV2 building. Out on Karl Johans Gate, the main street in Oslo, anything goes. In a way it was difficult not to be well dressed next to heroin addicts, prostitutes and tourists from Trondheim.

The whiteness of the reception desk was blinding, as were the backs of the computer screens, as were the receptionist's teeth. On the desk was a red bowl of sweets wrapped in white. The flat-screen TVs on the wall were showing the company's news channel, TV2 Nyhetskanalen. Steinar turned round and hurried out across the street to the first clothes shop he saw.

10 minutes later he was back in the reception, wearing new jeans and a dark blue piqué shirt, which he double-checked to make sure all the price tags had been removed.

'I've got an appointment to see Benedikte Blystad,' he told the Sensodyne man, who picked up the phone and passed on Steinar's message.

'Somebody will be down to fetch you. Take a seat for a moment.' He pointed at the red leather bench. Steinar had just turned to the second page of *Dagens Næringsliv* when a young man came up to him.

'Are you Steinar Brunsvik?'

Steinar nodded.

'Follow me, please,' said the man, leading Steinar over to the lift.

The doors opened into a large office area where a multitude of computers were ready to be used. The office was waiting for news. Steinar hoped the news wouldn't be him.

He was led past the small studio used by the news channel and along a corridor filled with workstations. There she was, leaning on a colleague's desk and resting on her left elbow while she pointed at something on the computer screen. Steinar couldn't help letting out the tiniest of sighs.

'I know, I know,' said the man who'd accompanied Steinar.

Benedikte spotted Steinar and came towards him.

'Come with me,' she said.

She led Steinar straight to a room at the back, a small meeting room simply furnished with a table and a laptop in the middle. He turned down an offer of coffee, but said yes to some mineral water, and sat down.

'Wondering about the way I contacted you, maybe?' asked Benedikte.

Steinar was becoming aware of the crease in his shirt, the one going across his stomach, as the shirt had come straight from the packet. He hadn't seen it in the shop, so now he tried to straighten it discreetly. He poured himself a glass of the mineral water, took a long sip and nodded.

'I've been working a fair amount on the Golden case over the last few days, and while I've been sitting here doing research, I started thinking of you. I put your name into an archival search together with Arild Golden's, and I found the raw footage for a planned investigation programme.'

'What?'

'It was a documentary about Arild Golden that was never finished, but I thought we could watch what's there,' said Benedikte. She turned off the light and pressed 'Play'.

Steinar saw a short summary of his own career: his years at Årvoll, being coached by Ståle Jakobsen, goals in the Amsterdam Arena, and then *VG*'s front page headline: 'HUNG UP HIS BOOTS AT HALF-TIME.' There then followed speculation about Steinar's relationship with Arild Golden, but the main topic of the documentary was Golden's vast finances and how Golden Boys had used dirty tricks to try and take the same kind of control over the African market as it had in the Nordic market. Steinar felt his stomach in knots, uncertain of what was to come, but he was really just on the margins of the story as one of many Norwegian pros who'd gone abroad and come up against a wall. Then Steinar saw Vlad Vidić in the background again. Perhaps Benedikte saw his reaction. She stopped the video and pointed.

'Do you know who this man is?'

'No,' said Steinar.

Had he answered too quickly? It was true, anyway, Steinar really didn't know who the man was. He only knew what he was good for.

They watched the rest of the footage in silence. If Benedikte and TV2 didn't know who Vlad Vidić was, with all their resources, how was he supposed to find out?

The documentary finished and Benedikte switched off the computer.

'Are these claims true, that Golden was your agent, and that he cheated you out of money?'

'I didn't have an agent. I used my coach from Årvoll, Ståle Jakobsen, who we just saw on the video, and negotiated together with him.'

'I thought you had to have an agent?'

'Not back then. It's a new requirement that's been introduced for some reason.'

'Why did you quit?' asked Benedikte.

'Why didn't they finish the documentary?' Steinar retorted.

'It was stopped after the scandal surrounding the documentary on the national skiing team. That one had gone to great lengths to accuse Norwegian skiing of being bottom of the class when it came to doping, but then it turned out that the evidence didn't hold up. TV2 didn't have the energy for another story about sports personalities straight away. It was too much trouble.'

'Why didn't the evidence hold up?'

'I don't know the details,' said Benedikte. 'We Norwegians are best in the world at double standards in terms of sport. If a Finnish skier wins, she's got to be doping, but we wouldn't hesitate to let the same skier take up Norwegian citizenship and let her puff on asthma medicine at 2,000 metres above sea level if it gave us a Norwegian relay victory or a European handball gold medal. It's career suicide to criticise these things. Imagine if star skiers like Petter Northug or Marit Bjørgen were exposed as dopers. If we wanted to show something about that, we'd need a video of them injecting themselves and we'd need a Supreme Court judge acting as cameraman.'

Steinar looked at his watch. It was almost 2 o'clock. He was relieved that the documentary had never been finished, but it was also nearly seven hours since he'd eaten breakfast.

'Why did you quit?' Benedikte asked again.

'Can't we get something to eat?' asked Steinar. He looked at Benedikte. She was strikingly beautiful. Part of him wanted to disclose everything to her, but she was asking about his closest secret. And he didn't know her well enough. Not yet.

Steinar let Benedikte choose a place, so she took him down to the Baltazar Restaurant. Shadows lay on the red bricks on the ground and across the walls outside the entrance to the restaurant behind Oslo Cathedral. It was an enjoyable place to eat outdoors, but Steinar insisted that they sit inside, where the dark interior meant Steinar could let his shirt hang freely. Benedikte also relaxed for a moment, or so it seemed. Steinar looked at a wine bottle up on a shelf. They'd used it as a candle holder, and white wax had congealed on the label. They ordered one without wax.

The waiter asked who would like to taste the wine, and gestures were exchanged back and forth across the table until Steinar had to pretend that he understood this business of sniffing it and letting it roll around his mouth. After what he hoped was a long enough pause, he signalled to the waiter to pour and took control of the conversation before Benedikte had a chance to.

'How did you get started at TV2?' he asked, taking another sip of wine. Benedikte looked at him for a few seconds before speaking.

'You know how some people irritate you from the very first moment you meet them?' she asked.

'Yes.'

'Well, there were a couple of girls who used to come into the petrol station where I worked for a while. They came to buy baby food. You know, those small jars of mashed up lasagne. These girls didn't have children, they just lived on baby food, and every day they stood there talking about some brain-dead rubbish. One day, I overheard them talking about a vacancy they'd seen for breakfast TV editorial staff on *God Morgen Norge*, and they were saying how cool it would be to work there and meet all the celebrities.'

'Baby food?'

'I think they thought it was healthy. Anyway, that's not the point. After hearing their conversation, I went in to see the boss, handed in my uniform and took the tram into town. I showed up at the TV2 offices and asked about the job vacancy, which it turned out wasn't vacant after all. But I refused to leave and they eventually let me do a trial shift as a studio runner.'

'What's that?'

'Someone who chats, serves coffee, makes sure people are miked up and takes the guests down to the studio at the right moment. Then off with the microphones once their pieces are done, and into a taxi they go. I got fed up after a while, started saying things I shouldn't have.'

'Like what?'

'A studio runner's supposed to reassure the guests. Make sure they perform, to use the sports jargon. But I started saying things that put them off. Have you seen that classic advert for the business school?'

'I'm not sure.'

'The one where there are people being made to feel nervous and out of their depth, who say "erm" before being reduced to their underwear by a puff of wind. It became my ambition to do that to people. Sometimes I was vicious. "Mind that step, a few people have broken a bone on that one." I said that to the new leader of the Pensioners' Association, who was already nervous. I once put off the prime minister so much that he offered me an internship.'

'So you turned down the prime minister?'

'I took time to think about it, and while I was thinking, along came Bertil Olsen.'

'Who's that?'

'The chief editor of TV2 *Sports Review*, but also the most frequently used handball expert on the breakfast show. He didn't turn up at the arranged time. I phoned him, waking him up at his hotel, then managed to rearrange the transmission schedule and organise things so that he could be on air before the 8 o' clock news bulletin. I think he was having a few problems with his boss at that time, and he was grateful I sorted it out for him. So grateful that he gave me the chance to be a reporter on *Sports Review*.'

'How come?'

'Between you and me, being a blonde woman is quite an advantage when you've got to interview male sports personalities,' said Benedikte, making a movement with her right ankle. Steinar noticed her ankles were bare above a pair of spotted pink and black high-heel sandals.

'Really?' said Steinar.

'The only problem is that we have to cover all kinds of sport. You've got no idea how much we have to look into some trivial stuff, sports that should be forgotten and that would be forgotten if a couple of Norwegian idiots hadn't found out that they were able to win at them. Not that hard when nobody else is taking part.'

'What's the worst?' asked Steinar.

'Skateboarding.'

'Skateboarding?'

'We did an in-depth report on Norwegian skaters. Everything from how many inches their trousers should sag to the special vocabulary on the skating scene. But the worst thing is that skating is so dull. We filmed skateboarders hunched over like ice hockey players, pretending they had wind in their hair, while our cameraman strolled along next to them. And then those lousy tricks, all of which are variations on jumping a couple of inches before landing back on the board. "Skate or die" is an easy decision, if you ask me.'

'So how did you go on to become an anchor?' asked Steinar. He liked hearing her stories. It helped him to relax. He still didn't want her to go digging into his past, but his fear was balanced by his curiosity, he wanted to get to know her better.

'It was a report on Birkebeinerrennet, the big cross-country ski marathon, that gave me my big break. I met a chemistry professor who explained how harmful ski wax is for the environment. As a former member of Young Friends of the Earth, I hit the roof. Tonnes of dangerous chemicals are left in the woods because business executives on their way to Lillehammer want to show that they're younger than it says on their passports. Then I got the manager of a well-known Norwegian company to promise that he'd never take part in the race again and would make sure his employees only took part if they weren't using ski wax, which caused a bit of an outcry.'

'Why?'

'Because the story was based on the idea that skiing could be harmful. Norway's sacred cow. Our religion. There's not much that means more to Norway than skiing does. But skiing was just an irritation at TV2 because it was the state broadcaster NRK's territory. For me, that story led to a promotion.'

'Chemicals might have something to do with the Golden case too,' said Steinar as Benedikte sat back a little. She immediately leant over the table again.

'Go on,' she said.

'I've got a friend who's a doctor with a professional interest in synthetic turf. According to him, there are major health risks linked to the use of artificial grass pitches.'

'Such as?'

'He mentioned MRSA, allergies, cancer.' Steinar noticed his words were making Benedikte uncomfortable. 'Is something wrong?'

Benedikte scratched her brow, shook her head. 'It's just that I hate hospitals. The very thought of how hospitals smell makes me retch, but carry on.'

'Another friend of mine has been admitted to hospital with lung cancer. My doctor friend Bjørnar is certain that he contracted it from an indoor artificial pitch, having been exposed to various contaminants over the years.'

'Let's go back to you and the documentary,' said Benedikte.

'Did you show any of it to the police?' asked Steinar, as Benedikte turned paler.

'Why should I? I'm looking for a story.'

'I don't trust the police,' said Steinar. He took a sip of the wine, which was going straight to his head. He wasn't used to drinking, at least not that early in the day and not having been out the previous evening.

Benedikte leant forward, looked him in the eyes and asked: 'Bad experience?'

'I think we're all like that. We're indoctrinated,' said Steinar.

'Indoctrinated?' asked Benedikte.

'It starts early. Just look at Postman Pat and Noddy.'

'What are you talking about?'

'Haven't you seen them?'

'I'm not sure, but what have they got to do with the police?'

'They depict the police as idiots. In *Postman Pat* there's PC Selby. He sleeps in his police car in the middle of the day. In one episode he can't do anything because he's lost his pencil. Pat has to remember everything for him and, as if that weren't enough, he cheats in a go-cart race against children. He uses a car with an engine, but that's not allowed! Then, in *Noddy's Toyland Adventures*, Mr Plod forgets to lock up the jail, and the way he investigates the theft of some pieces of cake is shocking.'

'I'm sorry, but I haven't seen those ones,' she said.

'What about *Pippi Longstocking*? Surely all girls have seen that. The police officers Kling and Klang. They try to arrest Pippi, an eight- or nine-year-old girl, to put her in a children's home, but they can't catch her. They also lose their bike to thieves and just cause trouble. Do you remember them?'

'Of course I remember Pippi, but maybe not all the details.'

'The point is that we learn early. Postman Pat's always up "early in the morning, just as day is dawning", Fireman Sam's "the hero next door", but the police are totally incompetent. The message is clear: we've got to fend for ourselves. The police are idiots.'

Benedikte smiled, then fell silent. Her eyes were sparkling green, a colour that reminded him of Glasgow Celtic. It felt like looking into them for too long would burn him. Her eyes pierced him as she leant closer, leaving him no escape.

'The police might be idiots,' she said, 'but Pippi's not. Pippi's tough, she gets straight to the point. She's not afraid to ask difficult questions. I think Pippi grew up to be a journalist. I like Pippi. I'm a fan. So enough of this bullshit. Why did you show up in a documentary about Golden? And why do you refuse to tell me why you stopped playing?'

Steinar stood up, he wasn't ready for this. He wasn't ready to tell her everything.

'I'm sorry,' he said. 'I...'

He ran out. He'd just remembered the most important thing of all, and he'd have to owe her for the lunch, this couldn't wait.

He ran across the street as fast as he could and up to the nearest taxi. He gave the driver the address and told him to step on it. The driver did his best, but the traffic ground to a halt at Carl Berners Plass. The new junction was completely jammed by a dislocated bendy bus. Steinar paid, jumped out and started running. He sprinted through the park in Torshovdalen with the tough climb towards Sinsen Station, on through the underpass below the ring road, over the grass to the path through Muselunden and up to the gate.

He leant on his knees for a few seconds, got his breath back and went through the gate. Jenna, the 22-year-old Swedish assistant, looked at Steinar disapprovingly, tapping her finger on her watch. When she opened her mouth, she spoke with a dialect that could have belonged to Pippi Longstocking herself, but her temper came from somewhere else. Still, all Steinar's agitation vanished when a two-and-a-half-year-old bundle of energy came running along with outstretched arms, shouting.

'Daaaaaddy.'

Part 3

23 July

Arild Golden never went more than two days without exercise. He laced up his shoes and went jogging through Smithfield, heading south towards St Paul's Cathedral. He then followed the Thames east, trawling his way through the streets of Whitechapel, then back to the west and his starting point, the Zetter Hotel in Clerkenwell.

Golden always stayed there when he was in London. It was an area with small cafés, advertising agencies, innovative restaurants and a wealth of interesting options for jogging routes. He loved jogging along the street and discovering a new neighbourhood. Besides, in this part of London he was spared having to bump into half-drunk Norwegian football fans digging to find out who he was going to sell next.

He took a shower, put on his suit trousers and shirt but left his jacket and tie in his room. He went downstairs to reception and into the hotel restaurant. The Everton chairman, James Sterling, was sitting there waiting.

Sterling was the complete opposite of Golden, as unfit as it was possible to be, and Golden wondered what had attracted him to the world of sport. Golden had pseudonyms for everybody in his work notes, and Sterling was referred to as 'Mr Gastric Bypass', but Sterling was also the executive ultimately in charge of Everton's finances.

Golden sat down, shook Sterling's hand across the table and ordered a bottle of water from the waiter.

'So, Mr Golden, will I be getting any money this time?' asked Sterling.

'Of course not.'

'Come on, how much longer are you going to use this against me?'

Golden felt nothing for the man but pure disgust. Not that this mattered at all in terms of business, of course. Sterling was one of two men he had to control in order to push through Diesen's transfer, but he felt no need to tread carefully with the man.

'They were under age,' he said. The pictures that Golden's partner had obtained were extremely revealing, what you could call perfect blackmail material, and Sterling had not done nearly enough for them to be handed over to him.

Sterling leant so far back he was practically horizontal in his chair. His voice trembled just a little as he spoke.

'But I wasn't to know that.'

'They were pretty girls. And I'm sure it's hard to distinguish a 15-year-old Ukrainian from one who's 20-something. But that's still what they were, 15 years old. And the pictures, they're extremely eye-opening. I just wonder whether it's the Sun or the Mirror who would offer the most.'

'I'm so ashamed about it. I would do anything to have it undone.'

'That won't make the girls any older.'

'How long are you going to punish me for?'

'Don't think of it as punishment. You're getting an outstanding player, after all.'

'Terribly overpriced, I suppose.'

'I've got three demands,' said Golden, leaning towards Sterling. 'Firstly, you'll support the transfer wholeheartedly. You've seen Diesen and you're convinced he's the man for you. Secondly, all the money will go via the Golden Boys office in Guernsey. None of it is to be transferred directly to the Norwegian club. And, finally, I'll act as Everton's official representative when we sign the papers on 1 August.'

As usual, everything would remain unwritten until the official signing.

In Shadow and in Sunlight

Steinar had taken Junior swimming on a Sunday at Tøyenbadet once before. They weren't about to go again. It had been so packed with people that it was impossible to stay in the water in any other position than vertical. Whichever way they'd tried to lie back, somebody was blocking them.

The theatre, cinema or soft play were the other options. Soft play would mean jumping around for three hours but, for some strange reason, Junior never got tired. He didn't need to go to bed earlier after an outing like that, and neither did it make him less active before bedtime. It really only acted as a warm-up.

The theatre was his favourite, especially the puppet theatre in the old tram depot at Torshov. But Junior had already seen the current play twice, while the cinema only had 3D films, and Junior refused to wear the glasses.

The boy toddled past Steinar with his hands thrust deep into his trouser pockets. He sighed, bowing his head towards the ground. Any further now and he might tip over.

'What do you want to do, then?' asked Steinar.

Junior looked up at his father and shrugged, sending his shoulders almost unnaturally far up towards his ears.

Steinar had decided as early as 1986 that, if he ever had a son, he'd name him after the Brazilian midfielder. Now it was Steinar who sighed.

'Shall we play football?' he asked.

'Yeah!' shouted Junior, jumping for joy. Steinar had the feeling that whatever he'd said after 'shall we', Junior would've shown just as much enthusiasm.

'Come along with Daddy,' said Steinar. They went to the basement door. Steinar opened it, switched on the light and looked down the steep, slippery stairs. Why hadn't he put down carpet, or at least some strips of tape to stop them sliding? He put on a pair of trainers and carried Junior down.

Steinar had taken over the house from his parents a few months before Junior was born. They thought it was nice that the next generation of the Brunsvik family would grow up there. It was also a matter of necessity, as Steinar's mother had a rheumatic disorder that meant she had to spend much of the year in a warmer climate. The bartering over their large flat in Calahonda, in southern Spain, had put another dent in Steinar's savings.

In the basement, there were tins of paint that had been there for 20 years. There were unpacked tools, and rolled-up architectural plans for a kitchen extension. All part of various projects that Steinar's father liked to plan but never had the energy to see through.

Over in the corner was a padlocked storage room made out of light-coloured wood. Steinar's father had eaten humble pie and got a joiner to put it up after years of nagging from Steinar's mother.

The key was in a crack in the wall down by the floor. Steinar bent down and teased it out. He moved his hand over the woodwork, put the key in the padlock and turned it. Junior had never been in the storage room and held on tight to Steinar's trouser-leg.

On one wall was a clothes drier, on which hung all the shirts Steinar had got in exchange after UEFA cup matches, internationals and decisive league matches. There were also football shirts going right-back to when Steinar was a little boy. He took down an old Brazil shirt and put it on Junior. It fit him.

Straight in front of them was a bookcase. There were scrapbooks marked by year: one for each year up to 2002. One shelf was dedicated to programmes from matches Steinar had played. Steinar had never sent any of them home, and his parents hadn't visited him that often either.

On their left hung the football boots, which also spanned the years up to his final season. Steinar took down a pair of Adidas Copa Mundial boots. The leather was soft. They'd been polished regularly.

'Look Daddy, a ball,' said Junior, who had his head buried in a large bag. He took out the deflated leather ball and went out of the room. Steinar checked the bag's contents, finding several more balls. Some small, worn-out plastic balls from his childhood, some tennis balls he used to juggle with, and a match ball from the Champions League clash with Hamburg in 2000, in which Steinar scored a hat trick and was given the ball to take home.

A loud clang tore Steinar away from his nostalgia. He ran out of the room and saw that Junior had hit the snow shovel, sending it crashing to the ground. Junior looked down.

'Sorry,' he said.

'It's alright,' said Steinar, putting back the shovel. Then he went to fetch a more suitable small plastic ball. He gave it to Junior and started to pile up the old paint tins into two stacks. Then he put an unused Jordan paintbrush extender over the top.

'Can you get it in the middle there?' asked Steinar, pointing.

Junior got the ball ready but, because the basement floor sloped down towards the drain in the middle, it started rolling away. He tried again. The floor was rough, so if he managed to put the ball down carefully enough, it might just work. Steinar watched him without interfering. Junior concentrated intensely, and eventually the ball stayed still.

He then took two steps back. His little body began to shiver. He ran towards the ball and closed his eyes just as he kicked it. The ball flew into the bottom of one of the stacks of paint tins, hitting it on the inside, and trundling into the makeshift goal.

'Goooooal!' shouted Junior, running around with his hands in the air.

Who taught him that? Who'd given the boy such a clear idea of what a goal was?

Steinar went back into the storage room. He fetched the smallest pair of boots. They fit Junior's feet perfectly.

'Let's try it on the lawn,' he said, carrying Junior, as well as a couple of plastic balls, out into the sunshine.

Football Xtra

'Arild Golden's death has left a power vacuum in Norwegian football. Who'll take his place?' asked Benedikte, looking at the panel on that day's edition of *Football Xtra*. There were two former Tippeligaen players, another who'd played professionally in England and a recently sacked top-division manager.

Her question was aimed at nobody in particular, and nobody chose to answer. Benedikte continued, but turning to face the man who'd once played in England.

'One of Golden's core business areas was developing astroturf pitches. Some people think the expansion in astroturf has gone too far. What's your opinion?'

'What do you mean?'

'Well, you've played in England where all the matches are played on real grass. Do you think synthetic grass will ever be on a par as an alternative?'

'The only thing that worries me about astroturf is global warming.'

'Global warming?'

'Because astroturf gets warmer than grass does, so that means the whole planet gets warmer, doesn't it?'

Benedikte nodded. He might conceivably have a point in that replacing large areas of grass with astroturf also meant less CO_2 would be absorbed. But how do you follow up an answer like that?

She heard a brief order in her earpiece: 'Pass to Tromsø now.'

'Something's happened up at Alfheim Stadion in Tromsø. Over to you, Stig Nilsen.'

'Fucking hell!'

'Stig, you're live on air.'

'I know, but can you fucking believe that idiot of a referee's awarded a penalty? Please excuse me if I'm being unfair by calling a referee an idiot, but come on, he must be totally fucking retarded.'

The last time Tromsø played at home, Nilsen had used the word 'dick' three times in some form or another within a 40-second item. It was only because of the numerous texts and e-mails they received about how 'genuine' and 'down-to-earth' he was that he was still on the air.

'I've never seen a more useless ref. That guy must have both eyes and half of his head shoved up his own arse. I mean, that so-called foul happened five yards out of the box. And there wasn't a bloody soul anywhere near. But wouldn't you believe it, it looked as if he'd been shot with a bazooka right in the forehead. Any normal ref would've given him a yellow card for diving and that would've been it, but no, this ref's given a fucking penalty. Sick bastard!'

The live pictures on the monitor on the studio floor showed the players crowding round the referee. It would take some time before the penalty could be taken, so Benedikte asked the studio guests if they thought it was a penalty. The interruption gave Bertil Olsen the chance to remind Stig Nilsen yet again about where he should sit. All the reporters should have the stadium in the background and look straight into the camera while they were live. That made for the best picture, but of course it did make it difficult for them to see what was actually happening in the match while they were doing their report. The penalty kick was near at hand. Benedikte handed over to Alfheim Stadion and, as expected, found herself staring straight into the back of Stig Nilsen's neck.

'Stig, Stig?!' she said. She glanced over at the live pictures. The player scored.

'Shit, shit, shit, shit, shit... shit...'

That last, meaningful 'shit' hung in the air. Benedikte handed over to the Color Line Stadion in Ålesund.

Then the break.

There was a message on Benedikte's screen from the controller of TV2. 'Get Nilsen to calm down before the second half!'

It was Benedikte who'd got to know Nilsen and had recommended him to TV2. He was her responsibility. He was like a little brother getting into trouble, one who didn't quite fit in, wasn't managing with school or life in general. That's what people from his particular background were like. Stig Nilsen was an ex-goalkeeper.

He'd played 15 seasons at Tromsø, turning down good offers from abroad three times. He was an eternal hero in the northern city, the gateway to the Arctic, and his intention was to follow his playing career with another as the club's goalkeeping coach.

His plans had changed suddenly a year before. In a huddle for a corner, Vålerenga's centre-back Marius Bjartmann had ended up on top of Nilsen, who landed with his knee in a very unfortunate position. Several ligaments, his menisci and other cartilage had been seriously damaged. Nilsen couldn't kick a ball anymore, and the only thing that still worked was his mouth.

'Hi there,' said Benedikte when she had him on the line.

'Have they been on at you again? Can't we just say that we've had a chat? That you've told me off and I've promised to pull myself together?'

'But can you, though? Can you tone it down a couple of notches?'

'Depends on the ref.'

'Give it a try. By the way, while I've got you on the line, do you know Steinar Brunsvik?'

'I knew him. We played together on the national youth team. Best player I've ever seen.'

'Do you know why he quit?'

'Can't say I do. What I remember most of all is that he was nuts!'

'What?'

'I've never even seen an animal with a temper like Brunsvik's.'

The guests came back into the studio after the advertising break, and the make-up artist, Karianne, gave them all an extra layer of powder. After a few rounds of questions, Benedikte handed back to Stig Nilsen in Tromsø, just as his old team's Finnish captain and midfield anchor, Mattis Niemi, caught his right foot on the astroturf.

'Oh shit. Mattis has injured himself. It looked bloody painful and I know all about what it's like to get injured on this pitch. One wrong step and you slide about like a cunt out there.'

Benedikte took over from the studio to discuss what a possible injury to Niemi might mean for Tromsø, but then a symbol on the screen started flashing. Something else had happened in Tromsø.

'Now the Tromsø lads are down to 10 men on the pitch, and Odd's just scored again. It's a scandal. The astroturf's new this year. I'm damned if I know how many times they've replaced the turf, but it just seems like they get a crapper brand every bloody time. I played all those wonderful years on proper grass here at Alfheim. Never a single bloody injury. Then along comes the astroturf, and I get injured. And now my damn ligaments flare up more often than seagulls shit on the hot dog stand. Poor Mattis. Bloody fucking astroturf. There'll soon be more synthetic grass than real grass in this country. Give it another couple of years and there'll be sheep grazing on the rubbish too. Or maybe that's where polyester comes from?'

Benedikte let Nilsen carry on. She was thinking about artificial turf and injuries, but also illnesses. And then she remembered the hospital. Those panicked trips there in the middle of the night. The injections. The nausea. And the stress. All those white coats running. At night they looked like ghosts.

She heard a voice shouting in her head but she didn't know what it was. Stig Nilsen got to carry on swearing for a few more seconds until Benedikte realised it was Bertil Olsen's voice in her ear: 'Geeet hiiiim ooooff! Nooow!'

She pulled herself together and said: 'We apologise for the poor sound quality from Tromsø.'

The opposing team, Odd, had brought their score up to 4–0.

At that same moment, a piece of breaking news scrolled along the bottom of the screen: 'Police have arrested a man suspected of the murder of Arild Golden.'

Upside Down

'What a nutter!'

Steinar pointed at the TV screen and at the back of his old teammate Stig Nilsen's head. He'd been trying to watch *Football Xtra* with his two-and-a-half-year-old propeller of a son, who was showing no signs of tiredness after three hours of intensive football playing in the garden.

Steinar felt uneasy as he sat down in front of the screen. He'd actually been feeling uneasy the whole time since he'd abandoned Benedikte at the restaurant, but when she started speaking about the Golden case on TV he only felt worse.

The plastic balls had ended up indoors. One of them was in front of Steinar's right foot. He stretched out, slipped down in his chair and stretched out some more. He just managed to get hold of the top of the ball to roll it closer. He sat back up straight. Then he put both of his feet on the floor and brought them together quickly from each side, his big toes hitting the ball at the same time, sending it shooting up into the air. He kicked it gently with his right foot, then with his left, before twisting his body in the chair so that the next kick came from the outside of his heel. The ball arced up high, almost reaching the ceiling before landing straight down in Steinar's waiting hands. He let the ball roll a few times over the bones in his right wrist, then he threw it up gently into the air.

Steinar thought back to what Vlad Vidić had said.

'Make sure you lose.'

And it was easier than Steinar would think. A sloppy backwards pass, a penalty, an own-goal. It didn't matter how.

Everything Steinar had trained for, everything he'd done until then, everything that had been imprinted in his head by Ståle Jakobsen was being challenged by four small words: 'Make sure you lose.'

Steinar had never thought that anybody would be able to make him quit football. That was a decision he'd make for himself. He'd seen several times the desperation of players who were forced to quit because of injuries; he'd seen grown men cry. But Vlad Vidić had put him in an impossible dilemma.

Junior came running in from the left, dragging a wooden dog on a string. He had his head turned towards the dog and was making straight for Steinar's footrest. Steinar gently put his foot by Junior's stomach. He slowed him down and hoisted him in the air, turning him upside down. He then ran a circuit of the living room with the boy, stopping and to blow a raspberry on the boy's bare belly. Junior laughed until he was gasping for air.

Steinar looked at the mantelpiece and the pictures of Junior's christening. The pronounced birth-mark on his forehead – the stork's bite-mark, as they'd called it at the hospital – had almost vanished. Now it only appeared when the boy became really angry.

Steinar had argued with Mette about the christening. He didn't want Junior to be baptised but Mette was determined and forced the point by citing her parents' religious background, which was far-fetched at best. Steinar eventually gave in on the condition that he wouldn't have to set foot in church himself. He'd taken the christening photos, but only on the church steps.

Mette had run off only a few weeks after that. Everything that had been so important was no more. She never said straight out that having a baby was a mistake, just that there was so much of the world she hadn't seen. The next he heard was a postcard from Peru. She left Steinar and Junior to fend for themselves.

The pictures also reminded him that he didn't take enough photos or videos. Junior was growing up at what had to be record speed. It seemed impossible that any other child could've grown that much in so little time, and he wasn't doing nearly a good enough job of documenting it. Steinar had even bought a new SLR camera. He had a small compact camera too, as well as the one on his mobile, but he also wanted to take really good pictures. He couldn't remember the last time he'd taken out that monstrous camera with its long, heavy lens.

The phone rang. Steinar held Junior upside down in one hand and the phone in the other.

'Hello.'

'This is Oslo Police District here. Am I speaking with Steinar Brunsvik?'

'Yes.'

'We've arrested a man named Taribo Shorunmo. He's being charged with the murder of Arild Golden.'

'And?'

'He'd like you to be his lawyer.'

The Black Adder

Benedikte looked over the partially green turf in Ullevaal Stadion. Even now, in the middle of summer, the pitch looked like a salad bar Jamie Oliver had given up on. If there was one place in Norway that should have astroturf, it was the national stadium.

Boltedal, the journalist from *Dagens Næringsliv*, estimated that Arild Golden and Golden Boys earned up to 1 million kroner for every new synthetic grass pitch. On top of that came the income from the so-called multi-use games areas and the seven-a-side pitches, as well as the constant need to replace worn-out surfaces. It was obvious to Benedikte to seek out an insider in the NFF, the Football Association of Norway.

Birgir Holme, the NFF's facilities manager, opened the door to his office and waved her in. Holme had broad cheek-bones that blocked his nerves, so large parts of his face appeared void of expression. He was dressed completely in black, from his sweater to his shoes and trousers. Benedikte shook his hand, which was cold and clammy.

'You were a little vague when you asked for a meeting,' said Holme after they'd sat down.

'I'm working on a background story about the development of training facilities at Norwegian clubs.'

'I hope I can be of some help.'

'Can you tell me about the number of astroturf pitches that are being built?'

'We're aiming to build a hundred new ones each year,' said Holme.

'Does that include multi-use games areas and seven-a-side pitches?'

'On top of those. We're talking about a hundred full-size pitches a year.'

'How often do the pitches have to be replaced?'

'I don't actually know,' said Holme.

'Why aren't you listening to the people using the astroturf, the players?'

'What do you mean?'

''96 per cent of top Norwegian players claim that the switch from real grass to synthetic leads to a greater risk of injuries.'

'No, no, no, there are studies showing that synthetic grass doesn't increase the risk of injuries.'

'And there are others showing the opposite to be true,' said Benedikte. 'Over 70 per cent of players claim that they've had injuries due to the artificial turf. Shouldn't you slow down the rate of expansion?'

'I repeat, our reports...'

'And what about the Finnish team that was used as a case study in one of those reports? Only their home matches, 13 games, were on astroturf. For the rest of the year they trained and played their matches on grass,' said Benedikte. This was only a rumour she'd picked up on, but Holme was looking guilty.

'But we live in Norway...'

'82 per cent of them report bad air quality around indoor pitches. They're complaining of headaches and respiratory problems.'

'Surveys...'

'Is there anything to prove the long-term effects of using astroturf? What happens to a child's knees, hips and back when he or she grows up after having been on it for hours every day?'

Holme squirmed as he sank deeper into his office chair.

'You don't know a thing about those effects, do you?' said Benedikte.

'As I said, we base our policy on studies showing that artificial turf doesn't cause any increase in injuries.'

'Studies carried out on the best artificial pitches, with professional players in clubs with full-time physiotherapists. What about the ones training on worn-out, rock-hard pitches? They're the most common type, after all. Has any research been done on them?'

'I don't know.'

'How much did Golden Boys make from astroturf?'

'They won a few tendering rounds, but...'

'Who else won them?'

'Er. I...'

Benedikte leant forward, resting her palms on Holme's desk, and asked another question. 'Who's making money out of astroturf now that Golden's dead?'

Definite Red Card

Steinar and Junior always took their time in the morning. Choosing your own working hours was one of the benefits of being self-employed, and anyway it was a non-issue with no clients. Steinar loved those quiet minutes while Junior sat calmly, focused on his bread and *prim* cheese spread.

It was a bit more of a problem at times when Steinar was busy, like today. He had to go to Oslo Police District's main custody centre, where his client was in a security cell. He should've been there the evening before, but he hadn't been able to get a babysitter. The time was ticking towards 09:20. Junior banged his fists rhythmically on the table.

'Mooore cheese!'

Steinar put his copy of *Aftenposten* down on the kitchen table before preparing another slice of bread. His mobile started vibrating and crept across the table, just like Junior's electronic toy insects did. Junior munched away while Steinar checked his phone. Four missed calls now. Steinar had put it on silent after he'd started his day having to say 'no comment' to an eager journalist from the news website *Nettavisen*. Now *Dagbladet*, *VG* and *Dagsavisen* had all been on the line, as well as the website *ABC Nyheter*. Steinar didn't want to talk to anybody until he'd met his client. He called for a taxi, made a packed lunch and helped Junior to put on a clean T-shirt.

On their short journey to the nursery, Steinar read more about the murder weapon. *Aftenposten* quoted 'police sources' when speculating about what might have caused those centimetre-deep wounds on Golden's neck. Meanwhile, Junior was singing 'Old MacDonald Had a Farm' at full blast in his ear. His mobile vibrated in his pocket yet again.

The taxi stopped at the gate. When Steinar went in carrying Junior, he was met by Jenna's reproachful look. What was it this time? Was it because they'd come by taxi? Jenna had jet-black hair, freckles and red lips, and always wore red tights. She looked like that German singer Lena who'd won Eurovision when it was held in Oslo's Fornebu Arena. But there was one big difference between Lena and Jenna: he still hadn't seen Jenna smile. Steinar pretended not to notice, partially turning his back to her as he entered the building sideways.

In the corridor, two young versions of Captain Hook sped past. Three princesses too. Steinar remembered the poster he'd seen the previous Friday for 'Carnival in August'. He understood the reasoning that it was better to have Carnival in the summer, so the children wouldn't get colds from wearing thin fancy dress in February. Junior was the only one who wasn't dressed up.

Steinar helped Junior change from his outdoor shoes to his indoor ones and sat him down. By the time he let go, the boy had already managed to run three steps on his way to another room.

At 10:05, Steinar pressed the buzzer outside the green-tiled building in the Grønland area of the East End. He introduced himself and told them why he was there. He was let in and went through two doors and up to the counter, where he spoke with a dark-haired administrator who seemed too delicate for the job. He was more Tom Daley than Dirty Harry.

'Like I said, I'm here to meet my client, Taribo Shorunmo. Number one or number two?' asked Steinar, pointing at the meeting rooms allocated to lawyers.

'Take number two.'

Steinar went into the empty meeting room and waited.

The detainee was escorted in, wearing blue trousers and a green vest. He was extremely muscular, and the veins on his upper arms looked set to burst. His appearance was West African. They shook hands. The man sat down, folded his hands, rested his head on them and fixed his eyes on Steinar. His pupils could barely be distinguished from his dark brown irises. The white of his eyes was more yellow. There was something hypnotic about him.

Steinar spoke. 'Alright, so I'm Steinar Brunsvik, and I'll be your lawyer. I've been informed verbally that you're charged with voluntary manslaughter. I've requested the relevant files and expect to receive them shortly.'

'And I'm Taribo Shorunmo. Don't you remember me?'

'I saw you at the match at Nordre Åsen.'

'I was there watching my son, Stanley.'

'Is he your son? He's good.'

'Thanks. I saw you too. And I googled you later that evening. That's how I found out you were a lawyer. But I didn't think you saw me. You seemed too busy talking with that blonde woman. The one from TV.'

'I noticed you and your pal.'

'I was alone.'

'Okay.'

'But don't you remember me from before, then?' Taribo asked after a brief silence.

'Have we met each other before?'

'You met me here,' said Taribo, pointing at his ankle. '16 years ago. A crazy tackle. A definite red card but, guess what, the referee didn't even give us a free kick. You remember? The Norway Cup final. I was playing centre-back for Bayelsa United.'

Steinar had usually been a gentleman on the pitch, but he had black-outs when all his rage came at once. He was one of the very few players who'd been given more red cards than yellow ones. He could remember that they'd won the tournament, but he wasn't as clear about the tackle or the man sitting in front of him. He shook his head.

'I remember it as if it were yesterday,' Taribo went on. 'After we'd showered, I went with two other players across the fields at Ekebergsletta, down the hill and into the city centre. And that's where we stayed. We moved a bit around different parts of Oslo until we'd got a kind of network. Then one day I met Mona, from Kløfta. Stanley was born one year after that final.'

'Shame you weren't just as quick on the field,' said Steinar, immediately regretting it. 'Have you spoken with your teammates since then?'

'Sure, on Facebook. Several of them wish they'd dared to escape too, but the coach is still mad. And he's got my passport. He tried to sell it to me just last month.'

'Wow.'

'Nothing to be surprised about. Some parts of Nigeria are okay, but not mine. Foreign companies are robbing our oil, while we find ways to rob each other and everyone else.'

'You said that your coach has your passport. Haven't you got Norwegian citizenship?'

'Stanley was registered as Mona's son, with his father's identity unknown. As time went by, I didn't dare to apply for citizenship. One of our friends said that being an illegal immigrant would mean that my residency application would be torn up even if we had children, even if we got married.'

'You've got a point. What about the option of living together in Nigeria for a while and then applying for residency in Norway legally?'

'Far too risky. Bayelsa State is dangerous. Not just for a white woman: Stanley would've stood out too. Lighter shades of skin colour can lead to kidnapping. I would've had to sneak my way down there, but then there was still no guarantee that I'd make it back.'

'Is it really such a dangerous area?'

'How much do you follow Nigerian football?'

'Very little.'

'The same night that Bayelsa first won the championship, the captain was shot dead. If you run into the crazy ones, they don't ask. They just shoot.'

'So you stayed in Norway. What have you been doing?'

'We settled down in Holmlia and I did casual jobs. Carpentry, clearing snow, polishing floors, bricklaying. You name it. Nobody cared about work permits. So I've been here 15 years.'

'What about football?'

'I played a few matches in the Third Division with Oslo City, under a false name, but then another team, Strømgodset, started showing interest, and it became too risky. Football means supporting Stanley now. I know a lot of dads would say this, but Stanley's really gifted. He's got the best of both worlds. His physique's West African and his discipline's European,' said Taribo.

'I can see that,' said Steinar, pointing at Taribo's arms, although he doubted that the village Stanley's mother was from, Kløfta, could be the best of anything.

'This thing will take my son away from me for sure, you know. If I'm found guilty, it'll be prison. If not, I'll be sent to Nigeria. At least he can visit me in prison,' said Taribo.

'You need an experienced criminal lawyer. This is manslaughter we're talking about.'

'I'm going to end up in trouble anyway.'

'What do you want me for, then?'

'I want you to represent my son.'

'Your son?'

'I'm not going to be allowed letters or visitors. They've been talking about solitary confinement too. The only person I get to speak with is my lawyer, and a lawyer can also act as an agent, you know. I need a lawyer who knows his stuff about football.'

'Can't you just leave it until you're allowed letters and visitors again?'

'There's no time to lose. Stanley turns 15 on Sunday, and then he can sign a contract with an agent. I'm worried he could get tricked if he hasn't got his dad to look after him. I think that's why I'm in here. I think the police were tipped off about me to get me out of the way.'

'Tipped off? Who would do that?'

'That sneak of an agent, Ola Bugge. He came round to my place, but I sent him out. He's not a good man. Just another one trying to take my son.'

Steinar had heard countless stories of scams involving agents, especially targeted at African footballers. Stories that meant he never wanted to get involved in the business, but now, with a mega-talent like Stanley to sign and with his legal business not doing so well? He thought back to Stanley accelerating down the flank at Nordre Åsen.

Steinar's civil cases usually ended in out-of-court settlements, while his criminal cases had generally been of a less serious nature and involved pleading guilty. But he knew the procedures and he'd done the training.

'I spoke with the police. They said you'd already been questioned. Is that right?'

'Yes.'

'Why didn't you wait for a lawyer?'

'Why should I? I only answered a few simple questions.'

'Did you admit you were guilty?'

'No.'

'Okay. But if you want me to represent you, then listen to me.'

'My life's in ruins. It's my son that matters.'

Whore

Benedikte sat down with Ola Bugge in Burger King at Ullevaal Stadion. She'd treated him to a Whopper meal and hinted at a vague chance of an appearance on *Football Xtra*.

'How come you're listed on the electoral register as Alexander Bugge-Eriksen, yet your business card says Ola Bugge?' she asked.

'I thought it looked better to have a less pretentious name.'

'Why's that?'

'Most of my talent comes from the East End of Oslo, and the hyphen in my name seemed to snag on the last lamp-post every time I tried to cross over the river from the West End. Besides, all the biggest Norwegian agents over the years have had traditional Norwegian names like Lars, Leif, Per, Stig, Einar, Erik, Rune and, not least, Arild. Ola wasn't taken yet.'

'But neither Ola Bugge nor Alexander Bugge-Eriksen are licensed with the Football Association of Norway. So that means you're not even an agent, are you?'

'I am an agent, but if I want to sell a player, I need the assistance of someone who's licensed. The only difference is that I have to split some of the profit.'

'But you don't want to sell, do you? You're just going to take 1,000 kroner a month from every single player and pretend you're working,' said Benedikte.

'I want to sell players, it's just none of mine have been good enough.'

'So why did you let Golden take over your best ones, such as Otto Cana and Kalid Jambo?'

'He outmanoeuvred me,' said Bugge, sucking the mayonnaise off the end of one of his chips.

'How?'

'I was picked up by a chauffeur. It felt like I was being given a private audience, but most of all it felt like I was being given a chance. If I could get in with Golden Boys, then all the doors of the football world would open,' said Bugge.

'But Golden wasn't interested in you, was he?'

'He barely had time to look at me. He was on his exercise bike, wearing one of those T-Mobile shirts from the Tour de France.'

Golden was known to be an exercise addict and a distinguished participant in everything from cross-country ski races to the Oslo Marathon. Benedikte even remembered seeing a report on Golden taking part in the formidable mountain run at Skåla in western Norway.

Bugge continued: 'He was standing up on the pedals with his shirt half open, sweat running down his chest. Then he sat down in the saddle, looked at me and said: "Five minutes of slower pedalling now, that should be enough time to reach an agreement."'

'About what?'

'The price for Kalid and Otto's contracts,' said Bugge.

'And did you reach an agreement?'

'Four minutes later we stopped at 100,000 kroner. I had to relinquish all my rights to them. I signed and was escorted to the bus stop on the ring road.'

'100,000 kroner is good money.'

'Not really, but the incident taught me a few things about business and football,' said Bugge, unwrapping his cheeseburger.

'So are you after Stanley now?'

'He's the biggest talent in Norway. And I wouldn't even have to deal with all that passport mess that's usually involved with African players.'

'Passport mess?'

'Stanley's a Norwegian citizen. The really big talent is usually from African countries. And then you've got to work on their passports.'

'I still don't get what you mean.'

'In Africa, the players with the most talent stagnate when they hit 16. Their league systems are weak, and they haven't got the facilities or good coaches. Besides, it's illegal to transfer players from one continent to another before they reach 18. Ergo it's up to us agents to take the expense of buying new passports, so we can inflate their age and get them into Europe.'

'I thought you aimed to make them seem as young as possible.'

'Sooner or later, yes. When they're in their early twenties we need to bring them back down to 18. All clubs want to buy 18-year-olds.'

'And the 100,000 you got? I expect you used it to buy the rights to Stanley. Am I right?' asked Benedikte.

'All I gave him was a CD,' said Bugge.

'What CD?'

'Snoop Dogg.'

'Which one?'

'Can't remember the name. There was a blue picture on the cover.'

'*The Blue Carpet Treatment*? You went for the bargain section? You forked out all of 50 kroner. Just a guess, but you haven't nailed the rights yet, have you?'

'Hey, I didn't come here to be insulted. On the phone you said you could help me out with some screen time if I gave you the information you needed.'

'You've given me nothing of worth yet. Nothing that will help me to find out who might've killed Arild Golden.'

Bugge took a long look at Benedikte before he spoke again. 'I was sitting outside their flat at Holmlia yesterday when a young African boy knocked on my car window and tried to sell me a bike. I turned down the offer but carried on talking with him. For 500 kroner, he told me everything he knew about Stanley's family.'

'If you scratch my back, I'll scratch yours.'

'He told me a long story about Stanley's uncle, who thought he would become a pro too but was conned. His uncle had to live on the streets in Antwerp for years, until Stanley's dad went down there and rescued him.'

'On the streets, you say?'

'He'd been working as a whore.'

Golden Goal

Steinar sat in his office, reading through the arrest warrant and the charge sheet that the police prosecutor had faxed over. They'd also had a short telephone conversation in which he'd been told that the remand hearing would be the next day at 1 o' clock. The doorbell rang. Two cases in one day, or journalists who'd found their way to his office? He opened up.

Benedikte was wearing a beige top, a short, matching pleated skirt and brown high-heel sandals. She smiled. Did she like him? If so, would she still think the same if she knew the truth about him? Again Steinar looked at her for a little too long before he said anything, then eventually invited her inside.

She sat down and didn't even let Steinar get back into his chair before she started.

'How did you manage to get Taribo Shorunmo as a client?'

Steinar stopped short for a couple of seconds before he sat down.

'How...'

'Don't waste any thought on it, we get hold of information like that. I can guarantee that the papers are on the scent too.'

'Yeah,' said Steinar, 'I've had to give them "no comment" several times today.'

'But just explain to me how you managed to steal the most attractive and high-profile criminal case in Norway when, let's be honest, your business here in Sandaker isn't exactly booming.' Benedikte crossed her legs. The same combination of bare legs, sandals and chat. Steinar stood up and looked out of the window.

'I... er...'

'Relax. I'm here because we've got shared interests. We can help each other.'

'What do you mean?' asked Steinar.

'We both need Taribo Shorunmo to be innocent.'

'Why?'

'Wouldn't it make your job a bit easier if we found out somebody else had done it?' asked Benedikte.

'Of course. What's in it for you?'

'He's in custody. All of Norway knows that now, it's not news any more. So I'm going to keep working on it in the hope that he's innocent. I repeat, how did you get him as a client?'

There was something in what Benedikte was saying. He needed all the help he could get. He and Taribo didn't stand a chance on their own. Perhaps they could help each other, and perhaps it was worth taking a chance and trusting somebody. He told Benedikte about Taribo, starting with their first meeting at a Norway Cup final and finishing with Taribo asking Steinar to be Stanley's agent. He didn't give her any sensitive information, and the fact that he was going to act as Stanley's agent was not something that could be kept secret, or that he had to keep secret anyway. An agent had to work in the open market when a player was on offer, after all. Or was he just defending himself? Was he being unprofessionally open just because Benedikte Blystad was so beautiful?

'So it's a double jackpot for you, then,' said Benedikte.

Steinar had read through the rules that applied to agents. It was a gold mine. There were no regulations as to how much an agent could ask for. In a country like Norway, where most things were regulated, and where an employer couldn't even give his employees a bike without the gift being taxed, it was strange that it wasn't subject to certain rules. An agent could charge anything. 10 per cent, 50 per cent, or even 100 per cent of a 15-year-old's pay.

Stanley appeared to be a future international star. If his mother was unschooled in the world of football, like his father Taribo said, then there was basically nothing to stop somebody in Steinar's position from putting together a contract securing himself an enormous future income. But Steinar didn't want to exploit the situation, he wanted to have what he saw as reasonable compensation for work carried out, and Benedikte's words 'double jackpot' hurt him.

'Being Stanley's agent makes me vulnerable too.'

'How?'

'Stanley might have been the reason that Golden was killed.'

'Is there that much money involved with such a young boy?'

'Agents who are willing to exploit the lack of restrictions could end up making several million a year from representing Stanley. And of course there are people who would kill for that.'

'Are you thinking about Ola Bugge?' asked Benedikte.

'Taribo brought him up as a possible suspect. Taribo also thought it was Bugge who'd reported him to the police, so that he could sign a contract with Stanley without any interference. Who else do you think might have a motive for killing him?'

'Per Diesen. I've got several sources who claim that Arild Golden was having a relationship with Sabrina,' said Benedikte.

'Jealousy is a classic motive, just like money. Any others?'

'Bugge told me that Taribo had a brother, and the rumours are that he used to be a street prostitute in Antwerp.'

'A prostitute?'

'Apparently Taribo found out about it after a number of years, went down there and fetched him.'

'But what's that got to do with Golden?'

'We know that Golden's been an agent for more than 20 years, and that he's been working in Africa for just as long. Could Taribo's brother have been an early transfer for the Golden Boys system? A transfer that went wrong and led to him ending up on the streets? It happens all the time. We're talking about thousands of African footballers living like this.'

'I'd go for revenge as a possible motive too.'

'We've also got the other Norwegian footballers. In the top division alone, Golden Boys has the rights to 134 players. It's obvious that some of them might feel passed over or poorly treated.'

'134 players. Are you sure about that? How on earth is one agent supposed to keep a personal eye on all of them?' asked Steinar.

'All agents work on a principle of "profit in numbers". By signing as many players as possible you increase your chances that one of them might excel and make you a profit.'

'So do you think that a player might have missed out on some income and taken Golden's life?'

'That's one possible slant. And money takes us further along the list. Kåre Jan Vasshaug, the TV2 news anchor, gave me a tip on how he used to approach a story. He always went looking for the money. If it was raining in the Sahara, you could bet that an oil company was making money by disturbing the ecosystem. Somewhere or another there's always a trail of money,' said Benedikte.

'And then there's the question of where there's the most money to be found.'

'That brings us back to astroturf. A hundred new pitches every year, pitches that have to be replaced every five years. Millions of kroner each time, millions that soon turn into billions. Golden had secured work through all kinds of channels. He was making money out of players, coaches, clubs, national teams, sponsorship, TV rights, but perhaps most of all out of astroturf. And since I met Birger Holme, the facilities manager of the NFF, my suspicions in that area haven't exactly diminished.'

Steinar had visited the increasingly frail Ståle Jakobsen again that morning, so he was keen to investigate that avenue further. That trail might provide some answers about who'd killed Golden as well as who'd slowly been killing Jakobsen. Besides, it might divert Benedikte's attention away from his own past.

'We've got to follow up on the artificial turf. That way, we'll find out who might stand to gain most now that Golden's not got a slice of the cake any more.'

'Speaking of cake, you owe me a dessert from last time. Let's go for a walk,' said Benedikte, getting up.

They strolled to a nearby café, Åpent Bakeri, where they pushed through a pile of pushchairs and found a table. Benedikte bought a croissant and a latte, Steinar made a fool of himself by ordering toast. It had to be made so he had to sit there keeping the conversation going while she ate.

Had Benedikte reminded him of the dessert because they hadn't finished their conversation at the Baltazar Restaurant, was that where she was heading? How long would it take before she started digging into his past again?

'Have you heard that Jonathan Franzen's working on a new book?' Steinar said.

He'd been skimming through the culture pages in *Aftenposten* and had seen a short note about it. In actual fact, Steinar hadn't read any of Franzen's previous books, nor had he any intention of reading his new one, but that was the kind of thing people chatted about.

Benedikte didn't answer.

Steinar was about to say something else when she leant forward over the table. She dried her mouth on a white napkin and said: 'I don't give a shit about Franzen. Why do you want to talk about him?'

'Huh?' said Steinar.

'It makes me suspicious. I'm starting to wonder why you ran off and why you change the topic to trivial things like Noddy, Pippi or Franzen.'

Steinar glanced at the counter, looking for his toast. At the till, a woman with far too many tattoos was playing with her hair.

'Either you're hiding something and are directly involved in the Golden case,' Benedikte continued, 'or you're nervous because you like me. So, let me ask, did you have anything to do with the murder of Arild Golden?'

'Of course not.'

'So this has to do with you wanting to sleep with me.'

'I...'

'Let's nip this in the bud.'

'How...'

'I think we've got to sleep together.'

'Wh...'

'You've got to stop stammering. Let's make a deal. You stop hiding things from me, we'll work together to find out who killed Golden, then we'll have sex. That way you won't have to think about pulling me as we go along. Consider me pulled. How does that sound?'

After some back and forth, Steinar stuttered: 'I look forward to it.'

Benedikte crossed her arms and leant back, melting the whole bakery with her warm smile.

Part 4

17 July

'I've made a breakthrough, Per,' said Golden.

'Have you?' Diesen put down a programme from the 1982 FA Cup and sat down again. He leant forward against the sleek mahogany desk. Golden put his right ankle up on his left knee and brought his fingertips together to form a pyramid. He always enjoyed these moments when he was just about to tell a young footballer what lay in store for him. It was the one pure moment of his life as a football agent.

'But before we get to that, how are things going with Sabrina?'

'Fine, but don't torture me. Tell me about the breakthrough.'

'Everton have registered their interest.'

'Everton?'

'If everything goes according to plan, you'll be a Premier League player starting from August.'

There was something symbolic about them each sitting on opposite sides of the desk, Golden thought. Because that's how it was supposed to be, in the eye of the law. And only like that. A football agent could only be on one side; as the player's agent, he couldn't represent either of the clubs. But in reality the trick was actually being in control on every side of the negotiating table.

Vålerenga wouldn't be a problem. Golden had sold players for the club time after time, and when he told them that he would lead the negotiations on their behalf, that's what happened. Like most Norwegian clubs, Vålerenga were in deep financial straits and needed to make a sale, so they weren't concerned about details like appointing an English lawyer.

For practical reasons Golden would officially be acting for Everton in the negotiations. He was licensed with the NFF, and they didn't have the courage to investigate what an English club was doing. In Norway, they had access to clubs as they knew the executives personally, but they had no such power in England.

The problem was the player. That's why Arild Golden handed Per Diesen a contract in triplicate.

'What's this?' asked Diesen.

'It's your agent's contract. We haven't needed one before, but we do now. We don't want any practical problems in connection with the signing. Everyone has to have one. Of course you and I trust each other, Per, but the NFF and Everton want all the papers in order.'

Nobody in the NFF had asked for such a contract, let alone anybody from Everton. Golden wanted it for himself. Regardless of how long he'd been working with Diesen and how well he knew him, Golden didn't trust anybody when it came to the big money.

'If you think it's best,' said Diesen, signing the contract where Golden had put a small 'X'.

'One copy's for you, one's for me, and I'll deliver the other to the NFF.'

After Diesen had left, Golden took down a trophy that a tired former Lillestrøm player had sold him a few years ago. Golden had to protect himself in every way possible, he thought, with the contracts in his hands.

Now Diesen would think he couldn't allow himself to be represented by anybody else. He would only deal with Golden as his agent, he was bound by his contract. A footballer would never wonder why it was the agent's lawyer who signed the papers in any potential transfer; he would only be happy that such details could be dealt with for him. And he would never check whether Golden actually delivered the papers to the NFF.

The people Golden had to protect himself against were those who might find a paper trail. That meant the British or Norwegian broadsheets, but it could even get as serious as Økokrim, the Norwegian authority that dealt with financial crime, so he had to make sure the paper trail was cold. Golden had to make sure that he was only listed as Everton's representative in the negotiations.

He tore up the contracts and stuffed them in the trophy. Then he poured some lighter fluid on top and lit it. He turned the cup, moving the pieces of paper about, and let them burn until there were only ashes left.

Walkover

At noon on the dot the case documents were ready at reception on the sixth floor of Oslo Courthouse. Steinar looked at the man on duty and thanked him.

'No problem,' he replied, holding the pile of papers tightly. 'Would you like the closed files too?'

If Steinar wanted access to those, he'd have to sign an agreement that he wouldn't share the information with anybody, not even his client. Steinar had heard of others in his profession who wouldn't take closed documents for that reason. Personally, he wanted to know as much as possible and saw laziness as the reason many lawyers chose not to see the closed files. He signed the confidentiality agreement.

The files were several hundred pages in total, and Steinar had 58 minutes. In that time he would have to tease out the most important points and meet with his client in the basement. He went into the canteen and sat down at a free table.

His body recognised the feeling of pressure from his days as a professional footballer. He used to play better in important games. If he had to take a decisive penalty he might miss, but he never hesitated.

He rushed through the pile of documents. The police had indeed questioned Taribo before Steinar had been able to speak with him. Taribo had admitted to them that he'd met Golden at his office on the day he was killed. They'd had a disagreement over money at the meeting, particularly in terms of the percentage that Golden would get out of Stanley's future deals. The police also had a witness who claimed Taribo had threatened to kill Golden. This had allegedly happened in the toilets at Bislett Stadion during the second round cup match between Skeid and Vålerenga.

The documents also included a letter from the Norwegian Directorate of Immigration confirming that Taribo didn't have a residence permit, and a report on a seizure made by the police. They'd taken a weapon that, according to the reports and pictures taken by the first response unit, could be a potential murder weapon.

In order to justify pre-trial detention, there had to be a 50 per cent probability, or just cause for suspicion, that the accused had committed the crime in question. Another old football expression came into Steinar's mind: the prosecutor seemed to be heading for a walkover victory.

At 12:30 Steinar scurried down two flights of stairs only to be told by the floor guard that Taribo's transfer from the lock-up to the courthouse had been delayed by a few minutes, the guard had just spoken with the driver. Steinar walked back and forth and read through the files while he waited.

At 12:52, eight minutes before the remand hearing, Taribo arrived.

'Are you alright?' asked Steinar.

'Yes.'

'We've only got a few minutes. I've gone through what I could of the files. When the judge asks, you should appeal against detention and plead not guilty,' said Steinar, who went on to explain what would happen.

Taribo nodded repeatedly.

Steinar took a deep breath, just like he used to do as he stepped onto the pitch at Amsterdam Arena. Then he opened the door to courtroom number 152. The room was furnished with simple, light-coloured wooden fittings. The judge's bench towered over the small courtroom. Directly above the judge's bench hung the state coat of arms, a lion rampant armed with an axe.

The prosecution's desk was to the right, beneath the judge, with Steinar and Taribo's on the left. They all faced the witness stand, where Taribo would sit when giving evidence. The judge's elevated position was usually intimidating for the accused, on this occasion, though, it was the judge who seemed intimidated as he looked at the mass of muscle in front of him.

At the back of the court there were a few chairs for the public. A lawyer might slip in now and then to learn from a senior colleague, or a law student might come if the case was relevant to their studies. Sometimes there were friends and family supporting their loved ones, but usually nobody could be bothered to come and watch as countless human fates were sealed.

Today, though, room 152 was packed. Journalists fought for seats and elbow room. Both NRK and TV2 had their hand-held cameras, and chairs scraped on the floor as cameramen rearranged the furniture to find the best possible angles, while also checking their sound connections.

The prosecutor requested that the hearing proceed behind closed doors out of consideration to the investigation process. The judge passed the request on to Steinar, who instinctively wanted to object. He knew that the prosecutor might see it as a sign of weakness if he agreed but, when he glanced across at the pack of hungry wolves, he realised that conducting the case in front of the cameras wouldn't do him any favours. He seconded the request.

The judge summarised the request made by the prosecutor and Steinar before stating his decision that the doors should be closed. His eyes met a row of annoyed journalists.

The courtroom was emptied.

The judge proceeded to confirm the identities of those present before turning to Taribo.

'How do you respond to the police's application for pre-trial detention?'

'I'm appealing against detention.'

'How do you plead to the charge against you?'

'I plead not guilty,' said Taribo, in almost perfect Norwegian. Steinar felt stupid. 'Say no… say no…,' Steinar had instructed him, as if he'd been speaking to a 12-year-old.

'Are you willing to make a statement?' the judge continued.

'Yes.'

The prosecutor was a woman in her late thirties. She had her hair tied in a tight ponytail, a couple of wrinkles on her forehead, and she was wearing rectangular glasses with wide metallic arms, a white blouse with the top button undone. She stood up, raised the adjustable desktop to a suitable height and lay down her papers. She went through the charge and the evidence before concluding.

'We request four weeks' detention. Due to the serious nature of the charge and the risk of evidence being destroyed or tampered with, we also request two weeks' solitary confinement and a ban on letters and visitors. Thank you.'

The prosecutor lowered her desk again and sat down.

'And what does the defence counsel have to say?'

Steinar raised his hydraulic desk too, although not quite as effortlessly as his female opponent. He sensed her slight twitch of a smile when he needed to make a second attempt. Steinar spoke.

'Your Honour, I won't speak at length about whether the grounds for reasonable suspicion are met. It has been ascertained that Taribo Shorunmo was present immediately prior to the killing, but he denies having had anything to do with the act described by the prosecution. I refer you to his testimony in court and his police interview. The body of evidence is tenuous. The police are relying on a witness who supposedly heard Shorunmo threaten Arild Golden on a previous occasion. The seizure of a weapon is also mentioned, but there's nothing to prove that this was used in the murder. The police claim that Golden and Shorunmo were also arguing on the day of the murder, but this is a daily occurrence for a football agent, so if that's a criterion then many people will stand accused.' Steinar shifted his weight from one foot to the other. He glanced up at the judge, unsure of how clearly he should insinuate that the police had got the wrong man.

'As for the risk of destroying evidence, I would like to point out that Shorunmo gave the police a relatively long and detailed interview immediately after his arrest, without availing himself of his right to have a lawyer present. It's too late for Shorunmo to co-ordinate his account with those of any other potential suspects in the case. Shorunmo also claims that he was on good terms with the victim and that Golden was alive at the time Shorunmo left him. As for the proportionality of the prosecution's request, Shorunmo risks losing his job. Having built up his customer base with a 16-year-long unblemished record, he's afraid he'll lose that if he's detained. Detention would be a disproportionate measure. I move to support the request by the accused to be released or, failing that, alternatively that the length of his pre-trial detention be reduced to two weeks,' said Steinar, smacking his hand too hard on top of the desk, which started to descend. Steinar just managed to add a 'thank you' before the desktop reached the bottom.

The judge looked at the prosecutor. 'Any reply?'

'The counsel for the defence mentioned the work situation of the accused. This is work carried out without a residence permit, so it cannot be considered.'

The judge looked at Steinar. 'Any response to that?'

'But it's paid work, and Shorunmo's family depends on it,' he said.

'Alright. I'll consider the case and give my ruling in 20 minutes.'

For the first time since he'd stopped playing football, Steinar was really being affected by the seriousness of a situation. He'd been nervous when Junior was born, but there were doctors, midwives and nurses at the hospital who knew what they were doing. Here in court he was back at the centre of events. He was pleased, but had no idea how it would go. Taribo was taken down to the court cell while Steinar went out to get some fresh air. He stopped at the door when he saw the journalists waiting on the steps outside the courthouse, then sneaked back inside and sat down in the canteen with a coffee. He checked his phone, there was a text message from Benedikte: 'When can we meet?'

He wanted to meet her again, but he also needed time to read and think. He texted her back: 'Lunch tomorrow. 12 o' clock?'

He'd barely pressed 'send' when the reply came: 'At the Delicatessen tapas bar in Grünerløkka.'

The judge's ruling came after 20 minutes, as promised. Taribo was remanded in custody for four weeks, and was given two weeks of solitary confinement as well as a ban on letters and visitors. Steinar hadn't stood a chance.

He'd suffered bad defeats on the football pitch too, but he always believed he'd win beforehand. He had to find that faith again. He had to find another murderer.

Astroturf Grows Fast

Benedikte was in the green room waiting to go on TV2's *God Morgen Norge*. She looked over at the sofa where that day's pop group were sitting. They were scheduled to give two performances, and the musicians always lay about on the sofas while they waited. Businesspeople paced back and forth while they scalded themselves on their coffee. Politicians were relaxed, like the musicians, but they sat on the sofas instead of lying on them. The studio runner gave Benedikte the signal that it was her turn.

It was Benedikte herself who'd asked to go on. The programme's producer had agreed, even though he seemed sceptical when Benedikte didn't want to tell him the details of what she had planned.

'Coffee or water?' asked the studio runner, when they'd got to the bottom of the stairs that led into the studio.

While the presenters were going through the newspaper review, Benedikte swapped places on the sofa with a child psychologist. She sat down and adjusted her cushion. The presenters were laughing at a crude article from *Vårt Land*, a newspaper with a traditional Christian outlook.

'Now, you're here to tell us the latest news on the Golden case, are you?' said the male presenter, putting down the newspapers.

'That's right,' said Benedikte, putting on her best morning smile.

'It's a terrible tragedy, isn't it?'

'Yes.'

'It's hardly what you'd expect in the world of sport.'

'No.'

'For those who don't already know, the football agent Arild Golden was found murdered at Ullevaal Stadion, and Benedikte Blystad here is the reporter from our channel who's been working most closely on the story.'

'That's correct. The police have arrested a man for the murder, and he was remanded in custody yesterday for four weeks. He was identified as having been at the crime scene, but it's difficult to see what his motive might be.'

TV chef Wenche was stirring her pot in the background, with the channel's wine expert next to her, corkscrew in hand. The breakfast show was really supposed to have a cosy atmosphere. Nevertheless, the male presenter had his journalistic instincts intact, and it was as if he was waking up from hibernation as he sat up straight on the sofa.

'Are you suggesting that the police might have arrested the wrong man?' he asked.

'His motive is certainly unclear, and that's important in a case like this one,' said Benedikte.

'What might the motive be then?'

'Money's one obvious possibility. Arild Golden and his company, Golden Boys, were making enormous sums of money in all areas of the football business.'

'We know him best as an agent though. What else are you thinking of?'

'Golden had gradually taken control of most things. He sold everything from TV rights to training camps for Second Division teams, but he probably made most money from astroturf.'

'Astroturf?'

'Golden practically had a monopoly on the market. If a hundred new pitches are being built a year, it goes without saying that there are huge amounts of money in the picture, so that means there will be people who are willing to cross almost any line.'

The female presenter was staring at the ceiling. Benedikte first thought it might be because she wasn't interested in football, but then she realised that she was probably being told something through her earpiece. Just as the male presenter was about to follow up, she interrupted him.

'Those are interesting thoughts Benedikte, but we have to move on now. Thank you for coming. After the break we'll be in the kitchen. What's on the menu today, Wenche?'

Benedikte spent the next few hours doing research. She was more and more convinced that she was onto something. She read through what she could find on Google, leading her to various pages with research on synthetic turf, rubber granules and high-PAH oils. She read documentation on MRSA, allergies and cancer, as well as about a baseball team from Kansas that played on artificial grass and had experienced a disturbingly high cancer rate. To her surprise she discovered that Norwegian researchers had also emphasised the dangers, but this hadn't been widely publicised. Their statements had only led to small notices about bad air quality in indoors sports halls and environmental pollution from granules made out of recycled tyres. She also read about benzene. She had visited similar websites before when she wanted to find out exactly why she'd fallen ill. Benzene had been one of the many possible factors then too, but she'd never been especially exposed to it. Her interest in the Golden case had been sparked by her journalistic ambitions, but now it had triggered something in Benedikte that had lain dead for a number of years. She was reading about delocalised bonding in benzene when a voice interrupted the monotonous sound of the computer fan.

'I need to speak with you,' said Bertil Olsen, without any of his usual introductory small talk. Benedikte's eyes remained fixed on the screen.

'What about?' she asked, but Olsen merely led her into a meeting room. Benedikte was puzzled, wasn't Olsen supposed to be in Bergen?

'You've got to leave off this stuff about astroturf,' said Olsen.

Benedikte looked over at her boss. It was part of her point to provoke a reaction, but she never thought in her wildest dreams the reaction would come from within. She'd expected that Olsen would want to discuss her next steps, as this was a big story, the more she read the more she felt sure that she was on the right track.

'Why?'

'Just do as I say,' said Olsen, leaving Benedikte alone in the meeting room.

She Wants to Sleep with Me

This was where it started. Steinar passed the 3.5 km mark on the treadmill. His heart rate was 190. He needed these tough gym sessions to process new information. He needed to push himself.

His body felt heavier with every step he took, but over the past few years he'd learnt to appreciate this kind of exercise and the pain that accompanied it. He always started his exercise sessions with 5 km on the treadmill.

The pain in his calf muscles was constant, but then it spread to the front of his quadriceps, just above his knees. The stiffness spread up like wildfire. He was running at 14.8 km per hour. His heart rate jumped up to 192. His breathing was getting louder, and the others on the treadmills glanced at him.

The people who went to the gym to drink water were one of Steinar's pet peeves. Some came out of the changing rooms already drinking water before they'd even touched a weight, before they'd put a single foot on the treadmill. He accelerated by another fraction. He passed the 4 km mark, now at a speed of 15.3. His heart rate was 194.

He let out a loud groan. A girl who had just started on the next treadmill got off and opted for the weight machine instead. 4.1 km. 4.2. At 4.4, his hip cramps started, every step sending waves of pain through his body. But giving up was not an option. Steinar would rather be injured than get off the treadmill before he reached 5 km. He pressed his thumbs into his hips, trying to keep the pain at bay. 4.5 km.

His heart rate reached 200 at 4.9 km, when he adjusted his speed for the last time. 16.1. He gritted his teeth and sprinted as fast as he could until the machine showed the magic 5 km. It had taken him 20 minutes and 15 seconds. He was getting closer, but he wouldn't see the number 19 today either. The treadmills next to his were deserted.

He found some paper towels and took a couple of minutes to catch his breath, then he went upstairs to the next floor and the free weights. He put 95 kg on the bench press bar. He used to manage 4–6 reps with 115 kg, but that was before he chose to prioritise the treadmill. His fingers met the cool steel. He squeezed the pole, then relaxed again, moving his grip a little. He closed his eyes and pushed the bar up until his arms were straight out. Then he lowered the weight to his ribs, time after time, thinking: 'She wants to sleep with me, she wants to sleep with me.'

4 reps with 95 kg. It was a start anyway. He sat up. He let his arms hang down and shook them. He turned his head from side to side, his neck cracking.

Myrens Verksted was an old factory building by the Aker River that had been converted into a gym. There was a high ceiling and space for a massive climbing wall. While Steinar waited for his body to get ready for the next bench press session, his eyes followed two girls scurrying like spiders up the white wall with its small climbing holds in all the colours of the rainbow.

He lay down and started lifting again. 'She wants to sleep with me, she wants to sleep with me, she wants to sleep with me, she wants to sleep with me...'

He'd just barely managed to lift number four. As he held the bar at the top with his hands shaking, he knew that he was taking a chance. He lowered the bar to his chest, trying to let it bounce off his rib cage and get it moving back up. He just managed a few centimetres before the whole thing locked in place. The bar hung there for a couple of seconds. He heaved on the pole, his arms shaking and the small of his back rising up from the bench mat. He turned so that he could get the maximum out of his stronger right arm. He stopped himself from letting out a howl before closing his eyes and relaxing.

The bar was stuck on his rib cage, and there was nobody nearby to help. The only people he could see were the two girls hanging on the wall with their backs turned. The weight was beginning to cause pain in his ribs. There was only one way out.

He leant to the right, and a 2.5 kg, a 15 kg and a 20 kg weight slammed to the floor. He was thrown to the other side, where the weights were still attached and then fell to the ground at full speed as well. Bang! He lifted the bare bar back onto the stand and breathed out. Then he put the weights back in place and worked on his back, arms and abs before going for a shower.

He got on his bike and coasted along the riverbank, having to slalom in between prams and pushers until he got to the Delicatessen in Grünerløkka, an up-and-coming part of town. His phone rang. It was the journalist from *Nettavisen*, calling for the third time that day. Steinar answered as politely as he could.

'Once again, I'm sorry, but I've got no comment to make at the present time.' He put his phone on silent and went up the steps into the restaurant.

Benedikte was sitting on one of the wooden chairs, her eyes fixed on her iPhone. She was wearing a sleeveless top in a multitude of colours, her sunglasses on her head. She noticed him approaching, stood up and gave him a hug.

'I knew it would be behind closed doors, so I didn't come.'

'How did you work that out?'

'Sports journalists in a courtroom? That's a bad fit.' She swiped her thumb over her iPhone screen. 'So what's happening to him now?'

'He's being transferred from the security cell at the city custody centre to Oslo Prison. I'm meeting him tomorrow.'

'From what I've seen on various online forums, it looks like he might need help. There weren't many people there who think he's innocent, let alone among newspaper commentators. Those right-wing populists from the Progress Party have gained 6 per cent in today's opinion polls. You've got some work to do.'

'I suppose so.'

'But it wasn't Taribo I wanted to talk to you about. It was you.'

She went quiet, something on her phone catching her interest. Steinar sneaked a peek at her arms. He would soon have to tell her that he had a son and that things were complicated. Or would he? He wasn't going to marry her, after all, couldn't he just shag her and keep his trap shut?

A waiter who, unlike most waiters in Oslo, wasn't Swedish, came over and gave them a couple of menus. Benedikte gave him the unopened menus straight back and asked him to bring some good tapas.

'To drink?'

'Sparkling water,' said Steinar.

'And you?' asked the waiter, looking at Benedikte.

'Answer yes or no. Have you got Tab Xtra?'

'Er, no.'

'Coke Zero?'

'No.'

'Diet Coke?'

'No.'

'Pepsi Max?'

'Yes.'

'So that's what you've got.'

'A Pepsi Max, then?'

'No, I'll have an apple juice.'

The waiter wrote this down, pushing his pen hard against the pad before turning and leaving for the kitchen.

Benedikte put her hand on Steinar's arm, squeezing it.

'You've got to tell me everything.'

Her squeeze sent a jolt through his body. Steinar looked down at the table, then back up at her.

'Well, I'm divorced, or actually just separated, but...'

'I meant that you should tell me why you stopped playing football.'

'Shit.'

'But, by all means, do tell.'

Steinar let out a deep breath. He opted for honesty. 'It started with a trip round Asia. I wanted some peace, but I kept meeting Norwegians who recognised me and wanted to talk football. When I was recognised on the streets of Kuala Lumpur by three drunkards from northern Norway, I'd had enough. I went to Langkawi and checked into the best hotel there for two weeks. All I wanted was peace and quiet.'

The waiter came with their drinks. Steinar continued. 'The first 10 days I spent drinking piña coladas and reading crime novels. On the eleventh day, I was tapped on the shoulder by a girl with dark brown, almost red hair. She said: "Can I join you?" We had a long chat about Langkawi and how beautiful it was, before we discovered that we both came from Oslo. I was from Grefsen, she was from Manglerud. She'd also needed to take a few days' break from a trip round Asia, but now she was ready to rejoin the group she'd been travelling with. She asked if I wanted to come along with them, and I said yes without a second thought. We travelled round Asia for a year. Our other travelling companions dropped off one by one, and for the last couple of months it was just Mette and me left to enjoy the beaches.'

Steinar cursed himself for getting bogged down in his history with Mette. And why on earth had he just told her that he came from

Grefsen, like his friend Bjørnar always said, and not from Årvoll?

'Go on,' said Benedikte.

'That same autumn we moved in together and both started studying law. Our student years went by quickly. She got a job in the Ministry of Foreign Affairs, and I got one in a big company at Aker Brygge.'

Steinar took a sip of his water. He could have done everything so much better. He'd walked away from his football career, he'd left a large legal firm and he'd lost the only woman he loved.

He looked at Benedikte. What would she think if she knew that he saw himself as a failure? Or that he longed for football like an alcoholic longs for the first drink of the day? She was only 26 with so many opportunities in front of her. There was a danger that he might push her away. And he'd still held back from telling her about Junior. Might the fact that he had a son mean that she wouldn't want to get attached to him? A separation was more or less a piece of cake, a child meant a lot more. Steinar felt old.

Their food came. Steinar spread some aioli on a piece of bread. It was so simple yet so good, as was the fried chorizo. Maybe he was just hungry, he thought, feeling his mood improve.

'I've been blocked,' said Benedikte, finishing off some marinated scampi.

'What do you mean?' asked Steinar.

'I was told not to investigate astroturf any further.'

'Who told you, and why?'

'My boss, in no uncertain terms, but I don't know why yet.'

'What next?'

'I can go after other leads in the Golden case, like his agency and his rumoured relationship with Sabrina, but it's best for me to leave the astroturf stuff aside. That's why I was wondering whether you might be able to do me a favour.'

'What is it?'

'Naturally this astroturf trail is even more intriguing now, and I've arranged a meeting with the chairman of FK Framfor, who knows a great deal on the subject. Would you be able to meet him?'

'That would be fine. I've got to get hold of Stanley and his mother, but I can get that done on the way.'

'Brilliant,' said Benedikte. She gave him a short briefing on the chairman of FK Framfor before finishing. 'I've got to go now, but can I pop by your place tomorrow afternoon? We can carry on our conversation then.'

There was something staccato, something stressed in Benedikte's voice when she said those last words. It wasn't like her to say 'brilliant'. Steinar didn't quite know why, but he thought it seemed like she had been making an effort to sound relaxed. It was also a bit odd for her not to push him a little further on why he stopped playing football. As for him, he'd neglected to mention Junior yet again. Why was he so afraid anyway? He brushed these thoughts aside just as quickly as they appeared, while Benedikte practically shot across the restaurant and out the door.

He twirled a chicken wing gently between his thumb and forefinger. So, she was coming round to his place the following day. The woman who'd said that she would sleep with him was going to meet him again. Not at his office, not at a restaurant, but at his home. Steinar put down the chicken wing. Honesty was overrated. What he had to do was clear away Junior's toys and squeeze in an extra weight training session the next morning.

Not Only in Italy

'Hi, Stig,' said Benedikte.

Stig Nilsen got up and gave Benedikte a big hug. The hug was slightly too long for Benedikte's taste, but everything about Stig was a little exaggerated.

'Do you know what this is about?' asked Benedikte when he'd finally let go.

'No, they didn't say anything. Probably something about me not swearing yet again. I watched the tape. I can understand it if that Båtsnes guy is pissed off.'

'Båtsnes? Who's that?'

'The boss.'

'He's not called Båtsnes.'

'Isn't he? Are you sure?'

'Positive,' said Benedikte. But she wasn't sure why she'd been summoned in person to the office of the controller of TV2. Was it even worse than she'd first thought? Had they been put under so much pressure that she'd have to go? And why was she there with Stig Nilsen?

The office door opened.

'You can come in now,' said Bertil Olsen.

The channel controller's office was spartan. He had the obligatory flat-screen TV on the wall. On his desk was a laptop and an award that the channel had won the previous year for the best TV documentary. In front of his desk were two chairs of a considerably simpler design than his own leather seat. Otherwise his office was bare and tidy, not a single excess piece of paper or Post-it note to be seen. The controller himself seemed to be reading something on his laptop screen, and Olsen signalled Stig and Benedikte to sit down.

The controller looked up from his laptop and closed it. 'I wanted to see you about *Football Xtra.*'

Benedikte was convinced now. She was going to get the sack.

'Let me start with you, Stig,' said the controller.

'Well, I'm sorry that I went a bit far last time, I didn't mean to swear so much.'

'Actually we've had nothing but positive feedback on you, the word "genuine" seems to be a recurring theme. I want to offer you a promotion. You'll take turns as the main presenter. And then there's you, Benedikte.' The controller took a pause before continuing. 'You'll have to work it out with Stig to decide who presents when. You'll take it in turns every other week.'

So it was Kristine who'd have to go, the 34-year-old mother of two who'd just fought her way back to the screen. Where would she go now? Benedikte was reminded once again how short a TV career could be, and how important it was to make a mark for yourself.

'I'll do it on one condition,' said Stig, bringing Benedikte back to reality. She looked across at Stig, just as surprised as the controller and Olsen were.

'Which is?' asked the controller.

'I'll do it on the weekends that Tromsø's playing away. I've got to be at Alfheim when the lads are playing at home. I don't mind having to do reports, but I've got to be there!'

'Like I said, you and Benedikte can discuss the rota between you.'

That brought a close to the meeting. There was something about the way the controller had presented the decision, as if the whole session were a warning for Benedikte. Normally, Bertil Olsen would've led a meeting of that sort.

Stig and Benedikte went out of the office and down along the corridor. Stig took hold of Benedikte's shoulder. 'I hope what I said won't be a problem.'

'You mean that my life will be run according to when Tromsø's fixtures are?' She smiled. 'It's no problem. We'll work it out. But why don't we go and have a beer or something this evening, since you're here in Oslo?'

'No bloody way. I hate Oslo. I'm getting out of here as quick as I can. I get lost in Oslo. And what would I tell the wife? She'd think I'd end up shagging you if I went out with you for a drink.'

Benedikte started laughing. She couldn't help it when Stig got going.

'But there's something else,' said Stig. He had a serious look in his eyes, and Benedikte had never seen him like that before. 'I hate to spread rumours, but you asked me about that Steinar Brunsvik.'

'Do you know any more?'

'I heard something about why he quit.'

'Do tell.'

'He just disappeared. Nobody knew what happened to him. The rumour was that he'd run off. Something happened that meant he couldn't stay in football anymore.'

'Why did he have to disappear?'

'I heard he was involved in match fixing, and that he was about to be exposed.'

Benedikte hadn't put enough pressure on Steinar. She'd backed off so he didn't have to explain himself. She'd been weak. As a journalist, she couldn't let herself be weak.

She bit off the end of a fingernail.

High Pressure

Steinar had to hold the phone away from his ear.

'What on earth was that?' asked his friend Bjørnar.

'That was the mother of the football player I'm going to represent. She's somewhat sceptical of football agents. She recently chucked out one by the name of Ola Bugge, who was advising her boy to leave school, as it was it distracting him from his football.'

'And his father's the one who was arrested for killing Arild Golden?'

'That's right.'

'And you've got to make sure the boy doesn't sign with any other agents?'

'Yup.'

'Doesn't sound like it'll be too difficult,' said Bjørnar, glancing over at Steinar, who had to break a smile. They were in the fast lane on the E6, heading to the Romerike district, north of Oslo, and to the home of the Second Division club FK Framfor.

'Since when have you been interested in astroturf?' asked Steinar.

'Ståle's condition made my interest grow, but I've had plenty of patients with torn ligaments and other serious sports injuries that could be related to the playing surface.'

'Have any been from other sports too?'

'Handball. Rubber surfaces have a much higher injury rate than wooden floors, especially with young girls. But the worst cases are with artificial turf. Just look at the shock pads.'

'What are they?'

'They're the thin rubber underlays beneath the turf that make the pitch softer. They lessen the impact, especially on the knees and the hips, but they're expensive. And nobody's got exclusive rights to the product, so there's nobody putting pressure on the NFF, ergo no requirement to use shock pads. Even though the long-term injuries would be seriously decreased.'

'How come?'

'Money, as always. So many young people are being allowed to spend so much of their time on surfaces that could be directly harming their health, with no proper studies being done on how this affects their bodies in the long term. Cancer and lung problems are one thing, but I'm afraid we might see plenty of people needing knee and hip replacements 20–30 years from now.'

The turning for the pitch came a short distance after a Shell petrol station. The road led onto a large flat expanse of gravel with goals at each end. Next to it was a synthetic grass pitch, the pavilion in between. A small wood and a winding river surrounded the site.

They parked outside the pavilion and the club's chairman, Asgeir Kringlebotn, came out to greet them.

Kringlebotn was wearing grey tracksuit bottoms and a T-shirt advertising the club's soccer school. His nose was far too large and far too red. He led them into the club room.

They sat down on a fabric sofa, with its old cushions sagging exactly where you might expect. Steinar slid down into one of the hollows. The walls were covered with treated pinewood panels, and old certificates told stories of local championships and triumphs in age-group tournaments.

A plate of freshly baked heart-shaped waffles was carried in, together with a pot of coffee. Steinar took a bite. They were fantastically brittle, with traces of the traditional sour cream. The coffee was burnt and as strong as dynamite, exactly how it gets after too many hours spent in the coffeemaker.

'So, tell me gentlemen, where would you have put the artificial pitch?' asked Kringlebotn, after having decked a waffle with strawberry jam and brown cheese.

Steinar and Bjørnar looked at each other. Kringlebotn went on. 'Out there we used to have the best grass pitch in Norway, but more and more people wanted to practise in winter. We needed an artificial pitch, and space wasn't a problem. All we had to do was roll out the astroturf on top of the gravel pitch. In the autumn of 2004 we had an inspection from the NFF, from their facilities manager Birger Holme, and he promised us funding on one condition, that the artificial pitch was laid on top of the grass one.'

'But doesn't it take a lot more groundwork to lay it on grass than on gravel?' asked Steinar.

'Yes.'

'So why should you destroy the grass pitch?'

'The answer the NFF gave us was how frequently it would be used. They want all grass pitches to be replaced because, in theory, gravel pitches are more useful in winter.'

'In theory?'

'Try to get the young ones to practise on gravel. Nobody wants to do that anymore, so the club will soon need a second artificial pitch. We have to get rid of the real grass. It's the real grass that's the competition.'

'So you mean the NFF is deliberately forcing clubs to switch to artificial turf?'

'Does that surprise you? It's in the media all the time. The NFF want to have a longer season. In 1993 the championship started on 1 May, but in a few years we'll be playing in February, because this forces the clubs to switch to artificial turf. Did you hear what happened with Ullensaker/Kisa a few seasons back?'

'No.'

'They were about to play their opening match in the Second Division, but the grass pitch was covered with snow. So the team suggested that they could play on the astroturf next to their normal pitch. It was fine by their opponents, but the NFF wouldn't let them. They preferred them to postpone the match.'

'Why?'

'The clubs are supposed to play all their matches on the same pitch. Of course, they should be allowed to play their first and last few matches on synthetic grass, and then use real grass in the middle of summer, but the NFF wanted to dispose with the option of natural turf. And it's working. Now Ullensaker/Kisa has a new stadium with artificial grass. Until I was sacked from the NFF, I was also part of the drive to introduce astroturf to Norway, but it was always intended to be an alternative for the winter.'

'You were sacked?'

'I probably argued a bit too much with the association president, it's a long time ago now.'

'Do you think artificial grass will take over completely?'

'I don't know, but it's even come to the point where the NFF has agreed, in principle, that there should be astroturf at Ullevaal. The national stadium. We'll be the laughing stock of international football. Brazil, England, Germany and the other big countries won't even pick up the phone in the future when we ask to play friendlies.'

'Aren't there any other international pitches with artificial turf?'

'The best known is probably the Luzhniki Stadium in Moscow. But when the Champions League final was going to be played there, the surface wasn't good enough any more. UEFA insisted that the artificial turf would have to be replaced with natural grass for the final, but afterwards they went back to the artificial stuff.'

'They replaced the whole pitch just for one game?'

'Ironically the final was decided when Chelsea's John Terry slipped and missed his crucial penalty. The turf hadn't stuck properly.'

'What do you think will be the next thing?' asked Steinar.

'Most of all the NFF would like us to play indoors. Soon there will only be indoor pitches in the top division, mark my words. It was Golden's last stroke of genius before he was taken out.'

'What did he do?'

'He bought the company that has a monopoly on building sports halls in Norway. It gave him yet another weapon in his armoury of coercion.'

'Coercion?'

'Golden built his empire through coercion. He pressured NFF executives to stop research, he forced new players on unwilling club managers and forced building projects on politicians who were inclined to leave things as they were. He put together a database with dirt on every single decision-maker, at club level, at the level of the association and in politics.'

'How did he get his information?'

'I've heard that he had people whose only job was to get this information for him.'

That would be Vlad Vidić, thought Steinar. 'What kind of information?'

'I don't know exactly what kind of coercion tactics we're talking about, but Birger Holme did whatever Golden said, and if anybody tried to bypass his system they'd end up at the bottom of the pile. Golden decided where the synthetic turf would go and who'd lay it.'

Kringlebotn took them out and across the warm, rock-solid carpet of artificial grass. The tarmac could be seen through the turf in several spots, parts of the penalty box were missing, and most of the rubber was in black mounds around the pitch.

'Our artificial turf had to be replaced just three years after it had been installed. And in 2008, the Softgrass company laid six artificial pitches in Akershus County. Today they're all useless. All the clubs have complained about the playing surfaces, but it turns out to be difficult to reslove. Softgrass is a subsidiary of Golden Boys.'

'But how can a company's reputation survive six useless pitches in one year?'

'The lowest bid wins, quality doesn't matter. The politicians can boast about making investments for the community, but they want to do it as cheaply as possible. So that means no shock pads, the worst kind of turf and pitches that are getting narrower all the time. Altogether this means enormously increased injury risks.'

Bjørnar looked at Steinar and raised an eyebrow. Kringlebotn asked them to follow him across the artificial pitch into the small wooded area where the ground sloped towards the river. Behind a shed, in which the club kept balls, cones and other training gear, there were huge quantities of rolled-up synthetic turf.

'This is our artificial pitch from 2005. Made by the same company, except it was called Topgrass then. A few days ago, there was somebody from Friends of the Earth here, who said there might be poisonous substances leaking into the river. But we can't get rid of the bloody stuff. No refuse tip will take it.'

'Do you know if anybody tried to take Golden's monopoly off him?' asked Steinar.

'I heard that Birger Holme and a couple of his colleagues from the NFF wanted to break free of Golden's iron grip. They were working on setting up their own company and taking over the exclusive rights on artificial turf. The NFF would be the main stakeholder, but the three of them were getting paid enormous sums for lending their services to football. It was jobs for the boys at its worst, but there are no checks in the NFF on this kind of activity. The only one who reacted to the plan was Golden. He was furious.'

Steinar nodded. He looked at his watch. 16:20. It was going to be tight to fetch Junior from nursery before 5 o' clock. He signalled to Bjørnar that it was time for them to go.

'Say hi to Benedikte from me,' said Kringlebotn. 'I'm surprised that she sent someone else, she must trust you.' He winked at Steinar, who didn't know how to react. 'You know, her aunt's married to a bloke who lives just down the road here. Benedikte used to spend a lot of time at the club as a child. Lively as dynamite, she was, although she didn't exactly have it easy.'

Monopoly

Were they all really that corrupt? Steinar too? Could the reason that he quit be that he was fixing matches and that he was on the verge of being exposed?

Benedikte was sitting at her desk. Ten days had passed since Golden had been killed, and still she was uncovering more questions than answers. She called Per Kristian Boltedal.

'You didn't tell me everything,' she said when Boltedal answered.

'What do you mean?'

'In a transfer like the one you described to me, there's at least one missing link on the pay list, the Norwegian club executives. Let's suppose that Golden ran off with some money and that the player and the manager in England got a cut, but then the Norwegian club still has to accept the transfer. Somebody there, such as the director of football, is also taking money under the table.'

'I can't tell you everything about what we're working on.'

'Come on, PK. Didn't we agree to help each other?'

'Each other, yes.'

'I promise to send you what I find out.'

'I don't want my story to be on the TV2 website while our paper's in print.'

'That won't happen.'

'I'm working on a story involving Norwegian club executives, and it's quite clear that a number of them were making money. Especially one. I won't give you the name yet, but there's one key club executive in Norway in particular whose exploits we're really trying to unravel.'

'What have you found out?'

'Like you said, Golden also needed the Norwegian clubs' blessing. And the clubs usually have one strong man. One man who can get the board to do what he wants. If Golden could get such a man in his pocket, he could easily have a monopoly on that club's investments, both in terms of facilities and, not least, player transfers.'

'But how? Surely he couldn't just transfer the money?'

'He could do it several ways. One's the classic brown envelope. That works with a few hundred 1,000-kroner notes that you can stick in a safe-deposit box, but there are still limits to how much money you can have without the tax authorities noticing. So there are other methods too, not least property and luxury holidays.'

'But surely those things are traceable?'

'They don't bother. Firstly, the NFF won't investigate anything like that. They haven't got the resources and, besides, they're afraid of the Golden Boys set-up. Secondly, the authorities aren't on to them, and thirdly, the media's afraid. I expect that TV2 would be cautious with a story like that.'

'Why?'

'Imagine if Golden started a press boycott, if he got his players not to talk to TV2. That would strangle the channel's output. Golden must have had 90 per cent of the top Norwegian players, the ones who featured regularly in the national team. Imagine if there was only one player who would speak after every international match, or if there were entire rounds of the top division championship when it was impossible to speak to the goal-scorers. The same goes for the big papers. Golden's reach extended deep into every corner of football.'

Benedikte hadn't been able to understand why TV2 didn't publish everything they had on Golden and his business dealings, especially in Africa. Neither had she understood why the papers weren't a bit tougher when covering football stories. So much money had gone in, and yet so many clubs had practically gone bankrupt, where had all the money gone? A boycott went a long way to explaining it. Was that also the reason why she'd been warned not to investigate artificial turf?

'But you're still looking into it?' asked Benedikte.

'*Dagens Næringsliv* doesn't have a sports section, so it was either up to us or the comrades over at *Klassekampen*. It's an interesting story, but it's also a difficult one to crack open.'

'What have you found?'

'The club executive I'm focusing on tends to travel to Spain. Four years ago he bought a tiny house there on a large plot of ground. The house was derelict and he got it for 100,000 euro. This was declared as a financial outlay, and he pays tax on the place. It's all out in the open. But nobody's gone down to see what the house looks like now. Nobody except me, that is. It's a palace. I got a local estate agent to estimate its current value. He said at least 2 million euro. According to the club executive's tax return, he hasn't spent a single krone on renovation, or on extending it to many times its original size. Neither did he submit a single planning permission application. Golden Boys dealt with it via foreign companies.'

'It's sheer corruption, basically.'

'Absolutely.'

'You say that you're focusing on one executive in particular. Are there many involved?'

'I also know of an apartment complex which is owned by executives from many different Norwegian clubs. As far as we know, none of them have declared this on their tax returns. They book their places on the cheapest unspecified charter tours, but they never stay in the mouldy old hotel. They stay in a luxury complex that they own themselves.'

'Why don't you just go for it, all guns blazing?'

'We need more time on the apartment complex. We haven't got any proof about that yet, but we're starting to get some about that one executive. His transfer dealings are so incredibly transparent. How many players do you think his club's bought over the past few years from outside the Golden Boys system?'

'You guessed it, they all came from Golden Boys. Football's answer to the state alcohol monopoly.'

Chit-Chat

'My client appealed against his detention, so that meant he was pleading not guilty.'

'It's not really the same.'

'No, but that's still how it is. He claims he's innocent.'

'What about all the evidence?'

'It's merely circumstantial.'

'What about the witness? What about the weapon?'

'I've no further comment to make,' said Steinar, hanging up.

Dagbladet, that bloody newspaper. The journalist wouldn't give up. And he also seemed to have read the closed files. How did he manage to do that?

Steinar had realised that he would have to answer his phone, otherwise the journalists would only get more and more insistent. He generally succeeded in politely dismissing them, but this guy from *Dagbladet* was getting more out of Steinar than he'd like.

Steinar had taken a taxi to Åkebergveien again, but this time he went a few steps east of the police's central custody facility. He was outside the main gate of Oslo Prison. He pressed the buzzer, explained his business and was let through the first gate up to the glass cabin where the guard sat.

'Can I see some ID, please?' asked the guard, who this time looked more like Dirty Harry than Tom Daley. Steinar showed him his driving licence.

'So you're here to visit Taribo Shorunmo?'

'Yes, he's in Department B. I called earlier and made arrangements.'

'So I see. Have you been here before?'

'No.'

'In through that door,' said the guard, pointing.

Steinar had to go through a metal detector, which he hadn't needed to do in the police custody facility. His mobile phone was taken from him, and he was accompanied into a visiting room. Taribo came in shortly afterwards.

Steinar studied the Nigerian giant. He'd only been in for three days but already seemed to be affected by it. Solitary confinement could leave a real mark, and Norway was considered one of the worst places in Europe for using isolation as a corrective measure. Steinar had heard of prisoners whose hair had turned grey overnight, and others who had become completely apathetic.

'Are you alright?' he asked.

'I'm fine.'

'Is there anything I can get you? A Coke or something?'

'Nothing. Just fix things with Stanley.'

'I need one more day. I've got to check something,' said Steinar, thinking that he'd better check how security worked at the prison. 'About that witness who heard...'

'I don't want to talk about the case. Not before you've got hold of Mona and Stanley.'

Was he hiding something? Or protecting somebody? Or did he just not trust Steinar?

'What do you want to talk about, then?' asked Steinar.

Taribo wriggled further down into his chair. He crossed his legs, put his hands together and placed them behind his neck.

'Tell me about the wildest football match you've ever played,' he said.

'Why?'

'Just tell me.'

'Okay,' said Steinar, scratching his nose. 'That would probably be in Turkey in the Champions League against Galatasaray. I don't think there's a crazier place in the world to play football than Turkey. Or maybe your Bayelsa is just as bad?'

'Tell me about Turkey.'

'It was madness. It was a warm autumn evening in Istanbul and darkness had fallen. The crowd was in its element. The score was 0–0. I'd been given a yellow card after an aggressive tackle.'

'Your usual,' said Taribo.

'I wasn't the only one doing some hard tackles that evening. Anyway, there was a break in the game. I looked up at the thousand Ajax fans

121

who'd travelled, they looked like frightened chickens in a coop. There was an empty section of the stand on each side of them.'

'Why?'

'For security. Not that it helped. The Turkish fans have good throwing arms.'

'What do you mean?'

'They lit flares and threw them over the empty areas into the Ajax fans' section. It reminded me of the footage from the Iraq War, with those missiles flying across the dark screen, almost pretty before they hit. It looked beautiful, but I was worried about the fans and what would happen next. The situation on the pitch deteriorated at the same pace as the commotion on the stands, but the match wouldn't last much longer for me.'

'What happened?'

'More throwing.'

'Were you injured?'

'No. I was about to take a throw-in. Just as I was standing there ready to throw, I was hit repeatedly by coins. It hurt, so I stepped onto the pitch to avoid it. I looked at the ref and pointed at my back. He misunderstood and thought I was wasting time. 0−0 in Istanbul would've been a good result for us. He gave me a yellow card, my second, and I was sent off.'

'Sent off?' said Taribo, laughing.

'Sent off.'

Steinar saw that as a good moment to leave Taribo. He seemed in good spirits, solitary confinement hadn't done him too much harm yet. Steinar went out to security and was given his mobile. More missed calls. But he also noticed that he wasn't searched on the way out. A plan was starting to take shape.

A Hundred Per Cent Chance

Steinar knew she was coming, but he was still shocked to see her standing there.

'Hi,' said Benedikte.

She was wearing a white blouse, with pleats that made it look like it needed to be gone over with an iron. Her denim shorts were very short, and her legs seemed longer than usual, plunging into her blue leather shoes, which were tied up around her ankles.

Steinar's whole body ached. He hadn't managed to do easy, relaxing gym work. Recovery sessions were a foreign concept to him. He was no longer used to doing two really tough sessions in two days. He brushed his right hand through his hair and scratched the back of his neck.

'Come in,' he said.

'Only if you promise to tell me absolutely everything.'

'What?'

'Did you take any money?'

'Come in first. I'll tell you.' He stepped back against the wall to make space for her. She went past and they sat down on the sofa. Benedikte scanned the living room before turning to him.

'Well?' she said.

'Do you remember the documentary you showed me?'

'Of course.'

'The connection between my story and the one about the national skiing team was stronger than you thought. The documentary was probably supposed to be part two of a series.'

'What do you mean?'

'What happened to me had to do with doping,' said Steinar.

'Were you doping?'

'Do you promise this will stay between us?'

'No.'

Steinar hadn't told anybody about this, and there he was sitting in front of a sports journalist, thinking about telling her the truth that he'd kept hidden for 10 years. A story that Benedikte, with all her ambitions, could either bury or run as the main story.

'Do you remember the man we saw in the video? The one you asked me if I'd seen before?'

'Yes.'

'It all started with him. It was an international match at Ullevaal. We were playing against Uruguay, and the score was 0–0 as we went into half-time.' Steinar felt a lump in his throat. 'When I got to my spot, I found an envelope. There were photos inside from my flat. Of the fridge. Of a hand dropping pills in some orange juice. In the orange juice I'd drunk at breakfast. A message was written on the photo in black marker pen: "Meet me in the players' tunnel now."'

Steinar met Benedikte's gaze, but she was giving nothing away. 'The manager wasn't ready to give us our team talk yet, so I slipped out. The man from the video was standing half hidden behind an advertising poster, and he beckoned me over. He said four words: "Make sure you lose."'

'What did you do?' asked Benedikte.

'I refused.'

'And?'

'He gave me two options. I could either make a sloppy backwards pass, cause a penalty, score an own-goal, anything to make sure that Uruguay won the match. Or, option number two, I would be caught doping.'

'After he tipped off the anti-doping officials?'

'Exactly. And I did have something in me. I'd been feeling different all day. Invigorated. Involuntarily, of course, but nobody's ever believed sportspeople who claim they've been doped against their will.'

'So you ran off?'

'I went into the changing room and told them I had kicked my last ball.'

'Didn't anybody try to stop you?'

'What could they do?'

'What happened next?'

'I walked past a journalist from *VG*, who looked perplexed when I said I was quitting. He got caught up in his own question as I disappeared. I took the Metro, wearing my full Norway strip. Nobody recognised me, there were no football fans on the Metro at that moment. I went home, had a shower, got changed and hailed a taxi to Gardermoen Airport. I took the first flight I could get out of the country. My career was in tatters.'

Steinar swallowed again, harder this time.

'Why didn't you go back to playing?' said Benedikte. 'Somebody like you must love football, and the maximum limit for doping cases is eight years. You look fit enough to play in the Second or First Division, anyway.'

It took Steinar a while to try to decide whether or not that was a compliment. He couldn't make up his mind.

'I love football,' he said, 'but doping and dopers are the worst of the worst, the lowest of the low. The fact I once had banned substances in my body, even if it was unwillingly, would have made me feel like a cheat if I played again. Maybe I loved football too much.'

'I've got a couple of other questions,' said Benedikte.

'Okay.'

'Are you two finished?' asked Benedikte.

'Are you talking about Mette?'

'Yes.'

'In that case, yes.'

'Where is she?'

'At the moment she's hiking with a couple of friends in Guatemala. She's a backpacker in her heart of hearts. She's a good person, but we're finished.'

Benedikte's bare calves stroked slowly over Steinar's thighs. She found a foothold and lifted herself onto his lap. She pushed him down until he was lying on the sofa, and moved too so that her mouth was above his. She turned her head, arched her back and pushed her breasts against him. He felt her breath on him. He saw the small birthmark by her ear. Then came the kiss.

'Maybe waiting wasn't such a good idea,' said Benedikte. The next kiss was intense.

So soon? Steinar was happy that she'd come round. He'd been looking forward to it, of course he'd been looking forward to it, but her promise had also made him relaxed and more focused. And now she was attacking him like this. There was only one thing he could do. He dug his hands inside Benedikte's denim shorts.

It felt so good, but something was still gnawing at him. One of Junior's Duplo bricks had been left on the sofa, and as Benedikte put even more weight on Steinar, he felt a sharp edge digging between two bones in the small of his back. He opened his eyes while he carefully wriggled his hand out of her shorts and moved the piece of Duplo. He carried on kissing her, but his gaze fell on the DVD player's digital clock display. It was 16:26. Time had got the better of him again, like at the Baltazar Restaurant, but he couldn't run off. He deliberated back and forth over whether or not he should slip his hand back into her shorts, but then Benedikte opened her eyes.

'What is it?' she asked.

'Shit.'

'Sorry?' said Benedikte, pulling back a little.

Steinar sighed. 'You'll have to come for a walk with me.'

'O-kay,' said Benedikte, frowning and leaving a long pause between the two syllables. Then she straightened her shirt and bent down to tie up the blue shoes that she'd somehow taken off without Steinar noticing. As she straightened her shorts, Steinar contemplated how he might be getting older, but still he was a fucking idiot. Bloody open goal.

It'd been so long since he'd last slept with a woman that, if he was honest, he hardly would've ruined anybody's schedule.

Steinar led her along Lofthusveien and then down Kjelsåsveien. He glanced at his watch, and then at Benedikte's legs, before swearing once more inside his head.

'Did you see Taribo today like you said you would?' asked Benedikte.

'Yes,' said Steinar, clearing his throat.

'Did you get any further with him?'

'Not really, he's evasive.'

'Next time you speak with him, turn up the heat.'

'Maybe I should.'

They turned by the low-rise blocks just after the Rema 1000 supermarket. The parkland at Muselunden came into view. A couple of grown men were throwing frisbees at a basket, a sport they called frolf. Steinar took a deep breath, then led Benedikte over to the gate.

The message went through the nursery at the speed of light. 'Junior, time to go home,' the keenest young girls shouted, in competition with each other. Then Junior noticed and shouted 'Daddy!' at the top of his voice, holding his arms up to be lifted. As always, Steinar's other worries disappeared.

Benedikte whispered so only Steinar could hear. 'Got any more secrets?'

Part 5

12 October 2009

'Hello. This is Per Kristian Boltedal from Dagens Næringsliv again. I'm still working on a story about your transfers and, as I'm sure you recall, we spoke last time about that Swedish keeper. This time I was wondering about the Nigerian striker from his local rivals.'

All that idiotic anonymous stuff. Sure, Golden used pseudonyms in his notes, but he had an obvious reason to do so, Boltedal didn't.

'Oh?' said Golden.

'I was wondering in particular about that aid programme.'

Fuck!

The project the journalist was digging into was a collaboration with the Nigerian agent Chukwudi. Bayelsa State in Nigeria was known for its oil deposits, but Golden had travelled round with Chukwudi and a couple of his pals, scouring the area for other commodities. By the time they were done, Golden Boys had the rights to seven 16-year-old talents. At least a couple of them would surely be good enough for the English Premier League.

It wasn't permitted to transfer footballers under the age of 18 from one continent to another. Besides, they would have to have played first-team international matches for Nigeria in order to get a residence permit in the UK. Luckily it was easier to get them to Norway, even before they turned 18.

The solution was the Norwegian school system. Golden put the boys in private sixth-form colleges. The headmaster was given a few thick envelopes, so he didn't ask any questions about why seven 16-year-olds from Nigeria should suddenly have their dreams fulfilled of attending a Norwegian school. Golden couldn't quite work out why the Minister of Education and Research let this exploitation pass, but if the politicians didn't react, then who would? PISA tests, or whatever they were called, didn't exactly keep Golden or his colleagues awake at night.

The Nigerian boys ate lunch in the school canteen now and then, but *otherwise they were never there, as the lessons were in Norwegian anyway. Their school fees still had to be paid though and, even if it was obvious that the boys were training with the Norwegian club, they couldn't let the school fees be traced back there. Golden Boys had to put up 400,000 kroner a year, so after two years it was high time for one of the boys to turn 18 and start seriously knocking in goals in the top division. So Golden sent Chukwudi down to Lagos with a fistful of dollars, and the required selection for the national team would soon be taken care of.*

'We've got an anonymous source who says that you've tricked the club out of millions in this transfer,' said Boltedal.

Bloody women. Golden was absolutely certain this leak had come from the club's board, and from one of the two sanctimonious female members who sat on it. Gender quotas on Norwegian football boards were madness. There were practically no qualified volunteers, and all clubs had to have at least two. It could only lead to trouble. They didn't understand how the economy of football worked.

Golden thought he deserved his agreed 20 per cent cut of the transfer fees, but when the sale price worked out at 79 million kroner, his agency fee was simply too much for the Norwegian club. 15.8 million kroner couldn't be swept under the carpet, the board wouldn't accept it.

'Our source also claims that you paid the Norwegian club's chairman under the table so that the money would go into a fund labelled "aid",' Boltedal continued.

Bloody women. Bloody journalist.

The club's board had suggested paying Golden 1 million kroner as his agency fee. 1 million! He'd already spent that much in expenses. What were they thinking? Breaking even wasn't how Golden had built his empire. He sat down with the club chairman and talked about the apartment complex Spain. They agreed that 1 million would be declared as the agency fee, and the rest would go into a so-called aid fund.

The argument was put to the board that, since the club now had lots of money and still had six other players for sale soon, part of the money could go back to the impoverished area they'd come from. The aid fund would go towards developing facilities in Bayelsa State.

This was acceptable for the board, but after a couple of online searches, none of them dared to travel to the rough region, so they agreed that Golden could keep them updated on developments with photographs. How difficult would it be to find a picture of an artificial grass pitch?

The money from the transfer was used to cover Arild Golden's travel costs, and the club chairman's private holidays. Honestly, do they really need artificial pitches in Nigeria?

It had worked out, but it was still messy. Loose-tongued board members were grumbling about it, and amateurs like Chukwudi were always a threat. From now on, only Golden's lawyers would have access to his deals.

'No comment,' said Golden. 'And if you carry on making insinuations like this, I'll sue you from here to eternity.'

"Posh" and "Becks"

First came the pink graphics, then two arrows flew by with Per and Sabrina's names embroidered on ribbons trailing below. From the opposite side came a heart-shaped football. The arrows hit the ball, penetrating it, and they all flew down towards Ullevaal Stadion. In the centre circle was an animated version of the young couple kissing in front of a capacity crowd. One by one, the letters appeared on the green grass: *PDTV.*

When life became complicated, Benedikte thought, there was only one thing to do: watch reality TV. She'd tried many times to justify her love for the genre. Call it mental pornography, escapism or whatever else, the truth was that Benedikte loved it. They worse they got, the programmes only seemed to get more enjoyable. Her current favourite was MTV's *A Shot at Love with Tila Tequila,* in which the bisexual presenter was chatted up by both men and women.

PDTV hadn't yet qualified for a podium spot in reality TV heaven, but there had been some priceless scenes, such as when Marius Bjartmann and his wife came round for dinner. Watching Bjartmann eating sushi with chopsticks was unforgettable. It looked like the centre-back was wearing windproof mittens. The item had been so popular that the producers were considering introducing a regular dinner feature. Norwegians couldn't get enough of watching famous people eat.

Football used to be shy and maybe even a little boring. That was until David Beckham married Posh Spice. Soon we would hear that Becks had taken a boot on the head from a hot-tempered Alex Ferguson, that Zlatan got into fights with numerous teammates, and that most coaches thought they were Al Pacino in *Any Given Sunday,* all stories that once would've stayed in the changing rooms. In any case, a reality TV series about a Norwegian footballer's life wouldn't have happened before

David met Victoria.

The fact that Beckham had gone on playing well while he became a public figure made it easier for Vålerenga to accept their highest-profile player marketing himself like this. Vålerenga had also had the opportunity for various product placements that they, in turn, had sold on to their sponsors. At the same time, they coached everyone from their own management on the importance of describing *PDTV* as 'good PR'.

Vålerenga had grown to become top of the class in financial terms, having once done their accounts on hot-dog wrappers. The club's great financial sobriety meant its accounts for the previous year had only marginally gone tens of millions of kroner into the red, and now they'd set themselves the unenviable target of actually balancing the books. They couldn't let any potential revenue sources slip away. The club knew that, if they managed to balance the books and have a Norwegian football club making money, they would be responsible for the greatest revolution in football since the invention of the goal.

But the rights to the concept, and to the big money, belonged to Golden Boys and the newspaper *VG*, whose website hosted the series, and they were already talking about expanding the idea to other top Norwegian players. Maybe they could even come up with the Holy Grail of Norwegian TV, something that would break NRK's stranglehold on Friday evenings, *At Home with the Riises*.

PDTV had started as a low-budget project, but then Diesen moved in with Sabrina, and his form on the pitch improved at the same rate as the number of views for his videos. For the sake of appearances, *VG* had taken a short production break in connection with the death of Golden, but now it was being rumoured that they wanted to put even more resources into the programme. Golden's murder was, on balance, good news. For ratings.

The camera panned through the living room. The interior decoration magazines that had done picture stories on their apartment had described it as 'hypermodern, but not without warmth and cosiness'. The flooring consisted of wide wooden boards painted gloss white, the furniture looked old but wasn't really, and even the mess looked planned. Benedikte imagined the interior designers arguing about the selection of magazines to put there and the angle at which to display them on the white wooden chair.

Dagbladet's Saturday supplement had also featured their home on its front cover, which was guaranteed to annoy their main competitors from *VG*, who had shown Diesen and Sabrina embracing, reflected in the bathroom mirror. An artistic black-and-white photo, accompanied by 14 occurrences of the word 'sex' in the text below. *VG* had wanted an exclusivity agreement, but it hit a brick wall in negotiations with Golden. Players, coaches, club managers and NFF executives, Benedikte had spoken with many people who'd dealt with Golden, and they all spoke of him like a god. If he entered a room with a few people in it, he'd own all of them. Who else could've made 100 million kroner out of a TV contract? 100 million kroner that should've gone to the football world itself. It was a contract that really belonged to the realms of fantasy, and Benedikte had never completely worked out why nobody had been sacked. It seemed as if people in football covered each other's back at any price.

The picture zoomed in on Diesen, sprawled out on the pink sofa. The camera zoomed in even closer, on his face, on his eye, past the blue iris to the black hole of his pupil. How did he manage to keep so calm? How did he manage to stay focused? Football was demanding its players to perform more than ever. The repercussions of the financial crisis were being felt as everybody cut back, and it was difficult to get new contracts in Norway or professional contracts abroad. The TV and newspapers were ready to give Diesen a hard time as soon as he stopped performing at his best, and now his Everton transfer had probably gone down the drain. Diesen blinked. Another wide shot.

Sabrina entered the scene, although it looked more as if she'd been thrown on. Benedikte wondered how Golden could've fallen for her. Why would he have risked so much for a pair of fake boobs? Golden was known for his style and sophisticated ways. Maybe it took a man to fully understand the fascination of such bazookas.

Sabrina was wearing blue-striped pyjamas, with a large number of buttons undone. She rolled around on the chaise longue, which matched the sofa. She then spent a small eternity piling up cushions so that the chaise longue could function more or less as a normal sofa.

Sabrina gave a deep sigh when everything was in place. She put her legs up on the stack of cushions.

'You could have helped me, you know?' she said, putting her MacBook Air on her lap. It annoyed Benedikte that Sabrina used the same laptop as her. Diesen was watching an on-demand episode of *Desperate Housewives*.

Sabrina's career had been on a vertical trajectory over the past few months. Even her unsuccessful appearance on *Paradise Hotel* last year had been turned into something positive. Sabrina had been brought in as a guest presenter for the last few weeks of the current series, a job that didn't require her to sleep with anybody, but one that let her wear skimpy clothing and be cheeky. According to the celebrity news website *Side2*, she was now towering at the top of the list of celebrities Norwegian teenage girls identified with most.

Sabrina's participation on the Norwegian edition of *Strictly Come Dancing* had also helped her to reach all age groups. Between them, the two programmes reached most Norwegian viewers, with the exception of the small group who were actually telling the truth when they claimed that they didn't watch reality shows.

As a natural consequence of these programmes, Sabrina was now an active participant in two separate 'blog wars'. While her *Paradise Hotel* blog posts were used as often as possible to call the others tarts, especially the male participants, the posts on her dancing blog were kinder, or at worst veiled allegations. The furthest she went was to suggest that Elin Hval, a female soap star, had put on a good few pounds after she'd stopped her intensive dance training.

Sabrina closed her MacBook and replaced it with a cushion, covering up her body. You could almost hear the producer groan. Sabrina put her hands on the cushion and crossed her legs even more. Diesen stopped watching *Desperate Housewives* and looked at her. The camera zoomed in on Sabrina's face. She had a natural beauty when her fake breasts weren't getting in the way of a good conversation. Maybe that's how Golden had seen her? Or was Benedikte reading too much into it? Was it just sex, and only sex?

'Have you learnt the lyrics yet?' asked Diesen. Sabrina had been used as a backing singer and dancer the last few times Diesen and Bjartmann had performed their mega-hit. Since Vålerenga were going to play that Saturday, the three of them would mime the words live on *Football Xtra* on Sunday, in what was probably the last appearance Golden had booked.

Sabrina was lost in her own thoughts. It took her a few seconds to digest the fact that she was being spoken to.

'Yeah, but I've got a question. I don't quite get the meaning.'

'What are you on about?'

'The chorus. You know, when it goes: "Bleed, bleed, bleed for the team. Hunt out that autumn dream." Why should we be singing about the autumn now, when it's summer?'

In an in-depth interview by the women's magazine *Henne*, Diesen had revealed that when he got home, he didn't have to explain why he'd messed up a pass or dribbled the ball too far. Sabrina asked if he'd won or lost and expressed an appropriate dose of happiness or disappointment accordingly. Sabina didn't know that the autumn hunting season in Norwegian football had nothing at all do with culling animals.

Sabrina was supposed to mime the lyrics and jump around as the heavy drumbeat sounded in between the words 'bleed, bleed, bleed'. Benedikte didn't think textual analysis was really called for.

'The lyrics point forwards to the future,' Diesen answered. 'The championship finishes in the autumn, so that's when everyone's hunting for the important points at the end of the season.'

'And what about the next line, "Red and blue, we're coming through"?'

'What's wrong with it?'

'Well I've got a bit of a thing for colours, you know. You're not red and blue. You're blue with a bit of red and a bit of white.'

'I see your point. And while we're on the subject, what are you going to wear on TV?'

'I'm stuck between a black or a brown top. Not sure. What are you and Marius going to wear?'

'Marius and I'll be wearing white shirts with open collars. Maybe it'd be best if you wear the black one?' said Diesen.

'Then I'll go for that. Are we still doing lip-sync?'

'Yes. Why?'

'I heard the original recording when we were in the studio that day. And Marius really can't sing. They didn't need to do anything with your voice, but Marius, good God, he sounded like he had some sort of disease, the poor guy.' Sabrina was whispering, not that it made what she was saying any less hurtful.

'Don't tell him. He thinks he sings really well. But that's probably why people have studios like those. No big stars use their own voices. It's all done by machines now,' Diesen whispered back.

'Even Engelbert Humperdinck?'

'Alright, maybe not him, but apart from him.'

'Well, Marius needs it anyway!' said Sabrina, giggling.

Diesen smiled cautiously. Then he kissed Sabrina on the cheek, said goodnight and went to bed. The episode faded out with Sabrina picking up her MacBook again and carrying on blogging about hula hoops and lip balm, and about how life as a football widow could be made easier by walking downhill instead of uphill when going shopping along Bogstadveien.

This was the most recent episode, so Benedikte didn't quite know what to do next. She stayed on the website to see the end of the video, skimming through the credits, where she spotted the name of Bettina Robertsen, an old classmate of hers. She had a source from within the world of Per Diesen.

Coma

'You said I should call you at any time if I had any news.'

It took Steinar a few seconds to wake up. He'd been dreaming about how to get it on with Benedikte again, and he'd picked up the phone by reflex. It was Bjørnar. His alarm clock showed it was 06:14.

'What's happened?' asked Steinar.

'He's fallen into a coma overnight. We don't think he's going to wake up again. I'm really sorry.'

'Thanks for calling,' said Steinar, dropping the phone next to him on the duvet. He stared at a knothole in the wooden ceiling.

Steinar had once heard that the happiest period in a man's life was the time after his first divorce. That must have come from a man who had done the walking out himself. For Steinar, the period when Mette's inner backpacker had reawakened had been full of anxiety. In the months after she'd left, Steinar had woken up every night, certain that Junior was about to die of cot death. Even though Junior had to be too old for that, Steinar jumped out of bed time after time, running into the boy's room and listening to check he was breathing. Time after time he'd felt relieved, tucked the duvet tight round the little poppet and sat there watching his sleeping child.

Steinar didn't run into Junior's room any more when he couldn't sleep, but he usually popped his head round the door to check on him anyway. He got up and turned his head to the right, cracking his neck and feeling his spine wake up. He rubbed his scalp hard for a few seconds and went towards the boy's room.

The cot was empty. What had happened? Junior had never climbed out of his cot before. If he woke up, which he sometimes did, he would start crying, but Steinar hadn't heard anything this time. He shouted, but there was no answer. Junior had gone. Steinar felt his stomach in knots and ran to the front door, turning the handle. Locked. He sped into the living room, but Junior was nowhere to be seen. He checked the kitchen, the utility room and the bathroom before running down the slippery steps into the basement. He cursed the stairs, but there was nobody down there either.

He ran back up, locked the basement door and went up to the first floor, where there were another two bedrooms and a bathroom. Junior wasn't in the bathroom, nor was he in either of the bedrooms.

Steinar ran back down to the living room.

Junior was reading on the sofa. Or rather he was flicking through a large pop-up book, which hid most of him from view. Still, Steinar should have spotted him the first time. He supposed that he was distracted because of Ståle Jakobsen. He wanted to lift up Junior and give him a hug, but there was something about seeing his son behind a book that pleased Steinar, and he didn't want to interrupt him. He stood there for a few minutes until Junior put down his book and stared at his father, waiting for him to say something. As if it were Steinar's responsibility, he thought, just because he was an adult.

'Breakfast,' said Steinar, and they went to the kitchen together. Steinar started making an omelette, while Junior ate a blueberry yoghurt. Steinar shook the pan so that the eggs wouldn't stick to the bottom. He put in some pieces of ham and some cheese. Shook it again. Junior, who'd had enough yoghurt, jumped down from his chair and ran into the living room. Steinar left him in peace. He took his omelette and a cup of coffee and sat down at the kitchen table, where he could see the boy in the corner of his eye. Junior had found another book. Steinar sneaked out to fetch the newspaper.

He was immersed in reading a piece on illegal workers when Junior came back into the kitchen, his shirt covered in yoghurt stains. Steinar looked at the time. They would have to hurry. He went to the utility room and fetched some clean clothes, took a good hold of Junior and pulled off his shirt. He suddenly stopped to stare at two blisters on his chest. Was it chickenpox? Damn. On any normal day this wouldn't have been a problem, but today he had another meeting with Taribo.

'Are you feeling alright?' asked Steinar.

Junior looked up at the ceiling. It was difficult to get any information from him at that moment. Steinar went to fetch the thermometer instead. No temperature.

How dangerous was chickenpox anyway? Wasn't it good to have

it when you were young? That's surely what the other parents would think too. They'd see it as Steinar doing them a favour. If he was honest, though, how many times had he suspected that the others had been lying too? With conjunctivitis or diarrhoea, symptoms were supposed to be absent for at least 48 hours before they took their children back to nursery.

Junior rarely came home wearing the same T-shirt he'd started the day in. The nursery staff would notice the blisters when they changed him. Steinar did the only thing that a single father with childcare problems could do on such an occasion, he rummaged through the things that Mette had left in the bathroom until he found what he was looking for. Concealer.

He couldn't fail to appear at the prison meeting because Benedikte was right. he'd been too soft at the previous sessions. This time he had to press Taribo.

Morning Star

'I saw you on that breakfast show,' said Arnold Nesje.

'*God Morgen Norge.*'

'What?'

'It's called *God Morgen Norge*,' said Benedikte, not quite sure why she was pointing this out. It came automatically. She'd worked on the programme for a long time and felt some kind of pride in it. Once, at a party, she'd even made a long speech in defence of the programme's red leather sofa.

The state broadcaster NRK's equivalent was called *Frokost-TV*, a programme that disappointed its viewers time after time. NRK would surely try to work on it at some point, but they couldn't get it right at the moment. *God Morgen Norge* wasn't the poor man's *Frokost-TV*, it was the other way round.

'I didn't call you to discuss TV programmes,' said Benedikte.

'I didn't think so.'

'I'm struggling.'

'What do you mean?'

'I've got no experience with murder cases. Hypothetically, how do the police look for a murderer?'

'Hypothetically?'

'If you'd found a body, what would you do next?'

'In that case I'd be what we'd call the first responding officer, and I'd write up a report on my observations. Actually, to start with I would've made sure that the body was dead, and if I had the slightest doubt I would call for a doctor.'

'Let's say there was no doubt.'

'Then I would've asked the control centre to send crime scene protection and the forensic investigation unit.'

'They're the ones in the white spacesuits, right?'

'Right. They investigate the crime scene and gather forensic evidence.'

'What about potential motives?'

'We don't look for any motives at the start. We look for evidence that might link people to the scene of the crime, or that suggest a timeline of events. Objective evidence like video footage from CCTV cameras.'

'Do you know if anything like that has been found in the Golden case?'

'No suspects were picked up on camera.'

'What happens next?'

'A police officer will be appointed to take over after the preliminary investigation has been carried out. He'll be given whatever information they've got, forensic evidence, in other words DNA and fingerprints, any witness statements there might be and police reports. Mobile phone data is also very useful.'

'What do you mean?'

'There might be data on the victim's phone showing who he's been in contact with. Base station tracking can also tell us where he's been. In many cases this has led to important witnesses or even helped find the culprit.'

'But let's say that there's no DNA, fingerprints or useful phone data from the killer. What would it be important to look for when interviewing witnesses?'

'Obviously we'd try to see if there's anything that sticks out. Did anybody threaten the victim? Debts: does he owe anybody money? Jealousy: is he having an affair? Might a jealous husband have something to do with it?'

'So money and sex, basically,' said Benedikte.

'Yes, if you want to put it tabloid terms.'

Money and sex. They'd both reared their heads while Benedikte had been investigating Golden.

'Why does this matter so much to you, anyway?' Nesje continued.

'The killing of Golden is the biggest story in Norwegian football for several decades, maybe even the biggest story ever. Doing a report on the transfer of a right-back from HamKam to Kongsvinger pales somewhat in comparison.'

Benedikte didn't want to expand on her suspicions about the health risks of astroturf for now.

'But the murderer's been caught. Taribo Shorunmo's been locked up.'

'What proof have you got against him?'

'Benedikte, you know that I can't...'

'Come on,' said Benedikte, interrupting him. 'I need some inside info.'

'I could get sacked for less.'

'You know that I won't do anything to expose you. There'll be no mention of "police sources" or anything like that,' said Benedikte.

'I don't have access to the case files, but I've spoken with the officer in charge. He's a good friend of mine. If any of the information I give you gets out, he'll immediately know it came from me.'

Benedikte didn't say any more. She'd reassured him that she wouldn't name him as the informant, and she'd keep her word.

'The door system kept a record of the number of visitors to Golden's office,' said Nesje. 'On the day of his murder, Golden only let somebody in from the street once. The witness statement also indicated that Taribo Shorunmo was in Golden's office that day.'

'Did he only have one visitor? I thought Golden was supposed to be a very busy man.'

'I suppose agents deal mostly over the phone.'

'There are other ways to Golden's office, though. It's a big stadium. For example, you could go in through the hotel and then into the conference suite. Then you'd have a safe route from there.'

'Not so easy on the day of the murder. The conference suite was closed off. A company had hired the restaurant for a seafood buffet. According to the general manager, the buffet was a bit more extravagant than the company's budget suggested, so they were very careful not to let in any uninvited guests. But, of course, it's Golden's office we're really interested in, and he was also careful not to let in any uninvited guests. There were surely quite a few of you journalists who might like to sneak in and have a look through his files. His office has an electronic lock. There was only one recorded visit at the time in question.'

'Have you got anything else?'

'We found a weapon at Taribo Shorunmo's house known as a morning star.'

Benedikte started Googling this while Nesje continued, bringing up many different illustrations of the weapon. It looked like a giant medieval cotton bud with sharp spikes.

'So you found the murder weapon,' said Benedikte. Maybe it was Taribo Shorunmo who had killed Golden after all.

'We won't know for sure until the autopsy report is done, and it might still be weeks or even months until that's finally finished.'

Benedikte looked up from the images on her screen. 'What about a motive?'

'They're working on several theories.'

'Which one would you see as most likely?'

'The murder was brutal, it was carried out with such force. I think there's something personal behind it. Real hatred.'

In or Out?

His mobile was taken off him again before he was taken into the meeting room at Oslo Prison. At least child welfare wouldn't be able to get hold of him, Steinar thought. Concealer make-up, what had he been thinking?

Taribo came into the room and they shook each other's hand. There was an air of exhaustion about him, but Steinar's hand hurt just the same.

'How's it going today?' asked Steinar.

'I haven't been able to sleep.'

'What's wrong?'

'The smell, the sounds, the bed. And then I keep thinking about Stanley.'

'I understand.'

'You know, for the first time since I came here, I'm missing Nigeria. We used to live by the woods in a simple brick house with a tin roof. It felt like sleeping outdoors. I've never wished to be back there before, but that's where I slept best.'

Steinar nodded then cleared his throat. 'We've got to talk about the matter of payment.'

'How much?'

'The trial won't cost you anything, I'm your court-appointed defence lawyer. But I will need payment as Stanley's agent, and I've come up with a formula I think is fair.'

'What would that be?'

'Young players who don't make much money shouldn't pay anything. I'll take 3 per cent of any earnings Stanley makes over 1 million kroner, up to a maximum limit of 100,000 kroner a year. If we can get the club to pay this fee, you won't have to pay me anything.'

Taribo just looked at Steinar, speechless.

'Do you think it's an unreasonable amount?' asked Steinar.

'Are you kidding? Golden wanted 25 per cent. Of everything.'

'25 per cent? Is that really how much he was after?' Steinar was genuinely shocked. For him, 100,000 kroner a year was the maximum an agent should be making from one player. He'd heard of extortionate fees from agents, but demanding 25 per cent of his salary was verging on criminal. If that's how Golden acted in all his business dealings, there was probably no shortage of volunteers willing to take him out.

'Like I said, 3 per cent,' said Steinar, 'but I need you to write a letter to your partner explaining that I'm on your side, so she'll trust me too. It's good that she's got a healthy scepticism of football agents, but it makes my job difficult. Strictly speaking, you're not allowed to write letters, so you'll have to keep quiet about this. Deal?'

'Deal,' said Taribo. He wrote a letter to his partner and gave it to Steinar. 'Won't they search you?'

'They didn't yesterday. I'm hoping it'll be alright,' said Steinar, leaving the letter on the table. It was time to press Taribo, try to find out the truth. He drew his breath and leant forward.

'Why were you at Golden's office that day?'

'Negotiations. That was when Golden made his demand for 25 per cent.'

'You realise that gives you a motive? Disagreements about money are often behind things like this.'

Taribo's eyes narrowed, his pupils growing as he leant forward too.

'Had you met Golden before?' asked Steinar. 'When you were playing in Nigeria?'

'No.'

'I need to know the truth. Did you kill him?'

Taribo took to his feet so quickly his chair toppled over, hitting the floor with a crash. He leant over the table, towering above Steinar, and slammed down his right hand.

'No!' he said, nostrils flaring. Then he turned and walked towards the wall.

'Do you know who might have done it? Are you covering for someone?'

'No,' Taribo said again.

Had he just hesitated before answering? Steinar wished he could have seen Taribo's eyes at that moment. He let the man calm down from his outburst before carrying on. 'When was it you said that Stanley turn 15?'

'On Sunday.'

'I know the race is on to protect him from other agents, but turning 15 also marks something else.'

'What do you mean?'

'It's the age of criminal responsibility. Stanley can't be punished for anything he's done before.'

'Get out!'

Steinar wondered whether he might have lost his client.

But Taribo let him take the letter with him.

An Accident

Benedikte took a window seat at Bar Boca, back in Grünerløkka, and waited for Bettina Robertsen. She had a sip of wine and felt the temperature rising in her cheeks. She fumbled to pick up the pages of an almost worn-out copy of *Dagbladet*. The large-print headline on the tabloid's front page read: 'HOW TO AVOID A HEART ATTACK.' Golden wasn't front-page material any more, now that Shorunmo had been locked up. The newspaper could let its usual fare dominate again, recipes for how to avoid cancer, cardiovascular diseases, stroke or diabetes.

In through the door came Bettina, Benedikte's old classmate from Bjerke Upper Secondary School. Bettina had been the quiet, shy and artistic one in the class. The girl who was always doodling, no matter whether it was maths or Norwegian they were supposed to be studying.

Bettina had the habit of putting her hands in her trouser pockets and pushing out her stomach. She stood there, eyes scanning the middle of the room, until she saw Benedikte. Her smile lasted approximately two hundredths of a second, more of a short twitch on the left side of her lip. Bettina still used the same amount of black make-up as she had at school, which made Benedikte think of Halloween just as much now as it did then.

For the first few minutes Benedikte had to drag the words out of her friend. For their next round, they swapped the wine for something stronger and, one hour later, Bettina was tipsy and had started to talk about her job working on the graphics for *PDTV* as well as a number of other video productions for the *VG* website. After another drink Bettina was quite eager to tell Benedikte all about a forthcoming programme on magic tricks, and Benedikte made several attempts to bring the conversation back to where she wanted it.

'Why are you so interested in *PDTV*? Do you need a new job?' asked Bettina.

'No, but I'm looking into everything that's got to do with Arild Golden.'

'Was he that large, pushy guy?' asked Bettina. It was almost beyond belief that anybody in Norway hadn't seen Golden's picture in the past few days, but that's what Bettina was like, focused solely on her own little world.

Benedikte tried to describe him anyway. 'Golden was a handsome man, always wore a suit. A mobile phone in each hand, always talking into one of them. He's only the one who's been killed, you know.'

'I usually block out names and other non-essentials. If you'd started by describing his cheekbones or shoulders, then I'd have known straight away. He dropped by the set a couple of times, but only for a few minutes. I wasn't always there, anyway. I do the graphics, so I don't need to see everything that happens. But that other guy also called himself an agent. It was so weird, people going round there calling themselves agents.'

'Did you get the other man's name?'

'No,' said Bettina, but Benedikte knew it couldn't be anybody else but Ola Bugge.

'Did anything ever happen that seemed odd to you? Anything suspicious?'

'There was some footage that disappeared. Deleted.'

'Why?'

'I don't know. We installed some cameras in the flat and filmed some test footage to try out the system. This was just a few days before the series premiere. We were seriously behind and I didn't think we were going to make it in time. I was supposed to get access to the footage so it would be easier for me to put together suitable graphics, but the footage wasn't there.'

'Did you ask anybody what had happened?'

'I went to the executive producer. He said he didn't know what had happened, but they'd have some new test footage ready in a few hours. They gave that to me, and I made the graphics. I didn't have any more time to spend worrying about it, it was non-stop stress right up to the deadline.'

'Who could have deleted the video?'

'It's quite likely it was an accident, but if somebody intentionally wanted to do it, it wouldn't be difficult. Most of us had access to the footage from the cameras, which had just been filming an empty apartment. It's only when we start full production mode that they really keep an eye on what we're filming.'

'So was it just an accident?' asked Benedikte.

'I don't know,' said Bettina, with a hiccup.

Hidden Transfers

As he rang the doorbell, Steinar realised he wouldn't be winning 'Dad of the Year' this year either. He was at a house on Dyretråkket, a street in the suburb of Holmlia. On the outside, it was painted an eggshell colour and had red cladding. It was impossible to guess how many flats there were inside. He was standing at the entry door, in the shadow of a large veranda.

He'd had three missed calls when he left his meeting with Taribo. No journalists this time, they were all from Jenna at the nursery. Steinar had called her back and was told to come immediately. She was threatening to exclude Junior.

Why were there so many Swedes working in nurseries in Oslo anyway? And in bars too? If it was true that only kids and drunk people told the truth, then the Swedes would soon have a monopoly on shaping it.

Changing nurseries was something Steinar absolutely didn't want to go through. It'd taken a lot of work to get a place for Junior at that place, and the boy loved it there. Steinar had poured out his troubles over the phone, being a single father and all that, and Jenna had thawed a little.

Luckily, Bjørnar's parents were more than glad to look after Junior for a couple of hours. They lived next door and had helped Steinar out before. They were usually able to help, unless they were on one of their many visits to Steinar's parents in Spain.

Steinar rang the doorbell again, and Stanley's mother opened the door.

'What do you want?' she asked.

'Read this before you say another word,' said Steinar, passing her the envelope.

She kept her eyes on Steinar for a long moment then slowly lowered her gaze, took out the letter and read it.

She opened the door and waved Steinar in. He sat down at the kitchen table as instructed, and accepted the offer of coffee. Steinar watched her while she served. She was in her late thirties and had a bit too much of everything, too many wrinkles, her hair a bit overgrown, and a bit too much padding.

'I'm sorry that I was a little abrupt just now. Let's start again. My name's Mona Johansen, and you must be Taribo's lawyer, right? I was told he was arrested, but since then it's been impossible to get in touch with him. How's he doing in there?'

'He's fine, all things considered, but he's in solitary confinement.'

'But you can bring messages?'

'I'm stretching the rules. I won't do it any more, but it was important for you to know what Taribo wanted for Stanley.'

'What do you think about the case?'

'I don't like the fact the police seem so pleased with themselves. They've more or less stopped investigations and are positive that Taribo's guilty. When that happens, getting a conviction is often a piece of cake.'

'The police can't be bothered to look any more once they've found somebody. Especially not when there's someone who fits the profile as well as Taribo does. Black, and an illegal immigrant.'

Steinar blew on his coffee, which was made with water from a kettle and two teaspoons of Nescafé. It was still far too hot. He knew how easy it was to make sweeping generalisations. Nescafé? He'd had slightly higher expectations when it came to coffee served in a half-African home.

'But can we afford to pay you? Aren't lawyers like you very expensive?' asked Mona.

'My fees will be covered by the state. Besides, this case has also given me two other sources of future income. A case like this will make my business better known, and I'll have the rights to represent Stanley.'

'At least you're honest. There have been several other agents here trying to court Stanley since Arild Golden died, and they made it out as if we should thank the Lord they would deign to have anything to do with our son.'

'Did you meet Golden?'

'Yes.'

'What impression did you get of him?'

'Definitely a capable businessman. He told us when we signed with him Stanley would get an immediate offer from West Ham's academy. He also presented a business plan showing how Stanley would make it rich within the next few years. But that bastard was cynical to the core.'

'In what way?'

'Stanley had a number of physical problems. Pain in one of his knees and in both Achilles tendons. You know, Stanley was lured over to Skeid two years ago. Vålerenga, Lyn, Stabæk and Skeid were all begging for him, and when it turned out that Holmlia's own team couldn't offer him good enough training, we decided that he could move clubs, but we let him make the decision for himself. He chose Skeid because he knew a number of players there. We organised everything so he could get from school to his training sessions and matches. Everything went fine until Stanley began to complain of these injuries.'

'What did you do?'

'I took him along to our GP. He's got a son of his own who plays on Holmlia's junior team and played with Stanley before he went to Skeid. He diagnosed Stanley with the early stages of jumper's knee and chronic Achilles tendonitis.'

'Did you tell Golden?' asked Steinar.

'He was furious. He said that we had to keep it to ourselves. He also wanted to send Stanley to a specialist he knew. Well, after Golden's death, we found out what that miracle doctor was doing. Naturally, he wouldn't see Stanley again once Golden wasn't paying him, so we took Stanley back to our GP. He spoke with Stanley, examined him again and became suspicious. Golden's doctor had been giving him cortisone injections. These helped with his knee and tendon problems in the short term, but they could give him enormous problems later in life. His tendons might snap in a few years' time. Our doctor called it madness to use cortisone in treatment like that, especially with a young boy.'

'Do you know why he did that?' said Steinar, wondering whether that was the reason Taribo had threatened Golden.

'Golden had struck a deal with West Ham. Stanley was due to go to them in August, and these days there's big money to be made by agents. The clubs where he played before can't claim anything more than some small change if he goes to an academy.'

'What do you mean?' asked Steinar.

'Golden called them hidden transfers, because Stanley wouldn't be sold to the professional part of the club. First he would go to the academy, where they can only pay him board and lodging, plus a few scraps of pocket money, so West Ham wouldn't need to buy him. But there was an agreement under the table that he would graduate from the academy into their first team squad. We would share a lump sum payment for the transfer with Golden Boys, which West Ham were only too happy to pay, because it was a lot less than the sum Skeid and Holmlia would've got from a professional transfer.'

'And Golden told you this?'

'We had to give him our consent, after all. He said it was normal. In cases when the clubs were especially keen, as they were with Stanley, they were willing to give the agent several million kroner under the table. Golden promised us half of the money, but we didn't know about that business with the injections.'

They heard the door close and Stanley came in. He took off his red hoodie, pulling up his grey T-shirt in the process, revealing a six-pack. Stanley put his hoodie on a chair and pulled his T-shirt back down, then took out his MP3 player and shook Steinar by the hand. He was almost as tall and muscular as his father.

'How's it going?' asked Steinar.

Stanley looked Steinar up and down before giving a shrug.

'Can we have a chat?' asked Steinar. Stanley didn't answer but came and sat down.

'I'll go into the living room, so you two can speak,' Mona said, leaving the kitchen.

Stanley and Steinar made small talk for a few minutes. Stanley didn't seem very interested to start with, but he gradually started to listen once he realised Steinar had been a good footballer, an international professional.

'Your dad wants me to be your agent,' said Steinar.

Stanley's face lit up.

'Yes!' he said, slapping Steinar on the back.

Steinar had spent the past day reading about young Norwegian players lured to various big teams' academies. Almost without exception, they came back like slaughtered animals and spent years trying to build up a fraction of the career they might have had, wrecks as footballers, and wrecks in terms of their education too. The educational side of foreign football academies seemed a bit of a joke. Stanley would have his breakthrough at home in Norway before being sold. If he was going to be the boy's agent, Steinar would build him up both as a player and a person.

'But the most important thing is to get you into a proper secondary school where you can get some good exam marks. However you do as a football player, your education will always be useful.'

Steinar heard the floor creaking and looked up to see Mona standing in the doorway.

'I think we might be able to work together,' she said.

Steinar was glad to have gained their trust, but his happiness was short-lived. Stuck on the fridge, behind a magnet, was a picture that Steinar hadn't noticed until now. A picture of Stanley and his dad, Taribo, at a football match, flanked by another bundle of muscles over 6 feet tall. They had their arms around each other and were smiling. Maybe they were celebrating a win. They were certainly happy. Especially the man that Steinar had seen together with Taribo at Nordre Åsen. The man that Taribo denied knowing. Taribo, who he had to defend in a murder case, had lied to him. How many other lies had he been telling?

Zizu

It was after 10 o' clock. Benedikte walked through the last part of Grünerløkka to a corner of another part of town, Sagene. She crossed over the inner ring-road and went along Vogts Gate, through the neighbourhoods of Torshov and Sandaker and up to Storo. The busy junction there was a jumble of tram lines, tarmac and paving stones, so Benedikte took the cycle path towards Grefsen Station, which for some reason had a window shaped like a Star of David. Then she walked under the outer ring road and up Kjelsåsveien. The walk made her more or less sober again, but she was still heading quite clearly towards Steinar's house.

She wanted to laugh at *PDTV*, maybe show Steinar some of the highlights and ponder what might have happened to the tapes Bettina had spoken about, and what might have been on them.

She was also curious about how the relationship between Steinar and Taribo was developing, and whether he'd got any further with Stanley. Or had other agents joined the fight?

And then there was that business with the Astroturf. She couldn't stop thinking about it. Some online research had given her further shocking relevations that she would have to investigate more closely. She needed help and wanted Steinar to be the one to help her. But most of all Bendikte had gone there from Bar Boca because she wanted to.

Her determined footsteps stopped two paces away from Steinar's house in Lofthusveien. She looked through the kitchen window and found herself staring at Junior's tear-stained face. Steinar was rocking him gently like a baby.

Junior raised his hand towards the window. Benedikte waved quickly and walked out of sight. The boy was clearly sick and needed his dad, she couldn't just come barging in now.

She walked down Lofthusveien until she came to Skeid's football pitch at Nordre Åsen. She went in through the black metal gate and over to the astroturf. She leaned against the fence and watched a couple of young lads knocking the ball to each other. One of the lads was tall, dark and West African. He was wearing rolled down socks, shorts that were far too long and a Barcelona top with the UNICEF logo on it. The other boy had lighter skin and was a little shorter, probably North African. The Barcelona boy called him 'Zizu', after Zinedine Zidane. He did resemble him, without a doubt. He was wearing a white football top with the number 5 on the back. They kicked the ball as it fell, giving it as much spin as possible. The organised matches and training sessions had finished for the day, but there was still enough light for a kickabout.

Benedikte stepped onto the synthetic grass which was hard, like green tarmac. Pieces had started to flake off the pitch, as if it had psoriasis.

One of the lads kicked the ball as hard as he could. It hit the crossbar, looped over the goal and bounced away. Zizu slapped his thigh and pointed at his friend, laughing at him for having to go and fetch the ball.

Benedikte took out her mobile and scrolled down through her contact list. She couldn't deal with the Golden case seriously without following up on every bit of information, and maybe it was best to keep Steinar out of it, he might try to stop her. This could cost Benedikte her job after all.

She scrolled until she came to the number of the NFF's facilities manager, Birger Holme.

Part 6

5 October 2009

Arild Golden stood in his office on the phone with Per Kristian Boltedal, the journalist from Dagens Næringsliv. He looked across the pitch at Ullevaal while trying to avoid answering Boltedal's questions. Still, he also needed to find out what the journalist was getting at.

'We've heard rumours about money being passed under the table in a transfer deal involving a well-known Swedish keeper moving from a big-name Norwegian club to an even bigger-name English club. What can you tell me about that?'

'No comment,' said Golden. Snotty brat, he thought. Bloody punk journalist, with his 'Swedish keeper, big-name Norwegian club, bigger-name English club'. If he was going to accuse Golden of something, he should do it properly and name names.

Golden knew which transfer the journalist was alluding to, it had happened in a moment of pure Golden inspiration. He'd been at a match and was impressed by the keeper. At the same time, he saw a well-known English talent scout in the stands and sat down next to him.

The English team didn't really need a new keeper but the match was so terrible, and there were no other players near international standard, so the scout and Golden started negotiating.

By midway through the first half they'd agreed on 600,000 pounds. Not as the transfer fee, but as the sum Golden would have to send so that enough people would persuade the club's all-powerful manager that they needed a new keeper.

40 minutes after the end of the match, Golden had his first meeting with the keeper. He hoped that the keeper would have an anonymous little agent or, even better, a humble brother or father taking care of business dealings, but no, he had one of Sweden's biggest agents. Of course, having that agent wouldn't stop the transfer, but it would cost Golden extra.

'We've spoken with a Nigerian agent who claims that you paid him to be an "on-paper" agent,' said Boltedal.

This was the first time Golden had used Chukwudi for a transfer. Chukwudi was resident in Norway but, since it's the individual agent's own national association that issues a licence, Chukwudi was subject to Nigerian rules. In terms of football, that meant 25-year-old players on the national under-17 team, all of whom were born on 1 January. The Nigerian association was even more lacking in scrutiny than the Norwegian one.

Golden wouldn't dare let the Swedish agent into the negotiating room, so he'd represent the keeper himself. The English team had their own agent, so Golden would need one more person to represent the Norwegian club.

Still, Golden couldn't quite understand why he'd given this job to Chukwudi. Africans were muscle. When playing football, they shouldn't stand in goal or take penalties, and Golden couldn't think of a single African economy that was in good health. A generalisation? Well then, thought Golden, show me a decent goalie, penalty taker or accountant from Africa.

Of course it was an idiotic thing to do. Of course it was manna to the press. Why should this unknown Chukwudi represent the club in their biggest transfer ever? It was a good idea to use him to bring young Nigerians to Norway, but it had been madness to use him to represent a Norwegian club.

The money had been siphoned off in too many directions. Golden Boys were left with just 3 million kroner. A big transfer, but a terrible payback. Was he really going to be grilled about such trivial deals?

Golden answered: 'No comment.'

'I'll speak to you again soon,' said Boltedal.

Golden hung up.

XYZ

'Yes?'

'Benedikte Blystad to meet Birger Holme.'

'Come on up.'

A small click. Benedikte opened the door and went into the NFF's reception at Ullevaal Stadion.

Nobody was using Ullevaal that day. Vålerenga had played an away match against Start in Kristiansand the day before, and it was a long time until the next international. But the main reason it was empty was that Holme and Benedikte had agreed to meet on a Sunday morning.

Ahead of the entrance door was the changing room area. When she'd started working as a reporter for *Sports Review*, Benedikte had hung around after matches with the other journalists there in the mixed zone, where they waited for over-dramatic statements from young footballers or angry coaches leaving in protest. It wasn't that difficult to judge what state of mind footballers would be in.

But this was also where Steinar Brunsvik had been presented with an impossible choice to make. Benedikte thought for a moment about the young *VG* journalist who hadn't understood what was going on when the national team's highest-profile player had left the stadium during half time.

She went up the stairs and into the long corridor where the NFF offices were. The association's logo was woven into the carpet. She skimmed through some of the names on the two large plaques in honour of those with 50 or more caps. The plaques looked like two giant beer labels. She walked past a display case with some kind of Ming vase inside. It was surely an innocent gift, but it reminded her of what Boltedal had said about them all being corrupt.

Outside the window she saw the empty rows of plastic seats. In the east stand, the *VG* Stand, blue seats spelt out the word 'Ullevaal' amongst the red seats.

Benedikte had been to all the Tippeligaen and First Division grounds in Norway. The TV crew always arrived several hours before the match started, so the sight of an empty football stadium was nothing new to her. What always surprised her was that clubs managed to sell seating as advertising, with hundreds of chairs spelling out a company's name, even though the name could only be read if there was nobody at the match. It was advertising space for companies who wanted to sponsor losers.

She looked at the other side of the stadium, where Arild Golden's office was. There was just one stand separating her from the crime scene. She carried on to Holme's office.

His office was empty, so Benedikte took out her mobile but like so many times before at Ullevaal there was no sign of a signal. How was the NFF supposed to pick up what grassroots Norwegian football was saying if they couldn't even get a phone signal?

Benedikte tried sending a text: 'Where are you?'

She sat down and took out a plastic folder with some print-outs she'd made of reports on research into synthetic turf.

Then a noise, as if somebody had closed a door. Benedikte leant forward, craning her neck so she could see down the corridor, but everything was silent. She sighed and went on reading a report about the use of a specific type of synthetic grass, called XYZ.

For prestigious facilities like top division pitches, Golden had made sure to get the best types of artificial grass. The real scam was aimed at the smaller clubs, where the rock-hard XYZ was used, like at Nordre Åsen.

XYZ was also used in the vast majority of the country's indoor arenas, large and small, including Årvoll. And the developers, both in the public and private sectors, had done everything they could to save money on something as important as ventilation. Was that such a lethal combination that it might cause cancer?

She was going to force answers out of Holme. If TV2 found out she was still investigating the story, she'd need something heavy to slam on the table, a story so good that they would have to show it.

She walked along the corridor and into the boardroom. The floor was covered with wide, brown wooden panels, blue upholstered chairs around an oval table. All the old association presidents stared down at her from black-and-white photographs on the walls. Apart from them, this room was empty too.

What if Holme had suffered a heart attack? Maybe he was lying down the corridor fighting for his life. There had to be something, as he'd let her in after all. Or had the voice on the entry phone belonged to somebody else? The sound had been crackly, but she'd just assumed it was him. What if it was somebody who altered their voice so that she'd think it was Holme?

Benedikte's phone beeped as a text message arrived, making her jump. She unlocked the keypad and read the message from Holme: 'But I thought you'd cancelled?'

She ran towards the exit.

Back then, long ago, all her trouble had started in her bone marrow and spread through her blood, so from then on she'd always been in a hurry. She wanted to do everything. Life could be so short. Now she was being chased again. The monsters were back.

She was grabbed from behind, a cloth over her nose and mouth. She couldn't help trying to breathe. Then she passed out.

Vroom

Steinar put down the phone.

His eyes were wide open, even though he hadn't slept more than a few minutes that night. Junior's chickenpox had been itchy, and the boy had been crying, it all felt like one big hangover. The lack of sleep dulled his senses, but he had to get to the police station as soon as possible.

Junior was sitting quietly at the computer, watching a cartoon that Steinar couldn't remember putting on. He must have nodded off after all. He walked across the floor and, unable to hold himself back, gave Junior's racetrack a kick. Technically the racetrack was a three-storey car park, but it was easier to call it a racetrack. 'Shall we play with the car park?' sounded a bit dull.

It was blue with yellow stripes showing the direction of travel. It had a car wash with water and brush sounds, and a helipad with loud rotor blade noises. There was a lift that went 'ping' when the cars reached the top, and a photoelectric sensor that set off a powerful engine noise every time a car went past on its way back down. The photoelectric sensor was very sensitive.

The car park play set was normally part of Steinar's evening checklist. He went around checking that the door was locked, the coffee machine was switched off, the oven dials were pointing to zero and this toy was unplugged. That night he'd had more than enough trouble lulling Junior to sleep, and once they'd both finally managed to get to sleep, the car park came to life.

'Vroooooooom!'

Junior had woken up and started scratching again, which meant another three hours of wandering round the house.

Steinar took Junior and lifted him up with his right arm while carrying the laptop under his left. He walked over the road to Bjørnar

Ramstad's parents' house and rang the doorbell. It was Bjørnar's mother who opened up.

'Would you mind if Junior sits with you for a couple of hours and watches a video?'

'Of course not. Come on in, Junior,' said Mrs Ramstad.

Steinar felt relieved. He'd known Bjørnar's parents all his life and trusted them a hundred per cent, but it was still so hard to ask, so hard to have to depend on other people.

Steinar got in the taxi, which drove him quickly past the Sinsen junction, along Trondheimsveien and onto Grønlandsleiret, the main artery through Grønland, where every building was either a snack bar serving halal meat or an old pub of the all-brown-interior sort. Nowhere else in the Western world could have a higher density of kebabs, khat and Carlsberg than Grønland.

Steinar got out at the police station and reported to reception. He was escorted to the fifth floor and the red zone of the Section for Violent and Sexual Crimes, where Inspector Håvard Lange was based.

Lange was waiting for Steinar. He shook his hand briefly and showed him into his office. Lange undid the buttons on his shirt cuffs and rolled them up.

'Do you still think Taribo Shorunmo's innocent?' he asked.

'Why do you ask?'

'He's run off.'

... And Now It's Over to Ullevaal

Benedikte couldn't move her body, only her eyes. She looked to the right, then to the left, making out a pair of black, polished leather shoes, some white tape and a floor of green tiles. She would recognise that shade of green anywhere. She was lying on her stomach in the changing room showers at Ullevaal. Something was blocking her mouth. Benedikte bit down on something soft that tasted like glue.

She heard a click. Water gushed over her face and into her mouth. She swallowed and spat, but the water was too much. Then it stopped.

She coughed up water and tried to bite down again. The man must have forced a roll of tape into her mouth. That was why it tasted like glue. And, just as she heard another click, she pictured the hole in the middle of any roll of tape.

Another burst of water. She kept fighting against it, but she could feel her energy fading. She'd heard that water torture was the worst thing you could do to a person, but she hadn't believed it until now. She thought she was going to die. She was going to die here at Ullevaal.

She remembered in her mind's eye a scene from when she was seven years old, but it was not at the hospital. It was from after that, when she thought she was free. Some older boys had decided they were going to bully the delicate little girl who had reappeared in the neighbourhood. They chased her, and she escaped by running inside the nearest block of flats.

She didn't think the boys had seen her run inside, and she went up to the first floor. Then she heard the door. One of the lads was coming up behind her. She crept to the second floor, hugging the wall. Then up to the third and top floor. Could she slide down the rubbish chute? Should she knock on the nearest door?

She lay down. He wouldn't bother to come all the way up, would he? The boy came closer, and by the time their eyes met when he was four or five steps away from her on the top floor, Benedikte had started sobbing uncontrollably. The boys were so much stronger than her that they could do whatever they wanted.

The boy looked at her for a couple of seconds, then he turned and went back down without saying a word.

The water stopped.

Benedikte coughed up what she could through the opening in the tape. The man must have ripped off the shower head to make the jet of water so strong. It felt as if every drop was shooting into her mouth. Could she take another round of this? She looked at the tiles and concentrated.

'Please,' she said, but ity just came out as a grunt. She tightened every muscle in her body.

Click.

She couldn't spit the water out anymore. She felt everything go black, but she managed to count down. She knew how long it would last now. Five, four, three, two, one, now. The water stopped. She knew how long it would last, but she also knew her own body. She couldn't take another burst.

The man doing this still hadn't uttered a word.

She felt the sharp nail of her little finger and dug it into the fleshy palm of her hand, but she could barely feel it. She tried to press it hard into the sensitive area next to her thumb, but she couldn't reach. Then she jammed her ring finger into the join between two tiles and twisted it as hard as she could. It started to hurt. Finally. Pain.

Click.

The water was coming again.

She twisted her finger until it was almost out of joint. The pain rose higher and higher.

The water struck her on the back instead. The man had turned on the next shower along. He then lowered an iPhone straight in front of Benedikte's face. Two blue balloons danced on the screen together with a lop-sided smiley face. He pressed a button, and out of the loudspeaker came a recorded message with a distorted helium voice.

'This is your final warning. Forget everything to do with the Golden case. Next time I will kill you.'

Unstoppable

Steinar read a copy of the press release the police had just issued. Why had Taribo done something so idiotic as to run off? Was he guilty after all?

Taribo had lied about the man in the picture on the fridge, now he'd escaped from prison. How could Steinar possibly defend him? High-profile cases were problematic and demanding enough without this.

'What happened?' asked Steinar.

'He jumped over the wall,' said Inspector Lange.

'How is that possible? What about the guards?'

'Taribo was in solitary confinement, as you know, separated from the other prisoners, so he was just there with a single prison officer in the exercise yard.'

'But didn't the officer try to stop him?'

'Your client is a mountain of a man. The prisons in Norway, just like the police, are seriously understaffed. What was he supposed to do?'

Steinar always felt annoyed when people passed the buck, he'd asked about what happened, not whether their budget was enough.

'Have you found any trace of his movements?'

'He flagged down a car just outside the prison on Åkebergveien. Since then he's been seen together with his son, giving him a hug before he drove on.'

'Stanley, his son, turns 15 today.'

'Then Taribo drove out to IKEA at Furuset. He left the car in the car park and proceeded on foot, but we don't know where. And that's where you come in.'

'What do you mean?'

'Do you know anything about this?'

'Of course not.'

'Taribo might try to get in touch.'

'My loyalty's to my client.' Steinar got up. 'I don't suppose there was anything else?'

Steinar left the police station and walked towards Grønlandsleiret, wondering whether they were going to keep him under observation now. He looked at a Mercedes SUV parked on the other side of the road. The driver rolled down the window.

'Get in,' said Vlad Vidić.

I Left My Heart in Bergen

The sun stung Benedikte's eyes when she managed to open the door and walk out of the NFF offices. She moved her head back and put her hand over her eyes as she staggered along, her socks drenched with water.

She walked straight into the road at the roundabout, a taxi heading towards her. The driver waved his arms angrily, making threatening gestures, but Benedikte just concentrated on getting across the road.

She stopped on the footbridge over the ring road and leant against the railing. One by one, the cars sped by. She wanted to speed away too, away from Oslo.

She could feel that her T-shirt was still wet as she walked down the ramp on the other side of the ring road, past Sogn Upper Secondary School and along to the petrol station.

There was a display of football gear at the petrol station. Benedikte grabbed a dark blue Chelsea cap and matching shirt, and went to pay. She went into the toilet, where she had to fight with an uncooperative lock for a few seconds before managing to close the door. Her hands wouldn't stop shaking. She put down the toilet lid and sat down. She cried her eyes out, burying her head in the Chelsea shirt.

Her friends and colleagues teased her for supporting Chelsea. It was a team that bought its glory, and nobody who knew anything about football was cheering about the influx of new Russian money. And there were other teams to avoid as well. Real Madrid could never be forgiven for its connections to Franco, and nobody other than Berlusconi could love AC Milan. It was more morally and intellectually proper to support teams such as Inter or Barcelona or, perhaps even better, obscure clubs such as the Dutch team AZ Alkmaar.

Benedikte had supported Chelsea ever since her father bought her a cap back when she needed it the most. He'd explained to her in his grown-up but trembling voice about the little soldiers of the body, and that she just had too many of them.

Now, once a year, she combined shopping, drinks and football in the London club's fashionable West End district. A Caramel Frappuccino from Starbucks on the King's Road seemed infinitely far away at that moment.

She threw her socks and T-shirt in the bin. She'd have to live with her shoes and trousers. She fished out a hair band from her trouser pocket, put her hair in a ponytail and pulled the cap down at the front. Then she left the petrol station and hailed a taxi.

'Gardermoen Airport,' she said, sinking into the clammy seat. She felt hungover, like after a really heavy night on the town and are tormented by a repetitive noise. In this case, the noise was that childish helium voice. 'Next time I will kill you.' Over and over again.

'What do you do for a living?' the taxi driver asked.

'I'm a flight attendant,' said Benedikte, grateful that there were Pakistani taxi drivers who didn't watch TV2.

The driver didn't ask anything else, just kept his eyes on the road. Signs with the Maxbo, *Dagbladet* and DHL logos vanished in quick succession as they drove past.

Benedikte thought about Bergen. She'd never grown fond of the city, but she liked the mountains there. Oslo didn't have any mountains, only insignificant rocks on the city's outskirts.

She wanted to get far away from this stupid and dangerous investigation. From now on, she'd stay in Bergen and work on her normal, harmless sports stories. There could never be too many 'at home with...' reports on Brann players.

She would bury herself in routine stories, and she'd go mountain running in her spare time. It was a long time since she'd gone up the track to the top of Ulriken, and she loved it when it was pouring with rain or when the fog meant that she had to feel her way to the top.

She rubbed her chin, which was still sore after being pressed against the tiles.

She arrived at the airport just after 12 o' clock, went over to the SAS ticket desk and bought a one-way ticket to Bergen before getting in the queue for security, her eyes fixed on the floor. She pulled her cap even further down over her face as she put her Visa card, some coins, her iPhone and her dark red lipstick on the plastic tray and sent it through the X-ray machine. She was sure she didn't have anything metallic on her, but the detector beeped when she went through.

The security officer already had his eyes on her. He asked her to put her hands out to the sides while he passed a metal detector over her body. His hands touched her trousers. Had he noticed that they were soaking wet? 'Please,' she thought, 'just let me through without any questions.'

'You'll have to put your trainers through,' he said. Benedikte did as she was told and stood there in her bare feet while she waited for her shoes to catch up with her at the end of the conveyor belt. The security officer had turned his attention to the next blonde female terrorist.

She put her feet back in her shoes, bending them at the heels. She thought she heard one of her shoes' heel tabs snap, but she just moved to the stairs that led to the Sinnataggen restaurant on the first floor. She practically started running when she spotted a young boy outside the security area holding a helium balloon from TGI Friday's.

It was a surprise to her that she might be in danger. She realised that she might be risking her job by continuing her investigations into Golden's links with astroturf, but she would never have believed that she was risking her life. She took off her shoe and straightened the heel. Then she took off the other and lifted up her feet, sitting on a sofa bench while looking at the crowd of people below.

An hour later, Sabrina turned up with a young man in tow. She was wearing jeans stuffed inside a pair of brown leather boots, a white T-shirt with a picture of Michael Jackson and some large, black sunglasses that looked like insect eyes. Hanging on her left arm was a small, gold handbag. Benedikte recognised the man from the weekly magazines as Sabrina's PA. He was wearing a light blue Tommy Hilfiger piqué T-shirt and made gestures accompanying every word he said. Benedikte had completely forgotten that Sabrina was going to appear with Per Diesen and Marius Bjartmann on that day's *Football Xtra*. The boys had probably stayed in Kristiansand after the game the day before and would be travelling straight from there. Benedikte watched Sabrina from where she was sitting until the departure screen read 'Boarding'.

Benedikte was last to get on the flight and she glanced up the cabin past the shoulder of the man in front. Sabrina and her assistant were sitting halfway up the plane. Benedikte was in seat 23, so she'd have to go past them.

Benedikte didn't want Sabrina to recognise her. For all she knew, Sabrina might decide to blab on air about seeing her, or maybe she would mention it to somebody else, then it might seem as if Benedikte were following her. The man in the showers at Ullevaal had been crystal clear, she should stay away from anything to do with the Golden case.

Luckily, Sabrina and her PA were too busy talking to each other. Immediately behind them was a young man in an army uniform. A soldier on his way home on leave, perhaps?

As Benedikte went past, she partially covered her face with her right hand. She took out a 500 kroner note and the stub of her boarding pass and gave them to the boy in uniform in seat 17C. He lit up when Benedikte winked at him, as he realised what was going on. He took the money and the ticket, and disappeared towards the back of the cabin.

Benedikte sat down and listened for the whole flight.

'Kalid was my first,' said Sabrina as they were approaching Bergen. Benedikte sat up. 'We were together for a year before I broke up with him. It made him crazy.'

'He's been in touch with the agency. He wanted to know about your diary, he was asking like totally flat out.'

'Jeeeeez! He plays on the same team as Per. You know, I've actually wondered whether it might be him who's been calling up and breathing down the phone over the past few days.'

'About that, we've got to have a word about how we're going to spin it.'

'I'd rather forget about it. Such an invasion of my privacy, it's horrible to have something like that happen to you.'

'I know it's not easy, but it sells. It's sexy, girlfriend. That's why I've exaggerated it. I leaked it to *Dagbladet* that you were assaulted and that it's really traumatic for you to appear on TV. We've just got to think about how big to make the black eye we'll give you in make-up when you go on air.'

Sabrina paused for thought. 'But will I look sexy like *that*? With a black eye?'

'Honey, you'll always be sexy. You're fabulous. But we've got to exploit the situation. It'll give your online hits a real boost. The advertising revenue will hit the sky if we play it right. The tabloids, the glossy magazines. They'll be outbidding each other to get the rights to reconstruct Sabrina's week of terror.'

Benedikte saw the PA using his fingers to make air quotes around what he clearly imagined the tabloid headline would be.

'But it'll be a lie,' said Sabrina.

'Sabrina darling, we all have our challenges. Your career's going fine at the moment, but you're not getting any younger. There'll always be someone ready to take your place. We've got to think about what's next? We've got to keep people interested in you. There's no doubt that your music career does best when you've got an active role on TV. After guest-starring on *Paradise Hotel*, you're sort of in limbo at the moment. It's difficult to get a break on quality reality shows these days. And *PDTV*, I mean I totally love it, but it is mainly Per's show. If we're not careful, you might, like, end up as the cook for the food section of the show. But if we play our cards right this PR might keep you on top for weeks to come.'

'Should I let out any hints that I think it's Kalid?'

'No, no, it's more important to play on how awful it's been. How hard it is for you to go on TV live. Traumatised, sweetie.'

It was strange to notice a generation gap at the age of 26, Benedikte thought, feeling grateful for the silence that always accompanied the final approach.

They'd barely landed when Sabrina shot out of her seat. She was one of the few people who were able to stand up straight under the overhead compartments. Her PA stood bent over next to her for the remaining few minutes it took the crew to prepare to offload the passengers. Benedikte pretended she was sleeping, her cap over her face. Next to her, an older woman was starting to become impatient. Benedikte wished she'd just relax.

Once they were inside the terminal, Benedikte didn't dare to follow them. It was too difficult, somebody could have their eye on her without her noticing. She decided to take a taxi straight to the TV2 studios instead.

She had lost count of how many times she'd driven along the road from Flesland Airport into Bergen. On the way, she would see Fana Stadion and, just before the centre, Krohnsminde sports ground. She would also always crane her neck from the back seat to see Troldhaugen, the home of composer Edvard Grieg, and Gamlehaugen, the royal residence in Bergen. Today was no exception, and seeing those familiar sights calmed her nerves.

Benedikte had a small flat within walking distance of TV2. She'd spent every other week in Bergen and its reputation for eternally rainy weather was justified. She looked out of the window towards the main square in Torgallmenningen while they drove on at high speed along Vaskerelven. The taxi roared over the cobblestones past the theatre, and they just caught the green light before turning the corner and driving towards Nøstet, where the studios were.

She went into reception, made up an excuse that she'd lost her key card and luggage, and took the lift up. She took out an outfit from the wardrobe and changed in the make-up room. Karianne put on a light layer of make-up for her and fixed her hair. She was feeling better and started chatting.

Then she went over to Stig Nilsen, who was checking over the programme schedule for the day. As usual, she was given a long hug, but today she felt like she actually needed it. Then she put her arm on Stig's shoulder as nonchalantly as she could.

'Can you do me a favour?' she asked.

'Yes?'

'During the break, can you trick the lads into keeping their microphones on?'

'Why?'

'I'm just curious.'

'Fine.'

'Good luck for your first programme,' said Benedikte, letting go.

'Shit, thanks!' said Stig, shrugging his shoulders.

The B-Sample

'Are we going to fly somewhere?' Steinar asked, as they pulled off the E6 towards Gardermoen Airport. No answer. Vlad Vidić looked straight at Steinar in the mirror.

The car stopped. Vidić inserted his Visa card in the yellow machine, and the barrier went up. They drove into the car park, parked the SUV and went into the terminal.

Vidić was wearing a thin, white V-neck jumper that revealed his shaved chest. He was a little shorter than Steinar remembered, but he still resembled a bloodthirsty Serbian centre-back. His skin was even more wrinkled than before, and his shoulders even further apart. He'd probably been munching on his own steroid supplies since that fatal day at Ullevaal.

At security, Vidić grabbed a red plastic tray and held it so that Steinar could put in his belongings. They both made it through the metal detector without any trouble. Steinar was given back everything except his mobile. They walked along the terminal until they found an empty waiting area and sat down.

'How did you manage to disappear?' Vidić asked.

Steinar watched a lone man standing on the moving walkway.

Quitting football had been the toughest decision Steinar had ever made, but disappearing was easy. He was puzzled by sportspeople who complained to the media about having too much attention, who arranged press conferences to say they were fed up. When journalists got hold of Steinar, he'd just been plain with them: 'Not interested.'

Steinar had run off and never needed to explain himself. He might handle the ball in the penalty box, he might grab an opponent's shirt, and if the referee gave a throw-in to the wrong team, he wouldn't say anything. That happened in the heat of the match, when anything was allowed as long as the referee didn't see it. But when Steinar saw the photos of the tablets being mixed into his juice, he knew immediately that football was dead to him.

'What do you want from me?' he asked.

'You're to stay away from us. Golden Boys will carry on as before without any interference from you. Arild Golden's dead, that's all.'

'Did you kill him?'

A small airport buggy drove past. Vidić sat back in his seat. A man got off the buggy and picked up two plastic bottles. Vidić gave no sign of answering.

'Oh, come on,' said Steinar. 'You can't turn up again after all these years and not say anything. I'll give it to you, you're a pretty smooth operator. You take me to Gardermoen, you don't say anything until you've eliminated the possibility I might be recording the conversation, and then you tell me to stay away. Just like *Scarface*, just like *The Sopranos*, hell, just like the whole Camorra all at once. But you've got to give me something. If I'm supposed to stay away from you, I've got to understand why.'

'I can tell you that Golden was, for a long time, the best front man Golden Boys could wish for. But a few rumours started circulating recently, especially within Vålerenga, that Golden was racist. He was giving more attention to players like Per Diesen and Marius Bjartmann than to Kalid Jambo, Otto Cana or other foreign players.'

'Is that true?' asked Steinar. Vidić's own origin was impossible to guess. It was even more surprising to hear his words come out without a trace of accent, without any clues as to a local dialect and not even a hint of class distinction. He spoke like a computer. But now he was silent.

'I've got to know this in order to defend Taribo,' said Steinar. 'If you tell me, I might not need to dig any deeper.'

'The most talented players in Norway come from Africa, so an agent must be able to deal with them,' Vidić said.

'So is that why he got Stanley pumped full of cortisone?'

'The accusations of racism annoyed Golden. He wanted to show that he could still make transfers with foreign players. He had to get Stanley ready.' Vidić lifted up his phone, which had just received a text message. He read it and answered quickly, using his thumb, before continuing.

'West Ham wanted to take Stanley for several weeklong visits over the next year until they could sign him aged 16. Of course, this was all supposed to be done under the table, so nobody else could snatch him.'

'They were looking to do some try-outs with him?'

'The club was having problems explaining things to their sponsors after several bad acquisitions at a difficult time financially. They needed more than Golden's word so, in the end, Golden let that quack treat Stanley. In a few weeks' time, Stanley was going to go over there and convince them. Together with Diesen's transfer to Everton, this would show that Golden Boys once again had control of all trade from Scandinavia to the English market. If you wanted to go to England, you'd have to be the property of Golden Boys. The market's like a house of cards. If one club falls away, others will follow and we'd lose our power. It was a panic reaction to inject Stanley full of cortisone, but it was also a sensible thing to do, in spite of everything.'

'Did Golden know that you threatened me back then?'

Vidić raised his shoulders and put out the palms of his hands, like Italian footballers do after faking their way to a penalty.

'How have you managed to stay anonymous all these years?' asked Steinar.

'I've always been there. Doing the dirty work, as you know from first-hand experience. A successful agency only needs one person on the outside. Only one face. We had Golden. Now I'll have to step up a bit more than usual until we get another front man. That's why I'm here to warn you. I don't give a shit about the case against Taribo. He can rot in jail. What I want is for you to stop nosing around in Golden Boys' business. You're to stay away from Stanley, Diesen, Bjartmann, Jambo, Cana and all our other assets.'

'And if I say no?'

'Then I might take more than your football career away from you.'

Steinar's impulse was to jump on Vidić and smash his head against the floor. He felt hatred bubbling inside of him, but there was a group of kids near them playing on a miniature plane. Steinar forced himself to sit still.

Vidić got up and gave Steinar his mobile.

'By the way, those were some pretty strong caffeine tablets we gave you,' he leaned over Steinar, 'but you were never doped.'

Football and That Little Xtra

Benedikte sat at the back of the studio control room, which was built like a gallery, rows of desks facing a wall of TV screens of various sizes and a red digital clock counting down to transmission time. Behind the wall was the studio itself.

As TV programmes go, *Football Xtra* was an adrenaline kick. The minutes leading up to live broadcast were nerve-wracking, and during the transmission it was pure fire-fighting. There were always technical problems and items that wouldn't play, guests who gave the opposite answer to the one they'd been expected to give, which could stifle any further discussion.

Per Diesen, Marius Bjartmann and Sabrina arrived at the studio just before transmission. Benedikte hid behind her Chelsea cap and her computer as the trio went past into the studio, where Stig Nilsen went through the programme schedule with them. Through her headset, Benedikte heard everything they said. Nilsen and Bjartmann had a short, awkward chat about the knee injury that put an end to Nilsen's career. Football injuries stayed with both the victim and the perpetrator.

As for Sabrina, she had her arms round Diesen's neck. They really looked in love. Benedikte wondered whether Diesen might have heard about Sabrina and Golden and forgiven them. Or was it the case, like so many times before, that the ones involved were the last to find out?

Stig looked at the young glamour model. 'Who the hell do you think you are, hanging all over him like that?' he said. 'Some kind of onesie?'

There was cheering in the control room. If that's what Nilsen's debut as a presenter was going to be like, it would be legendary.

Stig checked his chair, which was close to the edge of the high platform the studio furniture was on. Benedikte had also been worried the first time.

A Rammstein song led viewers through a montage of hard tackles from the previous weekend before Stig welcomed them to that day's action.

'On today's programme I've got Norway's new superstar, Sabrina, the tough centre-back Marius Bjartmann, and finally midfielder Per Diesen.'

Stig went on with the latest updates on injuries and match bans. Then he did the obligatory round trip of the football grounds. 10 minutes into the programme, the guy next to Benedikte shook his head. 'This is fucking boring!' he said. 'What's happened to Nilsen?'

Stig gave his analysis of how poor Start were at covering the space in front of the back four, something Vålerenga had only partially taken advantage of in the match the previous day. What was he thinking? He was supposed to swear. Had Stig Nilsen become too serious?

The programme went to a break after 22 minutes. Then they were back a few minutes later. A wide shot of the studio, then the camera zoomed in on Stig. 'Welcome back,' he said, before darkness fell both on the studio and on Stig's face. Benedikte grabbed hold of the intercom.

'Relax,' she said.

Smoke rose quickly from behind the J-shaped glass table, and loud hip-hop rhythms thumped out in the studio. Diesen and Bjartmann got up and crossed their arms, drumming along with the beat while thrusting their heads back and forth.

They were wearing white jackets on top of white linen shirts. The suit jackets had thin, barely visible silver pinstripes. Their shirts were open wide enough so that viewers could see a hint of the well-trained muscles on their chests. Diesen was wearing a silver piece of jewellery, hanging from a black leather strap, and a gleaming bracelet. He combed his fingers through his hair. They both looked good, but Diesen had that little extra. He looked like a real pop star.

In one synchronised movement, they pulled at their jackets so they tore up the back, then threw away the remaining strips of cloth. Sabrina jumped up on the table and started gyrating, while Diesen slid his hands down over his white shirt. He started miming the lyrics.

'You've got to bleed, bleed, bleed for our team.'

Bjartmann stood there with a steely expression on his face, looking sternly at Diesen before taking the next line.

'We're the ones to take you to the extreme.'

Sabrina performed an erotic dance lying on the studio desk. Then she jumped up on all fours, threw back her torso, shot up her right shoulder and mimed along.

'Hunt out that autumn dream.'

The song faded out with a long full-time whistle. Diesen and Bjartmann pointed both arms to the right, while Sabrina ended up horizontal.

Nobody had scored during the adverts or the song, and maybe that's why Stig didn't say anything. The silence was embarrassingly long. Benedikte heard Bertil Olsen over the intercom: 'You've got to give them some praise! Say something, man!'

Nilsen cleared his throat. 'Excellent stuff, folks. The single "Bleed for the Team" is on sale in most record shops, or you can download it free on the Internet if you think these lads make enough money as it is.'

'You idiot!' shouted Olsen. 'Ask about the assault, ask about her black eye!'

Once again the silence lasted too long. Bertil Olsen told Stig again, turning it into a direct threat. Stig looked at Sabrina, let out a sigh and finally spoke again:

'But it hasn't been very easy for you lately, has it?'

'No, it was a terrible thing that happened,' said Sabrina, touching the black eye that had been added to her face with make-up. 'Oslo, my childhood home, the city I love so much, isn't...'

'Sorry, something's just happened at... at Marienlyst Stadion in Drammen,' said Nilsen. He handed over to a bewildered reporter who said something about a semi-doubtful offside.

'What the hell are you doing?' asked Bertil Olsen. Nilsen didn't seem to be bothered and spent the rest of the programme's first half asking for updates from reporter after reporter.

The control room emptied during the break. A pizza delivery from Dolly Dimple's was on the way. Only Benedikte stayed. On the monitor, she saw Stig get up and cross behind Bjartmann and Diesen.

'I'll just switch off your microphones during the break,' he said. It had taken the production assistant three attempts to fix them back on during the short items between comments from the studio, so the lads didn't argue when Nilsen went on to explain: 'That way we won't have any more fuss in the second half.'

Very smooth, Benedikte thought.

'I've got to take a piss,' said Nilsen.

Diesen and Bjartmann followed out of the studio close behind him, while Sabrina sat down on the floor in a kind of lotus position, closing her eyes. Benedikte hid again behind her cap and her computer monitor. As the lads passed through the control room, she spotted a green light on Diesen's back pocket.

When Benedikte worked on the breakfast show, she'd got used to checking that the guests didn't take their microphones with them. It still happened quite often. The guests brought them back quite sheepishly and couldn't help asking if Benedikte had heard them at home or at work.

The truth was that the microphones' range was very limited. The signal vanished when the guests left the studio building, but it was strong enough for Benedikte to listen to Diesen and Bjartmann talking in the corridor.

Benedikte pressed the earphones as close to her eardrums as possible.

'I thought you wanted to go your own way now, that you were going to find an agent who would just represent you. And why Ola Bugge?' asked Bjartmann.

'I believe in him. We need somebody who'll get stuck in for us like Arild used to.'

Bullshit. Absolute bullshit, Benedikte thought. She was certain Diesen was lying, and she had to find out why. It would be cowardly of her to stay in Bergen now, and she couldn't live with that. Her dad had called her the world's toughest girl when she overcame her leukaemia. She'd been fighting it from when she was four until her recovery at seven. Fighting against billions of cancer cells trying to oust her platelets and red and white blood cells. She'd had to take one cytotoxic drug after another. She'd lost her hair and her friends. She'd been teetering on the edge of death, but she'd fought back.

Benedikte couldn't understand why anybody would choose to put their career in Bugge's hands, let alone why Norway's hottest footballer would try to persuade others to do the same.

Diesen was talking crap, and there could only be one reason for that. Bugge had to be blackmailing him, and Benedikte would have to go back to Oslo to confront him on that very matter.

To hell with the threats. She'd cheated death before, she could do it again.

Part 7

29 June 2007

'Local Oslo talent moving to Trondheim.'

Arild Golden stopped when he saw the headline in Groruddalens Avis. He was sitting in his office reading the most important Oslo papers, Nordstrand Blad to Østkantsavisa.

The article was about a young footballer from Veitvet who was going to start studying at the Norwegian University of Science and Technology in Trondheim. Apparently, Byåsen, a mediocre Second Division team, was interested in taking him on. The newspaper pages rustled as Golden tightened his grip.

The Swiss tennis legend Roger Federer had also been an unknown talent once upon a time. Arild Golden watched him playing against Jonas Björkman in the 2006 Wimbledon semi-final, the most brilliant performance Golden had seen at any sports venue. He'd taken special note of Federer's habit of blowing on his fingers. They were too hot for his racquet. Federer was too good and had to cool down before the next ball. The match ended 6–2, 6–0, 6–2.

Golden put down the paper. No outsiders should be making off with any players from the talent pool in Oslo's Grorud Valley, and nobody should be moving to the same city as Rosenborg without Golden's signature on their papers.

Rosenborg was Norway's best team of the past 20 years and had historically taken its players from local clubs. If somebody did well with Byåsen, they might soon find themselves playing for Rosenborg, and then a foreign transfer could be on the cards.

It was hard to predict who would be successful but most major transfers involved players who'd started off at small clubs. Golden worked in bulk, so the more talent he controlled, the better chance there was that one of them would make it big.

Golden found his number in the phone book. He couldn't help making the slightest of smiles as he blew on his fingers and dialled the eight-digit number.

'Hello, this is Edvart,' said the young footballer.

'This is Arild Golden. If you want to play football in Trondheim, you'll sign an agency contract with me. If not, I'll stop any transfers from taking place.'

'But...'

'Believe me, I can. And as your agent, I'll take 20 per cent of your pay.'

The player's monthly salary would be somewhere between 3,000 and 4,000 kroner. Arild Golden's work didn't come free, but he still saw the irony when he was going over his accounts that same evening and saw how much his professionals playing in England had sent him.

The Chief

No fucking way was he going to let himself be dictated to by Vlad Vidić. No fucking way was he going to give up the rights to Stanley, and you bloody bet he was going to check out the other sides of the Golden Boys empire. He'd let himself be frightened by that steroid freak before, and nothing good had come of that.

Steinar had sat there paralysed the first few minutes after hearing those four words at Gardermoen Airport. Had he retired without needing to? Had he thrown away the best thing in his life unnecessarily? Steinar had felt a strong impulse to get drunk, before becoming more constructive again and phoning Asgeir Kringlebotn. He set up a meeting with Jacob B. Iversen, better known as 'the Chief'.

The Chief blew on his steaming hot coffee, made by his hypermodern machine. Steinar also sat blowing on his double espresso. He'd been offered a latte, but he thought it a bit too much to ask the former president of the NFF to steam milk for him.

They were sitting in the Chief's office at Ullevaal Stadion. The Chief was wearing a smart brown tweed jacket, a white shirt and a black tie with polka dots. The tie was done up tightly around his collar. His face was tanned and chiselled, taut skin. He had a few lines on his face and silver-grey hair, but there was nothing to suggest this was a man approaching retirement age. The Chief was still an active player in the league system. Eighth Division, but still.

They'd gone through the obligatory football-related courtesies, and a goal Steinar had scored on the Chief's fiftieth birthday came up. The goal had sealed the result in the match between Ajax and Twente in the Dutch Eredivisie.

'Do you remember that goal?'

It had started with a lightning-quick right-left feint, leaving Steinar alone with the keeper. He looked down and moved his right foot towards the ball. The keeper jumped, guessing that Steinar was about to shoot, but Steinar's foot went over the ball. He'd missed it intentionally. The ball carried on forwards past the keeper, who was wriggling about on the grass. The goal was open.

Behind the goal was the section where the fanatical home supporters were, the so-called Ultras. Steinar spotted a placard with thick, black letters on a dirty, white background. At the bottom were a few smaller red letters.

The fluttering had stopped, the flags wilted and the banners hung down, slack and illegible. Steinar had all the time in the world. He even had time to smile at a supporter with a head so clean shaven that it might have been the inspiration for the Adidas Jabulani ball.

Steinar rolled the ball slowly towards the empty goalmouth. The Twente supporters still had a trace of hope that their keeper might get to his feet in time. Then Steinar turned round and stuck his arms in the air.

Steinar looked at the Chief and said: 'No, not in detail, I'm afraid.'

Steinar had been doing his best to keep football out of his life, but it was always there under the surface. He'd been instinctively more proud of Junior's first instep kick than his first three-word sentence.

'I remember it as if it were yesterday,' said the Chief.

Iversen had been known by that nickname since it was used in a *VG* headline in the early seventies. He'd become the NFF president at the early age of 22, following an unexpected death. Most people thought the young urchin would lose his position at the association's annual conference two months later. Instead, he became a legend of Norwegian football and spent 15 years on UEFA's Executive Committee.

'So you know old Kringlebotn, do you? I hadn't spoken to him in years and was quite surprised when he phoned yesterday.'

'I know him a little, but I'm here because I'm acting as Taribo Shorunmo's lawyer.'

'Yes, it would be hard not to know that. The media must be after you the whole time.'

'Well, I've had a few phone calls and interviews.'

'You've been making a good job of it.'

'Thanks. Shorunmo's suspected of killing Arild Golden, but there are others who had stronger motives than he did.'

'What motives?'

'Money from building synthetic pitches.'

'So that's why you've come to me. You think I get a cut of everything that gets built?' asked the Chief, who had started the job of carpeting Norway together with Kringlebotn. 'Have you heard the one about the Muslim in the NFF?'

Steinar shook his head.

'The NFF took on a former top Turkish player. He was Muslim and prayed five times a day. He left in protest when the NFF demanded his prayer mat be replaced with astroturf.'

Steinar smiled.

The Chief continued. 'I've heard the craziest stories and theories about astroturf and about us in the NFF, but maybe it's best if I show you something to illustrate the real picture.'

The Chief opened up his laptop screen and went through a standard talk about artificial grass, referring to the NFF's commitment to the Third World, astroturf pitches and multi-use games areas in developing countries, and soccer schools with an academic element too.

'There's an enormous amount of money in astroturf, but it's gone to the developers without any help from us in the NFF.'

'Why has the health risk been downplayed?' Steinar said. 'One of my best friends, Ståle Jakobsen, is on his deathbed because of this.'

'I know Ståle, and I'm very sorry about what's happened to him, but I don't agree with the explanation you're implying. Our job is to lay the groundwork so that as many people as possible can play football. It's up to the politicians to stop any health risks. We have a vision to build 1,000 astroturf pitches in Norway.'

'Whatever the cost?'

'Of course not. But you can't get away from the fact that playing football also has a positive effect on people's health, combating child obesity and decreasing the risk of cardiovascular diseases. It also means fewer young people end up in the crime statistics. Football is one of the best, if not the very best, tools for integration. We have a general social responsibility, so we have to live with the possibility that synthetic turf might lead to a higher rate of knee and ankle injuries.'

'So who's making money out of it?'

'Nobody in the NFF, I guarantee that. You'll have to look elsewhere.'

'Where?'

'Why don't you start at the crime scene? Have you been there?'

'No.'

'Come with me.'

They went downstairs and past the Thoresen box, named after Gunnar Thoresen and his son Hallvar, who had more than 100 caps between them for the national side. A unique feat. Just beyond that, Golden Boys had bought a large suite of boxes 10 years previously, which they had converted into offices.

The Chief took out a bunch of keys and opened the door. Pictures and framed shirts hung on the walls. Famous Norwegian and international players thanking Golden. Glass cases stood there, filled with treasures. There was a match ball from the 1970 World Cup Finals, a small piece of brick from the Kop, Liverpool's old stand, a pair of gloves that had belonged to Edwin van der Sar, and Michael Laudrup's Barcelona shirt. According to the small note next to the case, Laudrup had worn this when playing against Real Madrid in El Clásico. Pride of place went to a pair of football boots that belonged to Diego Maradona. Not from the 1986 World Cup, but from his season with Napoli in 1988. He's even bigger in Naples than he is at home in Buenos Aires, if such a thing were possible. The street traders still sell shirts with his name on them.

The trophy and medal collection was probably the most valuable asset, though. Golden Boys had bought up various championship medals, presumably from the many players who had gone off the straight and narrow once their careers were over. Not so much Norwegian players – although Steinar saw a couple of cups presented by the King of Norway – but mainly South American World Cup champions who needed the money more than they needed a piece of round metal.

The exercise bike in the corner was a departure from what was otherwise a football museum. Steinar had expected a minimalist office. Golden was one of Norway's best-dressed men and most eligible bachelors, after all. He'd been a model and had appeared, among other things, as the face of Varner-Gruppen, the largest clothing company in Norway. He'd been used as a more mature male counterpart to the female models employed by the Cubus and Lindex chains.

But with its football shirts, scarves and other memorabilia, his office was reminiscent of an old sports pub, and maybe that was a trick to make footballers feel at home. They felt they were in safe hands if they saw Maradona's boots nearby.

'I was surprised that the police were so interested in who came through the door here,' said the Chief, pointing at the electronic lock that counted the number of visitors over the course of the day.

'Why?'

The Chief pointed at the door next to Golden's desk. 'There's more than one way to get in here, but the police wanted to limit the crime scene to the office itself.'

The door was locked, and the Chief opened it with a master key. The door led into a box with 12 champagne-coloured leather chairs around a glass table, a fully stocked bar and an exit to the stand.

Steinar went out onto the stand and tried one of the seats, which was also made of leather. Dark blue. When he rested his head back against the comfortable headrest, he saw that the touch-line was just visible over the ledge where he could rest his feet. This was something else compared to the plastic seats the great unwashed had to make do with. Anybody who was demanding a new national stadium clearly didn't have access to these seats.

'But if the door out here was locked, like it was now, there would still be other ways in,' said the Chief, leading Steinar back to Golden's office. He drew the curtains.

The office had two large panoramic windows through which they could see the whole stadium. It was just beside one of these that Golden had been killed. This was the first time Steinar had been at the scene of a murder, and he was relieved that the blood had been cleaned up. He drew a deep breath then looked up.

One of the two windows didn't quite reach to the ceiling like the other. At the top was a ventilation window. Any reasonably athletic person could have climbed in.

And hadn't it been Oslo's hottest day of the summer on the day Golden had been killed?

Paranoia

Benedikte was on the train heading into Oslo from Gardermoen Airport. Her neck ached and she hadn't slept all night. She tried to give herself a massage, but if she pressed too hard, it only brought back the feeling of throwing up, lukewarm water pouring into her mouth and down her throat. There was no doubt that the man had been serious when he'd played back the message: 'Next time I will kill you.'

Outside the window the fields of Ullensaker sped by. She was sitting far from the door with her Chelsea cap pulled down. She took out her iPhone and flipped it round in her hand. They went past Åråsen Stadion where Lillestrøm played, the bright yellow seats shining at her.

Benedikte looked around the carriage. Was there anybody who stuck out, anybody keeping an eye on her? Was the man at the end of the carriage just pretending to read the newspaper? They rushed into the long, dark Romerike Tunnel. Her breathing stopped for a few seconds until she collected her thoughts.

She looked over at her suitcase. She had a full wardrobe in Bergen that had come into its own now, as she didn't dare to go back to her home in Oslo.

To begin with, the threat had convinced her to stay in Bergen and put everything to do with Golden behind her. But when she heard Per Diesen praising Bugge, she knew she couldn't do that. She had to find out what it was all about.

The train roared out of the tunnel at Etterstad, and the bright light startled her. She pressed the button on her iPhone, which came to life, and she made a couple of attempts to write text messages, but they became too long. Eventually, as the train was rolling along the last stretch into Oslo Central and the half-finished black-and-white tower blocks came into view, she sent Steinar a short text message: 'Where are you?'

The reply came a few seconds later: 'At home.'

'Can I pop by?'

She needed to tell Steinar about the attack. Maybe he'd be able to make her feel safe again. The phone rang, and she answered.

'Of course you can pop by. The only thing is that Junior's sick.'

'What's wrong with him?'

'Chickenpox. I thought it was going, but he got a lot worse again during the night. It's harmless if you've had it before, but it could be pretty bad if you haven't.'

'I had it as a child,' Benedikte said, although she didn't have a clue whether that was true or not.

'Then just come by whenever you want.'

She was the last person out of the carriage. She pulled her trolley bag up the short ramp to the station building and turned left outside, heading to the taxi rank. She stood a short distance away from the taxis, took out her iPhone and pretended to check her messages.

The other train passengers who needed a taxi had already taken one. There was still a long queue of black Mercedes waiting. Benedikte put her phone in her pocket and walked briskly towards the first taxi. The driver put her case in the back, while she stood there facing the station building. Nobody seemed to be showing any interest in her.

She got into the taxi and asked the driver to go to Lofthusveien. She sat facing the rear window, while he turned down the short ramp from the taxi rank, drove in front of the Hotel Opera and past Plata, which was empty just now, but was best known as a meeting place for drug addicts. Then they turned right alongside the tram line and over the narrow crossing, where the station square led onto the start of Karl Johans Gate. The bus shelters there were always filled with people who had no intention of taking the bus.

They drove round the corner between the two shopping centres, Byporten and Oslo City. Two skyscrapers, Postgirobygget and Oslo Plaza, hung over them, giving the impression that Oslo was a real metropolis. Then they turned round the back of the bus station, up to the roundabout and onto the main road leading to Gjøvik. They turned off towards Steinar's house, just north of Sinsen.

Nobody was following them, as far as she could tell. The roads were busier, so it would take a better trained eye to spot any potential pursuers. She sank into her seat, closed her eyes and allowed herself to feel how tired she really was. When they arrived at Steinar's house she paid in cash.

Steinar opened up before she could ring the doorbell. He was wearing a navy blue T-shirt and tracksuit bottoms that didn't match, as if he'd started to get changed but hadn't had time to finish. His hair was scruffy, and he looked the same way she felt. He clearly hadn't slept either. They twitched back and forth while they decided whether to opt for a kiss or a hug, ending up somewhere in between.

'Come in,' said Steinar, noticing Benedikte's suitcase.

'I've just come from Bergen,' she said.

Steinar lifted her bag into the hallway and led her into the kitchen. He put his finger to his lips and pointed at Junior, who was sleeping on the sofa with the computer on the table in front of him. A Donald Duck cartoon was playing with the sound on mute. Steinar shut the kitchen door.

'He finally fell asleep,' he said. 'He's worn out.'

Another one, thought Benedikte, but she didn't say anything. Steinar opened a container on the kitchen table. It was empty. Then he opened the red cupboard doors in the old-fashioned kitchen one by one, but he still couldn't find what he was looking for.

'There's been a leak at my flat. Can I stay in your guest room for a couple of nights?' Benedikte asked.

'That won't be a problem,' answered Steinar. He was craning his neck to see into the last of the cupboards, so Benedikte couldn't see the expression on his face.

'How are things going with your case?' asked Benedikte.

'Taribo's run off.'

'So I heard. What does that mean?'

'I've got no idea.'

'What happened?'

'He just legged it. Sunday morning.'

Taribo could have been at Ullevaal while she was there. Had the person who answered the entry phone had an accent? And had the iPhone recording been used to hide that very accent?

'I spoke with a source of mine in the police,' said Benedike. 'They said that they thought the murder weapon was a morning star, a kind of African club, and that Taribo had several of these at home.'

Benedikte hadn't seen what her attacker looked like. It could have been Taribo, but it could have been anybody.

Steinar went quiet for a few seconds, then yawned. He looked exhausted. She couldn't give him any more worries. She would wait to tell him about the attack.

'I've got to go out and buy coffee,' said Steinar. 'Can you keep an eye on Junior for a few minutes?'

'Of course.'

Benedikte locked the door as soon as Steinar left.

Deep in the Forest

Steinar's client had run off, Junior had chickenpox, and at the back of his head, Vlad Vidić was repeating those words: 'You were never doped.' Over and over again.

As if that wasn't enough, now he had Benedikte staying for a platonic sleepover, not long after she'd said they should sleep together. Steinar looked back on their kissing episode with perspective now. He analysed his own behaviour and yet again concluded: Yes, he was an idiot.

He slowly rolled his bike down towards the supermarket, Rema 1000. He stopped outside the shop on Kjelsåsveien, parked his bike, went round the uneven corner to the entrance and took the three steps in a single leap.

He took some coffee and a packet of sweet *lefser*, a sugar-filled flatbread. He glanced at *VG* and *Dagbladet* on the newspaper stand next to the till, they each had a large picture of Taribo on the front page, with a smaller photo of Steinar himself. The headlines were 'Fugitive' and 'On the run'. Steinar's back pocket was constantly lit up by his mobile, in silent mode.

He paid, went out to his bike and put in the combination for the lock, then heard somebody shouting. He turned round and saw an old, white Volkswagen van. Sitting in the van was a dark-skinned man gesturing to him, leaning out the window. It was the man from the picture on the fridge.

'I have important information for you,' he said. 'My name is Yakubu, I'm Taribo's brother. He said a whole lot of other things too, but Steinar couldn't understand everything. The man was speaking in African English at a furious speed, so Steinar asked him to slow down.

'Sorry. *Jeg snakker ikke norsk*. I don't speak Norwegian. I can understand a bit, but I prefer to English.'

'That's fine, just speak more slowly.'

'You've got to come with me to see Taribo. He wants to talk with you.'

He bore a striking resemblance to Taribo, they were cast in the same enormous mould.

Steinar sighed. 'Open the back so I can put in my bike.'

They spent the next few minutes chatting as Steinar managed to get to grips with Yakubu's English. Steinar had some experience of African players' pronunciation from the time he'd spent in the Netherlands. It was like when a Norwegian tried to understand Danish, if you tuned out the less clear parts and focused on the words that were stressed, you could work out the rest of the context. Now and then, Yakubu also pronounced the occasional word in a characteristically Norwegian accent. Steinar found himself having to interrupt less and less, while Yakubu went on speaking at pace.

'I was in Stanley's room while you were visiting him and his mum,' he said. 'I liked what I heard. I liked the fact that you were so open. It sounded like you meant it, not like that bastard Arild Golden. Did you know that he employed Taribo as a workman? Got him to redecorate his apartments. I'm paying attention more now, keeping an eye out. Both for Taribo and Stanley.'

They came to the Ryen junction, turned off south along Enebakkveien, drove past the Esso garage and through the neighbourhood of Abildsø. Steinar sent Benedikte a text message explaining the situation and asking if she could keep an eye on Junior a little longer. 'Be careful,' came the reply.

Yakubu continued. 'They're all bastards in Norwegian football. You know that guy from UDI, the Directorate of Immigration? The one who works with footballers?'

Steinar had no idea what Yakubu was talking about, let alone that there was somebody in the Directorate of Immigration dealing with footballers. He shook his head. Yakubu had used the Norwegian abbreviation for the Directorate of Immigration. UDI stood for *Utlendingsdirektoratet*, and he'd pronounced it in an especially Norwegian way: 'Oo-deh-ee.'

'Taribo and I know all the African footballers in southeast Norway. Whether they play for Lillestrøm, Pors, Stabæk or Ullern, we know them. We meet at African tournaments, both top players and cast-offs like us, and they've all run into that guy from UDI. He was Golden's inside man. He did whatever Golden told him to. If he wanted a player cleared, all he had to do was ask. Or he could have them stopped. If a club didn't want to pay, he'd get the UDI man to write that the player was *"ikke nødvendig for klubbens virksomhet"*; surplus to requirements. If the club paid, the player would be cleared within a few days.'

Yakubu raced through that phrase in Norwegian, which seemed out of place against everything else he said in English. It was clearly a phrase he'd learnt by heart.

Could the extent of Golden's corruption really reach as far as the Directorate of Immigration? Did he have a finger in every pie? Yakubu stopped the car in a car park and signalled Steinar to follow him.

'How do you know so much about this?' asked Steinar.

'Golden gave me a good reason to look into it. He was once my agent too. Africa's big, but the world of football is small. The biggest agents know where the biggest talent can be found. He promised me the world but left me in a hotel in Antwerp with no passport and no money. But God intervened and sent Taribo to me.'

Yakubu was confirming what Ola Bugge had told Benedikte, but why was he being so open? Did he think Steinar would protect them, even if they admitted guilt? Steinar had heard of the thousands of African lads who ended up as street prostitutes after football agents made money out of luring them to Europe, and he felt sorry for Yakubu if that's what happened to him, but that didn't give him a free pass to kill people.

They walked through a gate and along a tarmac road that soon became a gravel track. On their right was Rustadsaga, a large, red cabin where you could go for a bite to eat while walking or skiing in the woods. Yakubu led him up the track and into the forest, along the edge of Nøklevann, a small lake.

'My dad has a small shop in Nigeria. One day, three men came and robbed him. A few hours later, my dad's friends found them. My dad wanted to let them go once he got his money back, but his friends had other ideas. They cut the hands off one of them and made the second man drink fresh cement. Then they hammered a nail into the third man's head. You don't steal from a Nigerian.'

Steinar was familiar with the hilly terrain around Nøklevann, but a few hundred metres further on, they left the track and went through the woods, where there were no paths.

Yakubu led them further into the trees, constantly on the look-out.

Here was a man who was used to danger. Perhaps a man who was used to violence too. He had a scar on his face, was it from a knife fight? A fight to the death? What did Steinar know, other than the fact that Yakubu was leading him to Norway's most wanted man?

There were no bikes braking or children crying in their pushchairs, it was so unusual not to have the constant sound of traffic in the background. A bird, something rustling in a bush, a gust of wind taking hold of a birch tree, they were only the sounds until they heard a shout.

'Hot dog to start with?'

Taribo Shorumno was holding out a hot dog to Steinar. Behind him, hidden among the trees, Taribo had put up a tent. Inside the tent, Steinar could see a couple of bags of clothes, a portable radio, some newspapers and a paperback lying open upside down. On the large grill there were three chops cooking, some spare ribs and more sausages. Taribo had clearly planned his escape and had assistance. Steinar took the hot dog, sat down on the nearest rock and took a couple of bites before he said anything.

'What's going on, Taribo?' he asked.

The man whose face was on every newspaper, website and news programme flipped one of the pieces of meat and said: 'I saw a chance and took it. All I really had to do was walk out, and why not? My life's over as it is.'

'It's not. You've got to let me fight for you in court.'

'I'll be thrown out of the country even if I'm found innocent. I want to be close to my son.'

'They'll catch you if you meet him.'

'I'll have to see him in secret, but it's better than nothing.'

'Why am I here?'

'I still want you to be his agent. You're the only one who can protect him. Yakubu will also have to go into hiding now, he hasn't got a residence permit either.'

'Where are you going to live?'

'We'll stay here for now.'

'Why here?'

'Have you ever seen a black man in the forest here in Oslo? It's the last place they'll look.'

Steinar wiped off some barbecue sauce from the corner of his mouth. 'Why didn't you tell me about Golden and that business with Stanley's injections?'

'Because Golden said that such large quantities of cortisone might give a positive result in a doping test, so it was best to keep quiet,' said Taribo.

Steinar nodded, then he turned to Yakubu.

'Drive me back,' he said.

Steinar needed to think things through, work out how something like this could've happened, agents putting young boys' lives at risk. How could the world of football have become so dirty? But first he had to ask Taribo a couple of questions.

'Do you own a morning star?'

Taribo held Steinar's gaze but didn't answer. How much should Steinar push him out here in the wildnerness? He got up and started walking off with Yakubu. Then he turned towards Taribo one last time.

'By the way, do you remember that day whether or not the window in Golden's office was open?'

Back-Up

The sight of Junior sleeping had calmed her nerves, the rhythm of his breathing and his chest rising and falling. She wiped away a spot of crust from the corner of his eye.

Benedikte wasn't used to children, and she didn't know how much they could take without being woken. Carefully she pressed her finger against his chin. His head just drifted to the side. She lifted his arm. It was as if it had no muscles in it. The cartoon on the computer had long since finished.

She couldn't put it off any longer. She went into the kitchen, closed the door and dialled Ola Bugge's number. He answered on the third ring.

'Hi, it's Benedikte Blystad.'

'Hey baby, sorry it took me a while to answer, I had John Santio on the other line.'

Santio was one of the big international agents, and it was beyond Benedikte how on earth Bugge would know him. True, Bugge had been making the most of the void left by Golden over the past few days, signing dozens of his players, but Santio was in another league altogether. Santio was behind the really big transfers, the ones between Manchester United and Real Madrid, Inter and Barcelona.

'What can I do for you, my lovely little lady?' said Bugge.

'I want to meet you.'

'Didn't get enough of me last time, eh? Need a bit more "buggie wuggie"? I get you.'

'I've got a proposal for you,' she said.

'No problem, where should we meet?'

'Do you know St Halvard's?' asked Benedikte. The pub, in the old part of Oslo's East End, was just shady enough that nobody noticed who the other patrons were.

'No, no, baby, I'm done with places like that. I'm a respectable businessman now. Let's make it the roof bar at the Grims Grenka Hotel, 8 p.m.,' he said, hanging up.

Benedikte went back into the living room. Junior rolled over but didn't wake up. He wasn't seriously ill, but still, anything could happen, even with a child.

Her cancer had made Benedikte tough, but it also made her a cautious and thorough person. You couldn't take cytotoxic medication lightly. She couldn't fight the superior force of cancer all on her own. She'd taught herself to live life to the full, but when that life was under threat, she reverted to being that careful little child.

She was always afraid there were cells smouldering away, cells that came back to life and multiplied. The doctors had reassured her that wasn't going to happen, she'd been cured, but Benedikte knew that children who'd had leukaemia had an increased risk of cancer later in life. The risk was small, but she still insisted on regular check-ups. She didn't want to give cancer any extra chances, no advantage.

Similarly, she couldn't physically take on a large, strong man, so she didn't want to turn up at a popular place like the Grims Grenka Hotel to question Bugge without having someone in her corner. She'd wanted it to be Steinar, but not now, not while Junior was ill. She stroked the boy's head, went back into the kitchen and called her ex-boyfriend in the police, Arnold Nesje. She made it sound as if it wasn't anything special.

'Got any plans for this evening?'

Champions League

Steinar got out of Yakubu's car at the junction of Oslo Gate and Bispegata. Yakubu spun off while Steinar was heading to the back of the van to get his bike. He called after him, but Yakubu was already out of reach.

He took out his mobile and sent Benedikte a text message: 'How's it going?'

The reply came quickly: 'Fine. Junior's still asleep.'

'Is it OK if I go to a quick meeting?'

'Sure.'

'I'll be home ASAP.'

He walked past the medieval city ruins and the Ruinen pub. Steinar had his doubts about whether the name, which literally meant 'the ruin', was a good choice for such an establishment.

He walked down the slope, passing under the last stretch of railway before Oslo Central Station. The passageway reminded Steinar of Brooklyn, where he and Mette had gone on a break while they were law students. The landscape opened up with the big park in front of the prison and police station. Steinar walked up the path and through the door, together with four young people on their way to renew their passports. They were discussing an InterRail trip. Steinar went over to reception and asked to see Inspector Håvard Lange. A couple of minutes later, he found himself sitting in Lange's office.

'Of course we thought about that,' said Lange after Steinar had told him his theory about the window. 'But we also know that anybody climbing in there would most probably have been sighted.'

'Why?'

'Vålerenga were having a training session that evening, and they would've noticed if somebody was climbing in through a window up there.' Lange tidied some papers on his desk.

'What are you saying? Vålerenga were training at Ullevaal that day? They normally train at Valle.'

'Vålerenga had a Champions League qualifier, so they were doing some extra training sessions.'

'But that means there were a number of other potential killers in the immediate area of the crime scene.'

'We've got our man. Taribo fits the crime in every way. He's recorded as entering the door. We seized a morning star at his home, which we presume to be the murder weapon. Taribo's in Norway illegally and, when we questioned him, he admitted having an argument with Golden. Besides, he's escaped. I'm certainly not interested in investigating whether anybody else might have had a motive or opportunity.'

Lange could say whatever he wanted, but it was incredible that the police had leapfrogged over the fact that Vålerenga had been training at Ullevaal that evening, no matter how guilty Taribo might seem.

'Have you got any details of who was there at the training session?'

'Not exactly, but it's probably easy to work out. 20 players, some coaches, maybe a few people watching. Agents and some fans.' Lange drew some imaginary circles in the air.

'That morning star, have you got it here at the station?'

'It's in the evidence room.'

'Would it be possible to see it?'

Lange looked at Steinar for a few seconds before lifting the phone and calling the person in charge of the evidence room. Minutes later the weapon was brought up to them. Lange passed it to Steinar. One blow from that would surely be enough to kill somebody.

'Golden had holes in the back of his neck, about a centimetre deep, which could have been made with a weapon like this. Is that right?' asked Steinar.

'That's the theory we're working on.'

'But you're not sure that a morning star was used?'

'That's right. We've got to wait for the post mortem report before we draw any conclusions.'

Steinar ran his fingers over the sharp spikes. His eyes moved from the weapon to Lange.

'It wasn't a morning star that killed Arild Golden,' Steinar said.

We've Got Plenty of Time, Baby

Oslo's first designer hotel, Grims Grenka, was on Kongens Gate, right next to the Museum of Contemporary Art, and with a view of Akershus Fortress. The roof terrace, which deserved a better climate than the Norwegian, was getting full. Luckily most of the clientele was made up of couples, so Benedikte was able to sit and wait undisturbed.

It was past 8 o' clock and oppressively warm. Benedikte had sat farthest away from the entrance, on comfortable red cushions placed on a long wooden bench.

She rested her right foot on her left knee while she stirred her mojito with a black straw. Arnold Nesje sat at the bar, pretending to drink beer from a bottle.

Ola Bugge arrived at the end of the bar. He greeted the bartender, who nodded and smiled at him politely. He spotted Benedikte, put on a lop-sided grin, winked and pointed at her. Then he walked over, swaying an unusual amount from side to side. He was wearing an open shirt, sweat glistening on his partially hairless chest, and there was a cross hanging from his neck.

He flopped down onto his seat. The table shook. Benedikte's drink was about to tip over, as Bugge turned his head the other way and shouted: 'Waiter!'

Seconds later, Bugge got up, went over to the bar and got himself a beer. He'd already drunk half of it by the time he flopped back down into his chair. He was breathing heavily, sweat running off his brow.

'What can I do for you?' said Bugge.

'What are you using to blackmail Per Diesen?' asked Benedikte.

'What makes you think I'm doing that?' asked Bugge.

'Because Diesen's trying to persuade Marius Bjartmann that they should both sign with you. A player with such a high profile as Diesen could easily get a big foreign agency to represent him, so you must be using something against him,' said Benedikte, trying to read Bugge's expression.

'My theory,' she continued, 'is that you've got hold of compromising footage of Arild Golden and Sabrina from *PDTV* cameras that they didn't know were there. And now you're using those pictures to blackmail him. If it comes out that Sabrina was having a relationship on the side, it would ruin the whole illusion of them as Norway's dream couple. H&M are planning a Nordic campaign with Diesen and Sabrina as their models. They would lose millions in advertising revenue. It might be the end of their relationship, but they can't afford to let it happen in the full glare of publicity.'

'You might be onto something,' said Bugge.

'Help me out.'

'It's not as straightforward as just Sabrina and Golden having an affair.'

'What do you mean?'

'Getting the truth might cost you dearly, my love,' said Bugge, checking her out. 'Let me get you another drink. In the meantime, have a think about what you can offer me.'

Benedikte hoovered up what she had left of her drink.

Bugge came back with a mojito and a beer, but he still hadn't worked out how to sit down normally. He came down heavily and too fast without putting the drinks down first.

'Bloody hell. These cost me more than 100 kroner and then I spill half of them,' said Bugge, shaking sugar and mint leaves off his wrist. 'Good job I've just signed an international player. I need that money coming in, baby.' He rubbed both thumbs and forefingers together before drying the rest of the mojito on his jeans.

'Who's that?'

'Alex Mendy from Lillestrøm,' said Bugge.

Mendy was a left-back who had been on a couple of Norwegian national youth teams in the past year, but only on the subs' bench. He'd had Arild Golden as his agent.

'Have you signed many from Golden Boys?'

'Actually, I've been offered a position with the firm. If I want, I could be Golden Boys' new front man. We might even change the name to Bugge Boys.'

Benedikte realised that it would be impossible to keep their meeting a secret. Bugge was far too keen on name-dropping, and now he was even closer to the Golden Boys system, and therefore closer to the case. She looked across at Nesje, sitting at the bar. He was still only half facing them, but she was sure that he had an eye on them. She would be safe here, but she couldn't take Nesje with her everywhere.

'You've got to tell me what you know. I need all the information you've got. And I can help you. What about an appearance on *Football Xtra* this Sunday?'

Bugge took a long sip of beer, and it was clear that he was having trouble keeping a straight face. He laid down his glass and put his head back, while he scratched his neck with three fingers.

'I don't know if I need that exposure any more. Things are pretty much falling into place on their own. You'll have to offer me something else.' He put his hand in his pocket, pulled out a key card and put it on the table. 'We've got plenty of time, baby. I had to book the room right through to tomorrow.'

Benedikte leapt up. 'We need some more to drink,' she said.

She went over to the bar and ordered another mojito, a beer and three shots of vodka. After paying, she kept her mojito and mixed the beer and vodka for Bugge.

A couple of rounds later, Bugge was developing a slur. Benedikte hinted that they could go to his room. Bugge just nodded without any other expression. Had she got him too drunk? Was he going to fall asleep?

And was it wise to be alone in a room with a man who could be the killer? Bugge had a motive, his business had taken off since Golden's exit. But as they went past Nesje at the bar, she held up her hand in a disarming gesture. She'd manage on her own. Nesje also held up his hand. Benedikte interpreted that as meaning he would give her five minutes.

Bugge insisted on taking the lift from the sixth floor down to the fifth. They walked along a narrow corridor with a black carpet and white rectangular signs with the room numbers on them. Bugge also insisted that Benedikte walk in front. He took hold of her shoulder and stopped her at room 603. Once inside, Bugge made an attempt to break the bed by sitting on it. Benedikte fled to the bathroom.

Bugge had information Benedikte needed, information that might reveal who had killed Golden and that could guarantee her own safety, but how far was she prepared to go?

She sat down on the toilet seat. The bathroom was high-tech, with a shower that looked like it needed a manual, volume controls next to the sink and deceptive mirrors on the floor that gave the impression you were looking straight into the room below. The most creative feature, though, was the frosted glass separating the toilet from the bedroom. It was fixed high up on the wall, and you could see both in and out of it. Benedikte jumped when she spotted Bugge pressing his face against the glass. She ran out.

'I've got to pee,' said Bugge. He went in and shut the door. Benedikte sat on a bench next to the TV. She pressed her fingers against her ears to minimise the sounds from the bathroom. He came back out from the toilet.

'What are we talking about here?' asked Benedikte.

Bugge glanced over at the bed.

'Forget it,' said Benedikte.

Bugge looked hurt, but then he just shrugged his shoulders.

'One of my tits. You get to see one of them.'

'Both tits, and I get to touch them for one minute,' said Bugge.

'No touching.'

'Then I get to see them both for one minute.'

'One of them, I said.'

'Baby, you're forgetting I'm an agent. Negotiating is what I do. You've got to budge too. You've got to give me more than just one tit.'

'Fine. You get to see both. For 10 seconds. But that's it. That's all you get, and then you tell me everything you know. Agreed?'

Bugge nodded, crawled up onto the bed and put some cushions together to support his back. He put both hands in front of his crotch, like a footballer in the wall against a free kick. Benedikte got up, sighed and looked down at the yellow plastic alarm clock which had a second hand. Bugge had stopped blinking. She took hold of her top around the waist and lifted it up.

Benedikte kept her eyes fixed on the clock while she heard sounds from the bed that she wished to forget as soon as possible. Finally the time was up. She pulled her top back down again and looked at Bugge. He was like a still photograph.

'Now talk,' said Benedikte.

'Thank you,' said Bugge.

'Talk.'

'I've got to ask you not to disclose where you heard this information.

We don't take these things lightly in my profession.'

Benedikte wondered whether the tradition of protecting sources might not go back a little further among journalists than it did among football agents, but she didn't want to split hairs. She nodded briefly and Bugge continued.

'I got access to some computer files, and from those I found out that Golden had slept with more surprising partners than Sabrina. She didn't quite fit Golden's preferences, let's say.'

Benedikte wondered how she could have been so slow on the uptake. She knew where Bugge was heading with this. They were models. Male models. How could she have been so blind? It was so blatantly obvious.

She'd really hoped the motive would have something to do with synthetic turf and its health risks. When Steinar had started talking about Ståle Jakobsen, artificial turf and cancer, her own medical past had led her astray. She'd been so sure that there was a conspiracy behind this, but murders tended to be more straightforward. They tended to deal with small personal matters.

When Bugge finally said it, it was more like a confirmation of what she already knew: 'Arild Golden was having sex with Per Diesen.'

Part 8

6 April 2004

'Well, I understand you agents never take anything less than 5 per cent.'

Arild Golden looked across his desk at the president of the NFF. They were talking about negotiations for TV rights. The financial value of football was exploding all over Europe. It was Sky that had set the ball rolling in Britain, and the time had come for Norway to follow suit.

The current TV agreement, which would run out at the end of the year, had a combined value of 250 million kroner. The agreement was so far off the true commercial value of Norwegian football that Arild Golden could secure the same sum by sending just one e-mail, so the matter was quite simple. Was the top boss of Norwegian football really offering him 12.5 million kroner to send one e-mail?

It was Golden who had invited the president to his office to discuss the TV rights, but he'd been unsure whether the president would even be interested in meeting him. Golden was under investigation by the NFF, suspected of representing more than one party in a transfer deal.

The NFF could punish him in one of two ways, either by suspending his licence or issuing a fine. In themselves, these things were trivial. It would be no problem to pay another agent to put his name on the papers while Golden was suspended, and the fine would be an insignificant amount. The problem was that the penalty would attract the attention of the media and, worse, it might attract the attention of Økokrim, the authority that dealt with financial crime.

His plan was to help the NFF free of charge. If he negotiated a better deal for the TV rights, maybe the association would allow the investigation against him to be forgotten at the bottom of a drawer.

There were three potential partners to deal with. The state broadcaster NRK had long since indicated that they weren't interested, which left Canal+, TV2 and TV3. Golden had already arranged meetings with all three the *next day. And then along came this, a 5 per cent offer to start negotiations. If he got this deal, the football associations in Sweden and Denmark would also come knocking on his door. Soon he might be negotiating rights for the Olympics, the World Cup, skiing and handball. There were enormous opportunities to be had, and nobody had taken them.*

He cleared his throat. 'I'll need to ask for 12 per cent. Negotiations like these take a lot of work, and it's not clear how much money we might be talking about.'

'6.'

'10.'

'I'm sure that you're worth every penny, and if it'd been up to me, I would've accepted that. But I've got a board to deal with and they've authorised me to offer up to 8. No more.'

'Okay,' said Golden, shaking the president's hand and leading him to the door. He spent the next few minutes looking out across Ullevaal Stadion. Three TV companies to deal with, he thought. Norway was such a tiny country. There were three companies to set up against each other, and those three meetings would make him tens of millions. At the back of his head, he was already kicking about the idea of 100 million kroner.

Coming Out

Steinar was holding a white coffee cup with red, yellow and blue squiggles on it. Junior had made it at nursery.

The cup was also painted on the inside, and Steinar wondered what kinds of chemicals he might be ingesting. Before taking another sip, he wiped his finger over the rough surface where Junior had been so generous with the paint. The coffee tasted just of coffee.

A short distance away from the house stood a big pine tree. Most of the bark had fallen off, and the thinnest branches hanging down were grey. The tree looked like a old man, but in reality it had gone one step further. It had been standing there dead for as long as Steinar could remember. Every day he looked for the tiniest sign of life. He knew it was pointless, but he always checked while he was drinking his coffee.

The tree was on the agenda at the residents' association meetings. Steinar had taken on the task of getting an expert opinion as to whether it should be cut down and, if so, when. It was a task he'd been putting off, and he would soon run out of excuses.

Above the tree, dark clouds hung in the sky. There had been record high temperatures in Oslo that summer, with very little rain. Now it seemed as if all the summer's humidity had accumulated in the black clouds enveloping the hill above at Grefsenkollen.

Junior was sitting at the kitchen table, his yoghurt untouched. His fingers were busy pressing hard at Benedikte's iPhone. He easily manoeuvred his way into the various apps. He spent minimal time on each app before his fingers sped across the screen looking for something else. Technology had developed to such a degree that the gadgets would soon be too small for grown-ups. They were better suited to a child's fingers.

In Steinar's childhood, the Commodore 64 had been all the rage.

He'd learnt to write programs that would fill the whole screen with one word or one sentence, not to mention the joy he and his friends had when they got hold of Tetris or some other basic game. Now Junior was sitting there, aged two and a half, operating a touchscreen smart phone as if it were the most natural thing in the world.

Steinar heard a noise. He went out of the kitchen and saw Benedikte coming down the stairs. She'd crept in after Steinar and Junior had fallen asleep the night before.

Benedikte was wearing a Puma T-shirt that was far too big for her. As far as Steinar could see, that was all she was wearing. It reached down almost to her knees. She wasn't wearing any make-up. She stretched, leaning on the big toe of her right foot, put her head back and yawned slowly.

'Good morning.'

'Good morning.'

'Per Diesen and Arild Golden were having a relationship.'

'What?'

'Have you seen my mobile?'

'Junior's got it in the kitchen,' Steinar said.

Benedikte disappeared off looking for it.

That Golden might be gay was something that hadn't even crossed Steinar's mind. Had Golden and Diesen been an item? In that case, how would that work for Diesen, playing on a football team?

Steinar had spent much of his life in changing rooms. The kind of banter in there was still the kind he was most comfortable with, even after years of university education, countless study group meetings with challenging discussions and, more recently, a fair amount of experience as a lawyer. Even now, he knew that it was when he'd sat on those wooden benches and taken off his socks after a tough training session that he'd felt most at ease.

Dressing room banter was macho. That doesn't mean that girls and cars were all that they talked about, but it was a world of teasing, arguing over card games and throwing things across the room, with little space for talking about feelings. Steinar remembered a teammate who used to come in and shout '78' or '82' or whatever it was, updating them on how many women he'd slept with. He did it in such a way that the manager and any other uninitiated passers-by would hear it and wonder what the numbers meant.

In a culture like that, it's not that easy to talk about feelings, especially if it's feelings for another man. They had plenty to say about players from other teams, but Steinar could only imagine what they'd say about one of their own playing for *the other team*. It was hard to imagine any part of modern society where the word 'shame' had more currency.

Maybe gay men were being scared away from football. Maybe they preferred other arenas where they could feel safer around their colleagues. Or was the changing room closet really bursting with gay men?

If a player shied away from tackling or turned his back when setting up a wall against a free kick, he was often called 'gay'. In a Second Division match, Steinar had once been tackled to the ground, and the defender had held him down when he tried to get up.

'Let go of me, you bloody poof,' he shouted.

There were some young boys standing nearby. From that day onwards, Steinar's opponents would be 'bloody idiots'.

Steinar went into the kitchen where Benedikte was trying to retrieve her iPhone from Junior. He'd turned away from her and was holding his new favourite toy in an iron grip. Benedikte was trying to trick him with quick movements to snatch the phone from him. She looked at Steinar.

'The hottest example at the moment is a Welsh rugby star who came out as gay. It was a sensation,' said Benedikte. 'Another example is that the FA even had to set up a special group to combat the widespread homophobia in English football. But it's a hopeless task in England. We're supposed to be a lot more liberal in Norway, or so I thought. Why was there that absurd level of interest when an unknown handball player came out? There's only one Norwegian male footballer who's done the same, and he had enough and quit straight afterwards. Nobody reacts the same way with women's sport. Why is it so difficult for you men?'

How was Steinar supposed to discuss this without appearing like a Neanderthal? He remembered some old jokes about women's football, but steered himself away from them.

'Have you read about Brian Clough?'

'You mean the manager who picked on Justin Fashanu because he was gay? They found Fashanu in a garage after he'd hanged himself.'

'That's right, but Clough, with his boastfulness and incredible results, was still one of the greats. You know, they're still making books and films about the man. He was manager at Nottingham Forest for most of his career, and you'd have to be totally mad about football to know the names of any other Forest managers. Many years later, Clough said that he regretted the way he'd treated Fashanu.'

'So Fashanu's suicide has scared off footballers from coming out?'

'There's certainly a fear of not being accepted. Maybe it's easier to pretend nothing's going on. I might be wrong, as I haven't been keeping up with football that much, but I don't think any really high-profile players have come out since Fashanu.'

'Anton Hysén. It caused quite a fuss in Sweden. He's famous.'

'I've never heard of him.'

'He's the son of Glenn Hysén, a former Liverpool player. His brother Tobias plays for Sweden.'

'Which division does Anton play in though?'

'I think it's the Swedish Second or Third Division.'

'So he's famous because he comes from a well-known footballing family, not because of his own performance on the pitch.'

'How would you have reacted if you'd found out you were playing with someone who was gay?'

'I don't know.'

'Wouldn't you have encouraged him to come out?'

'I wouldn't have any problem with having a gay teammate. Many players would have accepted it. It depends on the atmosphere in the team, and some teams would probably fall apart or force the player to leave. But in a strong team, with players who get on well with each other, it could work. Especially if there's a good manager and a strong captain. The biggest problem would be the fans.'

'What do you mean?'

'Playing away at Brann Stadion in Bergen, at Lerkendal in Trondheim or, perhaps worst of all for a well-known gay player with Vålerenga, in a derby match against Lillestrøm at Åråsen. It wouldn't be good. The jeering would be too much. The taunting would go too far.'

'What about the NFF? Wouldn't they intervene?'

'I'm sure they'd launch a campaign like the one in England. They'd take the opportunity while they were at it to boast about their years of work against racism, but there are still bad cases of racism in football, even in Norway, and it is a bit more common with players who are black than players who are gay.'

'So you would've told him to keep quiet?'

'At least to wait until his career's over. It's important that some people come out, but it's hard to encourage somebody to be a martyr. Besides, even if it doesn't have to mean the end of their career, it's bound to be tough, so they'd have to be especially well-adjusted to carry on as usual.'

'Would somebody's status in the dressing room really be a reason to kill?' asked Benedikte.

'Definitely. The impression also seems to be that it's young Muslim men who are the most homophobic, so maybe it's even harder to come out in a diverse team like Vålerenga than one like Bodø/Glimt, which has far fewer Muslim players. It's certainly possible that's what Diesen was thinking, that he was terrified this would come out and what that would do to his position in the changing room hierarchy,' said Steinar, looking out of the kitchen window again. He thought he'd heard something, but all he could see was the tree and the clouds, still menacing in the sky.

'Imagine how much of their lives players spend in there,' he continued. 'They don't talk to each other much on the training pitch. The changing rooms are the most important place to talk. Losing your status there might force you to move clubs, and some players never recover from that. I've got no doubt a gay footballer who doesn't want to be outed might kill to keep it a secret.'

Steinar felt annoyed with himself. He'd heard that it was Golden who'd set up Sabrina and Diesen, and he knew how much that meant for their respective images and careers. He should have thought that Sabrina and Diesen's relationship might be fictitious. Steinar had read interviews with Diesen in which he'd said how important he thought self-development was, and that he often stayed at the end of training sessions to practise free kicks. Nobody would have seen him climbing into Golden's office.

More strange sounds. Had he heard somebody talking outside? He got up, went into the hallway. He opened the front door to check and was faced with a barrage of flashing cameras.

Spin It

Benedikte hid behind the curtains, peeking out at the journalists. Steinar had slammed the door shut when he saw them. They'd clearly had enough of Steinar repeatedly saying 'no comment' on the phone and were now laying siege to the house. Benedikte turned towards Steinar, who was pacing around the living room.

'Well, we've been trying to look at the murder from different angles,' she said, 'but I really hadn't thought about this. Gay sex.' Then she put her hand to her mouth.

Steinar picked up the plastic ball with Mickey Mouse on it and threw it across the living room, with plenty of backspin. The ball bounced right next to Junior and came to rest. Junior wasn't paying any attention, his whole world was Angry Birds on Benedikte's phone.

'Good ball control,' said Benedikte with a nod of approval. 'But are we certain it's Per Diesen?' she said.

'What's certain is that these pictures would cause a scandal in the media, and if this was a crime of passion, there are only two people who could have done it.'

'Diesen or Sabrina.'

'And out of those two it must be Diesen, because I know what the murder weapon was, and it wasn't this,' said Steinar, lifting up a copy of *VG*, with its photo montage of Taribo and a morning star on the front page.

'Oh?' said Benedikte.

'Golden had a fracture to the left side of his nose, which suggests he was punched. After that, he's supposed to have been killed with a morning star, leaving wounds on the back of his head about a centimetre in depth. But why would the killer punch him first instead of using the morning star to start with, which would be more effective? It had to be something else that left those marks, and that something needed the victim to be lying down.'

'What?'

'Name one of Norway's great inventions.'

'Golden was killed with a cheese slicer?'

Steinar gave a wry smile, went down into the basement and came back up with a pair of black-and-white Adidas boots.

'Are you seriously claiming that football boots were invented in Norway?' asked Benedikte.

Steinar turned the sole towards her.

'No, but it was apparently a Norwegian who invented screw-in studs. They could leave marks a centimetre in depth. Diesen could have stamped on Golden's neck, breaking it.' He pointed at the studs. Benedikte ran her finger over the cold metal.

'So Golden was struck down then stamped on?'

'I think Ullevaal Stadion must also be one of the best places in Oslo to kill somebody.'

'Because of all the DNA?' asked Benedikte.

'Vålerenga play 15 league matches there. Average attendance so far this year is 18,000. That makes 270,000 people. Then you've got three or four international matches with 20,000 spectators each, plus Norwegian Football Cup matches, Europa League matches, and concerts. Then there are all the people who work at these events. The police. It's easily somewhere near 600,000 people a year. People sweating, coughing, spitting, not washing their hands when they go to the toilet, throwing away the odd sneaky cigarette. And that's just outdoors. Inside there are also lots of people on guided tours, and right next to Golden's office is UBC, one of Norway's biggest conference centres.'

'What about the DNA on his boots or other clothes?'

'Diesen's worn his boots again in training and at matches. I'm sure he's changed his studs too. The kit man washes their kit every day, and he wouldn't have been surprised to see blood on it. Some people even get annoyed if no blood's been shed in a training session, that means it wasn't tough enough.'

'So what do we do? Do you think the police will arrest Diesen just because of our suspicions?'

'The police have got their man. If we're going to get them to reopen the investigation, we'll need proof. We've got to get Diesen to make a mistake.'

'What kind of mistake?'

'I've got some ideas. The most important thing is to psych him out, let him know we know about him and Golden, that we can take everything away from him.'

'How do we do that?'

'I've got a plan to threaten his position in the game. It's their careers that footballers are most afraid of losing.'

'And what about me?'

'You've got to trick him into coming to the studio. Get him to believe that it's a real TV programme. I'm imagining a hot studio with excessive lighting. An intro with Fashanu, Clough, Hysén, that rugby player and the Norwegian cases. And then over to him. You can press him on rumours, on his preferences.'

'Can you go first?'

'Do you want me to?'

'All the same to me,' said Benedikte, looking away.

'Fine. Can you look after Junior for a few hours in the meantime?'

'Of course. What are you going to do?'

'I'm going to start a media circus.' Steinar took his football boots and headed out.

Benedikte put her ear to the door and heard Steinar answering 'no comment' to yet another question about Taribo. Another journalist followed up by asking: 'What are you going to do now?'

'What I do best of all,' said Steinar, as cameras clicked away. 'I'm going to play football.'

Playing in Black and White Boots

'Are you fit enough?' asked the Vålerenga coach, but Steinar knew the coach couldn't turn him down. The journalists, the ones who'd followed him to the training ground at Valle and the usual sports reporters who were already there, would pour criticism on the coach if Steinar were turned down, he was far too big a name from football's past. Besides, there was unquestionable curiosity in the manager's eyes.

'I'm in reasonable shape physically, but I haven't been playing football.'

'Not since you left Ullevaal that day? I was at the match. Nobody could work out what had happened when you didn't come back out after half-time.'

'No, I haven't played since that match.'

'We'll be playing 11 against 11. It won't really matter if we've got a couple of extra players there. Actually it could be quite good. Go and see Hjalmar to borrow some kit. And hey, good luck.'

Steinar shook the manager's hand and went to the kit room, next to the changing rooms. There, in a narrow room with shoes and other kit, was Vålerenga's legendary kit man, Hjalmar Bakken. If you came from the East End of Oslo, you knew who he was.

He was wearing a Vålerenga tracksuit from 1980, his skin grey. His fingers showed years of close contact with roll-your-own cigarette stubs. What was more surprising was that the right side of his face was also burnt, the skin missing in places. Half of his hair was like a silver fox, the other half reminiscent of those things you used to scrub pots and pans when they were very dirty. Steinar couldn't help staring.

'Explosion,' said Bakken, combing the healthy part of his hair. Then he drew out a cough from the depths of his lungs.

'Explosion?'

'I've got chronic obstructive pulmonary disease and need to take oxygen. They said it would be dangerous to light up around it. They were right.'

Bakken smiled at his own story, a smile only used by a certain generation from the East End.

'What do you want, anyway?' he said.

'I'm going to train, I need some kit.'

'Going to train?' said Bakken, coughing again.

'It's been cleared with the manager.'

'You need boots?'

'I've got my own.'

'Good. The worst thing's when we've got try-out players who come along and borrow boots. Never get them back.'

'I'll be using these ones,' said Steinar, holding up his Adidas World Cup boots.

'Black-and-white football boots. Do they still make them? Everyone here wants neon colours. Neon boots, agents, models and all that stupid nonsense, that's what they want.'

Bakken picked out some socks, shorts, a training shirt and a lightweight rain jacket. The rain was lashing down outside.

'Come on, I'll take you to the changing rooms,' said Bakken. He walked out and Steinar followed. They came to a waiting room with chairs, TVs and video game consoles, then went through a door into the large first-team dressing room.

'This part's Africa,' said Bakken loudly. 'From here halfway up that wall is where the blackies sit. There are also some from Kosovo or Jamaica or some place like that, but we call the whole mishmash Africa. The part from here on is Europe. This is where the white players sit. And that's Switzerland.'

He pointed at the physiotherapist and his bench, then laid Steinar's kit down on a free space in the part he'd called Europe, as delicately as if it were porcelain. Steinar shook hands with Marius Bjartmann, Per Diesen, Hilmar Guðjónsson, an Icelandic player that nobody could believe Vålerenga had bought, John Duff, a Canadian keeper who'd been a great success, and the 36-year-old Danish centre-back Jim Elkjær, who was far too good for the Norwegian top division but who was now too old for the big clubs in the rest of Europe.

Steinar put on the dark blue training shirt and shorts. The shirt was tighter than it used to be, and Steinar quickly reminded himself that all sports clothing was a tighter fit now, it was the fashion.

Steinar took hold of the socks by the ends and stretched them behind his neck. He didn't know why, but it was just a natural thing to do. He put on the socks and his Adidas boots, and did up the laces. The boots were a little too tight, to the extent that Steinar had to squeeze his feet inside. Football boots were supposed to be tight. He noticed that most of the others were wearing orange or fluorescent green boots.

Kalid Jambo started arguing with Martin Hovdenakk. Hovdenakk was the only one from a Norwegian ethnic background who was allowed to sit in Africa.

He was holding up his mobile phone and pointing at Jambo's laptop.

'Why won't you let me borrow it?' he said.

'I told you, I haven't got my adaptor. If you want to charge your fucking mobile on my computer, I need my adaptor. I don't want the batteries to run out.'

'For fuck's sake, Kalid, the battery's fully charged. I only need to charge my mobile a bit so it doesn't die on the way home.'

'Then buy yourself a charger for your car, you sponging bastard.'

The language had got tougher and the dress code had changed. Steinar noticed that many of the foreign players, as well as the Norwegian ones from immigrant minority backgrounds, covered their genitals while they changed. It surprised him to see a couple of the youngest ethnically Norwegian players doing the same thing. The rest of them had shaved their hair down below.

The manager came in and spoke about the training session. He welcomed Steinar as a guest player, and several of the 'African' players started whispering.

The plan for that day was jogging followed by three 15-minute sessions playing eleven against eleven. The manager handed out bibs. It was going to be the first eleven versus the reserves. Steinar felt a twitch. Shit, he hadn't been given a bib, he was on the lesser team. He hadn't experienced that before, and it awoke the competitive spirit inside him. It wasn't enough just to take part in the training session, he wanted to do well.

They went over to the training pitch at Valle. Small puddles had formed on patches of the grass pitch they were going to train on, but it seemed as if the rain was about to stop.

They jogged round at the edge of the pitch. Steinar's thoughts went back to Ajax, where they always started with ball work. Galloping round the pitch like this had gone completely out of fashion in the Netherlands generations before Steinar arrived. He looked around at the facilities. Compared to here at Valle, Ajax had a competitive advantage in terms of its location too. On the Ajax training pitch, Steinar had always had the gigantic Amsterdam Arena in his field of view, where they all wanted to play. If you kept it up, you could end up in the stadium playing football, not just selling hot dogs or watching. Some players thought the sight of the stadium was unnerving, that it stood out in the landscape like an impregnable fortress. Steinar thought it resembled a gigantic hamster cage, with its glass-covered escalators on the outside. When he'd been worn out during training, the sight of the stadium in the background gave him new energy, like a spin-crazy little rodent. Here all he could see were blocks of flats and Vallhall, the indoor arena.

Thousands of thoughts were spinning through his head while the manager prepared to blow his whistle and start the game. Would he survive a training session like this? What if he sprained something and had to limp off after a minute?

Steinar's team was set up in a 4–4–1–1 formation, trying to mimic Vålerenga's next opponents, Odd. This meant that Steinar would be used as an offensive midfielder, or a hanging forward as some people called it. That meant he'd be playing in close proximity to Diesen and could try to psych him out. Steinar looked over at Diesen, who was standing with his hands on his hips and eyes on the ground.

The manager blew the whistle and the game began. Steinar's body was poised in anticipation of what would happen next. He was also thinking about those four words Vlad Vidić had said. Had he really given all this up for nothing?

Half a minute into the match Steinar found space. The ball came to him from a perfect pass, and he would have to stop it. It went through his body like an electric shock, he was so unused to being in contact with the ball. He got caught in the grass and stumbled. Kalid Jambo took the ball from him and moved upfield. It was as if Steinar had never played the game before.

Things went better from then on. Steinar made a couple of good passes, but his team were 1–0 down when they took their first break. Otto Cana had knocked in a rebound. Steinar took a couple of sips of water and half-listened to the assistant coach, who wanted to adjust the team's positions, but most of all he stared over at the first-team players. Partly to keep an eye on Diesen, but also because he couldn't help feeling annoyed that he was on the wrong team.

After another two minutes, the keeper on Steinar's team took a long goal kick. The striker in front of Steinar ended up in a running duel with Elkjær. The Dane pulled away from the striker under pressure, but he was far too nonchalant when he had to find a teammate. His unsuccessful pass ended up at Steinar's feet and the ball came to an immediate halt. Steinar's first touch was working again. He'd stopped the ball without thinking about it, as if he'd never been away. Jambo saw the danger coming. Steinar was 30 yards from the goal. Jambo came towards him. Steinar pulled to the left. Jambo threw himself into tackle, but Steinar saw it coming and jumped over him. He took his shot from 25 yards, with the instep of his right foot. The ball spun and slammed into the top of the goal. Marius Bjartmann came in late and collided with Steinar. He turned round and saw the ball lying at the back of the net.

'Played football before, have you?' he said.

'I suppose so,' said Steinar, heading back to his own half of the pitch. It was a struggle not to smile. He wanted to turn his shirt inside out and run around like Junior had done.

Another kick-off. The game moved back and forth. Steinar got the ball in the same position, this time he was mown down. Jambo had seen they were in danger again and wasn't going to miss his tackle a second time. Steinar landed on his back, knocking the breath out of him. It was unnecessarily hard but Steinar was mostly annoyed with himself, he'd reacted too late. He ignored Jambo's niggling remarks and went on playing.

Another long ball from the keeper. This time Steinar got an elbow in the chest from Jambo. He felt his blood rush and the sweat stinging his eyes. The inside of his left thigh was aching where a muscle was torn, the meniscus on his right knee was hurting a little and he had cramp on both sides of of his lower back. Steinar felt alive again.

Jambo got the ball. He came towards Steinar, feigning left. Steinar realised it was a feint and stuck out his shoulder and a foot as a counterweight, and Jambo ran straight into Steinar's shoulder. Jambo landed in the mud and leapt up with his fists clenched, but Elkjær took hold of him from behind and calmed him down. Bjartmann smiled at Steinar.

'Maybe you should try not to provoke him too much,' he said. 'He might explode. Kalid's an idiot, but he's someone you want on your team. He'll die for you when you're on the same team and hate you if you're wearing the other team's colours. It makes no difference whether it's a training session or a real match.'

Bjartmann was right. Every time Steinar had tried to get close to Diesen, Jambo had stopped him. It was his job to make sure Diesen could be the playmaker.

The second part of the match faded. It was still 1–1. Steinar was worn out. He wasn't used to all these fits and starts. Running on the treadmill, cycling or skiing all involved monotonous motion and couldn't be compared to the intensity of exercise on the football pitch. Steinar drank some more and saw the coach pointing his finger at Jambo and Diesen.

Halfway into the game's third 15-minute 'half', Steinar moved up behind Diesen's back. A short pass upfield. He pulled away, took the ball with the outside of his foot right in front of Diesen and dribbled back diagonally towards the touch-line. Then he turned quickly and kicked the ball between Diesen's legs. The nutmeg was a bit too hard, and he had to sprint round Diesen to catch up with the ball, which was heading towards Jambo.

Jambo was coming for him with fury at a raging pace. Steinar managed to get his toe on the ball and knocked it through Jambo's legs. Nutmeg number two. Steinar was now running straight for Elkjær, who was waiting for him. Big mistake. Steinar kept up his speed and switched the ball from right foot to left, a two-foot dribble round the outside of the Dane. Now Steinar was alone, facing the keeper. The same two-footed move and the keeper was also dealt with, but the ball was on its way off the pitch. Steinar caught up with it one yard from the goal line. He had an open goal. He caught a glimpse of Bjartmann sliding towards him out the corner of his eye. Steinar stroked the ball out the way. Bjartmann slid past and Steinar heard Bjartmann say 'shit' before Steinar rolled the ball into the open goal. Steinar was free again. For a few seconds, he thought about nothing. Absolutely nothing.

Then came the situation he'd been waiting for. Jambo lost the ball on his way forward. It was cleared by the centre-back from Steinar's team, and it ended up with Diesen. Steinar timed his tackle perfectly. He caught both ball and man, sending Diesen tumbling to the ground. From where he lay, Steinar passed on the ball to Guðjónsson, who moved on quickly. Steinar grabbed Diesen's wrist, pulled him up and said: 'I know everything. I've got your pictures.'

First Goal in 10 Years

If the glossy magazines caught wind of where Benedikte had spent the night they would have a hard time choosing which story to put as the main spread. But all the journalists and photographers had gone now, they had no idea.

She sat down at her Mac. She wanted to gather as much background information as possible, as soon as they got some proof, she wanted to go on air and nail Per Diesen as Golden's murderer.

Benedikte and Diesen were on nodding terms, but they hadn't ever really spoken to each other. He was far too vain for Benedikte's tastes, and the whole idea of metrosexual men annoyed her. There had to be some middle way, surely men weren't just either dirty mechanics who threw girls on top of car bonnets or the type who shared everything, including their moisturiser.

She checked the main news websites. The biggest clubs worked extensively with these sites. It wasn't because of Vålerenga's work on integration that *VG* automatically published the stories from the club's website. The aim was to increase the hits on the club's website artificially, thereby getting a bigger percentage of the NFF's media funding pot. This would then be split between *VG* and Vålerenga. It also saved *VG* having to pay journalists. It was a win-win situation, except in the case of the small clubs, who missed out on their slice of the media pie.

The main story everywhere was Steinar joining Vålerenga's training session. Short video clips were published as the training session went on, and it came as some relief to her to see that Diesen was also playing. She would be safe where she was for the time being.

She reloaded *VG*'s football page. A large headline read: 'Steinar Brunsvik's first goal in 10 years.' She followed the link to the short video clip and saw Steinar move past Kalid Jambo and hammer the ball into the net behind John Duff.

Benedikte had watched some archive footage from his time on the national team and at Ajax, but she thought this must be another Steinar. She watched the clip four times, it was a spectacular goal.

She clicked away from the sports pages and started looking at an online map. Vålerenga had been playing against Start in Kristiansand the day before she was attacked at Ullevaal. Diesen could have driven from Kristiansand to Oslo overnight. The team had gone there by bus, but Diesen and Bjartmann had probably stayed the night in Kristiansand so they could travel to Bergen for their appearance on TV2's *Football Xtra* the day after. As a player with both Vålerenga and the Norwegian national side, Diesen would know Ullevaal like the back of his hand. It would've been a piece of cake for him to get hold of some keys.

From Oslo, Diesen would've had several options, but it was probably safest to drive from there to Bergen. Benedikte hadn't seen him at Gardermoen Airport, and it was highly likely that somebody would have seen him there if he'd taken a later flight. A fan would at least have tweeted about it. The most likely scenario was that he'd driven over the hills himself. It was a six-hour drive, so he would still have been able to get to the studio just before 6 p.m. Maybe that was why the trio turned up so late, maybe Bjartmann and Sabrina had been waiting for him.

There were still several things she couldn't work out. How did Diesen find out she was going to meet Birger Holme? How had he tricked Holme into thinking that she'd cancelled? And how could he have threatened TV2 to stop her from investigating?

Of course, no single player should have that much influence, but she was afraid it might be the case. If TV2 found it credible that Diesen could get other players from Vålerenga and the national team to refuse to be interviewed, it was possible that the channel might be willing to bury a story like this.

The doorbell rang, making Benedikte jump. It couldn't be for her, she thought, as Junior ran towards the front door. She tried to grab him but missed. The boy dashed into the hallway and pressed his face against the window next to the door. It was hopeless to pretend there was nobody home. As she came into the hallway, Junior was reaching up as far as he could and just managed to turn the lock and open the door.

There stood Norway's most wanted man, Taribo Shorunmo.

What Goes On in the Dressing Room...

Steinar was drying himself after taking a shower, keeping his eyes on Diesen the whole time. Then a piercing whistle cut through the room.

Into the dressing room came Otto Cana, a Kosovan Norwegian, together with the other two young lads who'd been fetching the balls. They tossed the ball-net towards Hjalmar Bakken, who checked that they'd collected them all. But Otto Cana had found something else too, he was holding a sports bottle above his head.

'Marius, look! Kalid left his bottle on the pitch, that'll be a fine!'

Every football team had its own internal justice system, often in the form of fines. The players agreed how much it would cost to turn up late for a match or training session, to wear sports clothing from a competing brand to the team's sponsor, or to leave things out on the pitch. This encouraged them to grass on each other, and it was this, as well as the prospect of having to pay 50 kroner, that made Jambo snap. He leapt up and shouted at Cana.

'I'm going to kill you!'

Jambo was the type of player who never admitted he was wrong. If he missed the ball the pass was too hard, if he hit a pass over the touchline, it was the other player's mistake. He was famous all over Norway for being the only person who'd ever accused the ball of bouncing the wrong way on the indoor pitch at the Telenor Arena.

'Marius, I swear, somebody hid my bottle, I looked for it everywhere. They must have covered it with grass.'

Kalid was addressing Bjartmann, just as Cana had done. Bjartmann was clearly in charge of issuing fines. He pulled out a small, black notepad from his washbag, opened it, breathing in as if he were smelling freshly baked bread, and started to write.

'But...,' said Kalid.

'Kalidi Amin, you'll have to go and bring it back into the dressing room, otherwise there'll be a fine,' said Bjartmann.

'So it's alright to hide other people's bottles, is it?'

'I don't give a shit, you know the rules. Any appeals are to be lodged in writing.'

Bjartmann brought an end to the intercontinental discussion, but it went on over in Africa.

'It's always like this,' Jambo said. 'They look down on us foreigners. They never listen to us.'

'I hear you, bro,' said Cana.

'Shut up, Otto, fucking grass, blabbing to the Norskies like that. What the fuck do you think you are, integrated?'

The language was different in Africa from Europe. In Africa they all called each other 'bro' or 'asshole', or both, usually as terms of endearment. They also swore a great deal and took things out on each other. There were 22 players in total in Vålerenga's first-team stable, the nine players in Africa, making up a significant part of the team. There were three Moroccans, two Kosovans, a Russian, a Somali and a Nigerian, as well as Martin Hovdenakk, who was as white as a sheet but apparently had a 'black way of thinking'.

Diesen sat down in his place next to Bjartmann. Bjartmann had a Brazilian flag above his clothes pegs.

Brazil, with its five world titles, was the best national team of all time. Almost all Brazilian international players came from poor backgrounds, with the famous exceptions of Kaká and Socrates. True, there weren't exactly any favelas in Norway, but the national team would soon be dominated by players from the Grorud Valley and Holmlia, largely from less well-off families, and often from immigrant backgrounds. Would there soon be a class division in Norwegian football too?

Bjartmann pointed over at Africa, where they were still gesticulating as they discussed the bottlegate scandal, and shook his head. 'I can't believe they're wasting so much energy on that bottle.'

Steinar's mobile received a text. There were lots of conversations going on at the same time, loud outbursts too, but when his mobile beeped it caught everyone's attention as if a gunshot had rung out.

'Steinar doesn't know the rules,' said Bjartmann. 'We'll let him off a fine, just this once.'

Steinar put his mobile on silent before reading the message from Benedikte. Taribo and his brother Yakubu were on their way to pick him up. Benedikte had guessed there might be a few journalists there, so they would wait in the van by the side entrance.

The mood in the dressing room was still heated. Words such as 'the Norskies' and 'grassing' were thrown about, there was even lively discussion about how Steinar's text message had been dealt with.

The only one of the Norskies who said anything back was Hjalmar Bakken: 'Now just you calm down, you black buggers. Clean up all your tape instead.'

None of them answered back. It seemed they accepted Bakken.

The players put on their clothes, and the big iPod headphones they all wore in Africa. In Europe Diesen was wandering around humming a Coldplay song.

'Tssss. He's a poofter, you know,' Kalid told Otto as they gave each other a slap on the back. They'd clearly put the grassing incident behind them.

Then Kalid picked up that day's *VG*. The entertainment section had a big picture of Per Diesen and Sabrina from their appearance on *Football Xtra*. Jambo pointed at the picture and shouted.

'Aren't you going to sing for us then, Shawn Carter?' Kalid laughed, giving several of the others high fives. 'You could at least get Sabrina to come and dance for us.' Still no reaction from Diesen. Kalid then got up and raised his voice even louder.

'She danced for me first, you know,' he said, stressing the word 'danced'.

Kalid Jambo defended Diesen on the pitch, but here in the dressing room there were other social rules. Steinar saw Diesen's eyes narrowing. Kalid lowered his voice, but was still clearly talking to his midfield partner:

'Just say if she's looking for a man, won't you? Alright, little Per? Or is it Pervert?'

Diesen was Vålerenga's captain that season. He'd been given the job because he was their best player, probably in the hope that it would make him even better, even more happy with the club and even more valuable if a transfer came along. But a captain was also supposed to be like the central reservation on a motorway. In a dressing room with very different opinions around, people from different religious and social backgrounds, different age groups, it was unavoidable that the traffic would sometimes be heading in opposite directions. A captain was supposed to help the manager to avoid any frontal collisions, and make sure the lads were all heading in the same direction when they had a match.

Diesen picked up a roll of red sock tape lying next to him and threw it with full force at Jambo. The tape slammed into the wall just a few inches from Kalid's curly hair, and Kalid leapt across the room before the tape had hit the floor. Diesen leapt to his feet too.

Kalid shoved him. 'You fucking homo!'

'Oh, shut your trap for once, bloody couscous,' said Diesen, before taking a right-hander to the stomach. Diesen paused for a couple of seconds before he hit back, wrestling Jambo to the ground. Diesen had surprising strength in his sinewy arms, but Jambo managed to get the upper hand and sat up on top of Diesen, ready to hit him again before he was lifted off. Bjartmann had seen enough. He pushed Jambo down to the ground and gave him two short jabs in the thigh.

'Next time I'll take your knees,' he said.

Jambo kept quiet and, once Bjartmann had finally let go, limped over to the physio and asked for an ice-bag.

What a bunch, thought Steinar. He finished changing and left the dressing room. Hjalmar Bakken was standing at the door to the kit room.

'Heard a rumour that you did quite well,' said Bakken.

'It went alright.'

'I've got an Adidas catalogue ready for you, just in case. I've underlined the items I'd recommend.'

Steinar took the catalogue, shook Bakken by the hand and walked briskly into the indoor sports hall, with its synthetic pitch.

'Will we see you again?' Bakken shouted, as loud as somebody with lung disease could.

Steinar pretended not to hear him and hurried across the astroturf. He went out the door on the other side and over to the waiting white van. Nobody saw him get in.

Stars

Benedikte looked through the main news websites once again. The *VG* site had added another story about Steinar under the headline 'Steinar Brunsvik's super solo goal'. She clicked on the link.

Had he really been that good? Or was it years of pent-up energy coming out all at once against a bunch of worn-out footballers who only saw that day's training session as a chore?

Benedikte looked up from her MacBook and straight at Junior, whose face was straining, his head leaning forward but his eyes looking up at her. His lip was trembling. The smell confirmed her fear. The boy had done a poo.

She liked Junior, but she had to force a smile while she held her breath, took off his nappy, stuffed it down into the nappy bin, which was almost full, and took out the wet wipes. Junior was unable to stay still, and he wrinkled his nose when Benedikte grabbed tightly onto his ankles.

'Sorry,' said Benedikte, making her take a deep breath. The smell made her giddy, but she managed to control herself and stroked Junior on the cheek.

'It's alright,' she said. She took out a new nappy, put it on him, lifted him and put him down on the floor.

At least the change of nappy stopped his lip from trembling. He tugged at Benedikte's shirt while she washed her hands, he was ready to play. She let him drag her over to the cark park play set, just outside his room.

He showed her where she should sit and gave her a pink car. Benedikte thought he wanted her to let go of it on the ramp so that it came out through the exit.

'No, no,' said Junior, 'lady wait.' He drove his black car up the ramp, against the direction indicated by the arrows. Benedikte was amused to see him playing with it the wrong way round. She wanted to do the same, and started at the bottom.

'No, no. Lady stay there,' said Junior, turning his car round at the top. Now he was going to let his car roll down. Benedikte switched on the sensor that made the engine sounds. Junior's car flew down, went round the corner at full speed, then zoomed out the exit and across the living room floor. 'Vroooooom!'

'Yeaaaah,' he shouted, getting up. He bumped into the car park, knocking off a piece of plastic. Benedikte picked up the piece and pushed it into place. Then she did the same as Junior, drove the wrong way up the ramp and let her car roll back down and across the floor. Her car rolled about a metre further than Junior's.

'Vrooooom!'

Benedikte was worried for a moment that the boy might be disappointed. She'd beaten him. Her competitive instinct meant she'd tried to win, was that fair with a child? It didn't seem to bother him.

'Yeaaaaah,' he shouted again, this time running around the living room with his hands in the air.

Benedikte ran after him with her hands in the air too. They repeated the sequence fourteen times until Benedikte got tired.

'Do you want some ice cream?' she said.

Junior ran towards the freezer compartment with his arms in the air, shouting 'Yeaaaaaah' again. She helped him to find an ice lolly which disappeared at record speed.

Benedikte started writing Steinar a text during the short interlude, but she didn't have time to finish. Junior ran into the living room, took hold of a Captain Hook sword and ran back into the kitchen. Benedikte heard a terrible crash and went through. Junior was bashing away with his sword at the coffee maker, which was only just hanging on. When he spotted her, he opened one of the kitchen cupboards, took out a spatula and gave it to her.

'Fight!' he said.

She couldn't resist. Junior was soon standing on the living room table while Benedikte shouted: 'En garde!'

He scored a direct hit on her finger, so she moved her hand further down the spatula handle. Junior was swinging his sword wildly now. Benedikte ducked and Junior missed. He lost his balance and was about to fall off the edge. Benedikte grabbed him just before he tipped over, but she couldn't stop his sword from flying through the air and hitting a vase with a large sunflower in it. It started rocking and was on the edge for a second while Benedikte softened Junior's fall to the floor. She put him down, but couldn't catch the vase in time, which smashed onto the table, sending water everywhere, some of it splashing over her MacBook.

She turned it upside down and ran to the bathroom, taking a towel and starting to dry it. Not much of the water had gone in, so maybe she'd been lucky. When she'd dried off all visible traces, she went back into the living room, put it down and opened the file with all her notes in it. It worked. She sent a back-up copy to her iPhone.

Where had Junior gone? Had she scared him? She walked towards his bedroom door. It was closed. Maybe he wanted to play alone for a while, Benedikte thought, sitting back down at the living room table. She scrolled back through the file, relieved that the MacBook still worked. Then Captain Hook came out from the kitchen.

'Hi!' said Benedikte loudly, checking he wasn't upset.

'Fight,' said Junior again, holding out his plastic sword.

Benedikte was about to assume some kind of defensive position when she noticed that Junior's eyes were focused on something behind her. His car park made another 'Vrooooooom!' Something, or someone, had gone past the sensor.

An ice-cold voice pierced the air.

'I warned you.'

Benedikte spun round.

'You?' she said, before the leather gloves strangled her voice. She heard Junior crying as she was dragged down the steps to the basement, the back of her head hitting each step in turn. The last thing she saw, before everything went black, was what looked like stars.

Part 9

20 May 2002

Arild Golden unlocked the door to his office at Ullevaal Stadion. Even though he'd only had the office for a few weeks, he noticed that something was wrong. He wasn't alone. He took another step inside and saw the silhouette of a man in the dark, sitting behind his desk.

'I want to be your partner,' said the man.

'Who are you, and how did you get in here?'

'That doesn't matter. What matters is what I can do for you.'

Golden already had two partners. They'd come along in the early nineties when he needed somebody to open doors for him. With no football career of his own to speak of, he needed help to build a network.

His first partner had opened the door to Norwegian football, introducing Golden to club chairmen, managers, players and association executives. His second partner had arranged for those first important handshakes in the closed world of English football. Over the years, Golden Boys would go on to export a great number of players to the Premier League and, as a result of that, also to Spain, Italy, France and Germany.

'Does it look like I need your help?' asked Golden, putting out his arms.

'You're big, but you're still just an ordinary football agent. I can make you king.'

'How?'

'I make things happen.'

'I need an example.'

'I'll give you two. Let's say Golden Boys and another competing agency each have one footballer playing an international. A club's sent somebody to watch the two players, comparing them against each other. Wouldn't it be a relief if the other player got food poisoning on the day of the match?'

Golden looked at the man but didn't say anything. The man held up two fingers and continued. 'Secondly, you've got an interest in astroturf. Part of

Golden Boys' income derives from it. I can give you a monopoly. I can put pressure on entrepreneurs, clubs and people in the association, so that nobody would dream of building a synthetic pitch outside the Golden Boys system.'

'I've got no idea who you are or what fantasies you're talking about. All I know is that I need to upgrade my security. If I'm to consider working with you at all, I'll need proof.'

'I thought as much. Norway play Uruguay here at Ullevaal in two days' time. Put your money on Uruguay. I'll make Steinar Brunsvik lose the match.'

'That's risky business.'

'Nobody will ever find out.'

'A player might get injured and lose his influence on the result.'

'You've always been annoyed with Steinar Brunsvik, the best player not to be with Golden Boys, haven't you?'

'I have.'

'That's where my expertise will benefit your firm. If Norway don't lose against Uruguay, then Steinar Brunsvik will never play football again.'

Ballet

'Have you done anything for Stanley?' asked Taribo from the back of the van, partially hidden by a couple of cardboard boxes. Yakubu was at the wheel.

'I haven't had time. Shadowing Diesen is my main priority at the moment.'

'Does that mean you'll be able to solve the case more quickly and help Stanley?'

'I think so.'

'It's checkmate for me anyway, but if you promise to help Stanley after the case is solved, then we'll help you now. Deal?'

'Deal,' said Steinar.

Steinar showed Yakubu the way to the car park below the ice rink at Valle Hovin, where they could wait for Diesen without being noticed. Steinar texted an update to Benedikte, telling her she could take Junior to the neighbours if there were any problems. How he'd pick up his own car from Vallhall was another problem, but he'd have to deal with that later. He'd seen journalists waiting there, he'd played a bit too well at that training session.

Diesen was sitting in his white Porsche Cayenne. The car turned towards Fyrstikktorget, then sped up along the motorway into the Vålerenga Tunnel. He braked just before going past the speed camera. Many winters of cars driving past with studded tyres had kicked up dust from the tarmac, so the camera now blended in with the tunnel wall, but everybody knew about it and everybody sped up straight after it, like Diesen did.

But maybe not all drove quite as fast as him. Diesen swerved and passed other cars on the inside lane. Yakubu pushed the van as fast as it would go to keep up. The tyres squealed and the speedometer was redlining. Diesen got away from them, but they were saved by the slowing traffic in the Festning Tunnel.

Diesen drove along the motorway all the way to the Bygdøy junction. If he was heading home, surely it would have been quicker to drive through Solli Plass. Had they been spotted?

Diesen turned onto Karenslyst Allé at Sjølyst and parked in front of Høyer, a high-end clothes shop, coming out a few minutes later with a couple of bags. He stood calmly for a few seconds underneath the shop awning before putting the bags in the Porsche and going into the shopping centre along the road. He came back out with a smoothie.

With three cars between them Steinar, Yakubu and Taribo followed Diesen, up Bygdøy Allé, over the crest of the hill at Gimle Cinema, then down onto Niels Juels Gate. Diesen parked his car right outside number 48. After waiting for a few minutes, Yakubu parked the van further up the street, with a decent view of the entrance and Diesen's car.

'Guys, we can't just sit here like this,' said Steinar.

'What do you mean?' asked Yakubu.

'We're too black for this part of town,' said Taribo. They were in the exclusive West End district of Frogner.

Yakubu kept his eyes on Steinar for a moment before softening his expression and breathing out through his nose.

'Alright,' he said, climbing into the back with his brother.

Steinar gave him a hand, holding cardboard boxes to one side so that the enormous man could clamber into the back seat. He landed hard on Steinar's bike.

'Sorry,' said Yakubu.

'I'd completely forgotten it was in here,' said Steinar, checking his phone. No reply from Benedikte.

'Why did you leave football?' asked Taribo.

'I was forced out.'

'How?'

'I was tricked into thinking I'd been doped.'

'Did you give up that easily?'

He had a point. Why had he given up so easily? And why hadn't he beaten up Vidić at the airport? Why wasn't he hunting him down now? Why was something always getting in the way of him taking up the fight with the man he hated more than anything?

'I'm hoping to start afresh now. In more ways than one,' said Steinar.

'You really should.'

'How are things going in the forest, by the way?'

'We're on the look-out the whole time. People sometimes come past, and then we've got to hurry inside the tent. But the only thing that bothers me is how much I miss Stanley.'

'I can imagine how hard it must be.' Steinar thought of their little chats on the way home from nursery when Junior told him how his day had been. Maybe Junior could go back to nursery tomorrow. Things seemed to work best for Steinar and Junior when the boy was at nursery. That way, they missed each other enough to be happy the rest of the time.

'So what are we going to do with this Diesen guy?' asked Taribo.

'I hope I've provoked him enough to do something stupid,' said Steinar, pushing his left fist against his right elbow to stretch his shoulder, which was stiff.

'What do you think he might do?' asked Taribo.

'There's only one way I could've got hold of the evidence, and that's from Ola Bugge. Now that I've provoked Diesen, I'm hoping that he'll go after Bugge too. Then I'll catch him red-handed and hand him over to the police.'

'To the police? Are you sure?'

'What would you do?'

'Which one of us are you asking?'

'Both of you.'

'I've lost everything,' said Taribo. 'I'm a wanted man, I can't meet my son and I have to live in the woods. I hate him.'

'But he has done one good thing,' said Yakubu. 'I hated Arild Golden. He ruined my life, so I thank the man for killing him, but I also hate what the murder's done to my brother.'

'So what's your conclusion?' asked Steinar.

'If we get hold of the killer,' said Taribo, 'then I'll try to kill him, while Yakubu will try to stop me. It's hard to say what the outcome will be.'

It was hard to know with Taribo, but Steinar didn't believe he was completely joking.

'He's a good player, though, this Diesen guy,' said Taribo after a while.

'Yes,' said Steinar. Diesen was like a ballet dancer gliding over the grass, highly gifted. Nevertheless Steinar had outplayed him, briefly, earlier that day.

At his peak as a footballer Steinar had experienced a taste of happiness, when his body was performing even better than the sum of his training and talent. When he had no trouble running those extra few steps. When his feints were at their best, his pace was quicker and his opponents seemed more stupid and sluggish. When everything was working, it was as if he was a coach at a soccer school, joining in the game and having to tone down his abilities, so as not to take the pleasure away from the young ones. He'd just had another small taste of it again in the training session today.

Gliding over the grass. The image of a ballet dancer kept coming back. Maybe it was because they'd found out that Diesen was gay. Steinar would never admit it to anybody, but when he saw a male ballet dancer, he jumped to the conclusion that he was gay. Maybe it was the dressing room banter that had made him like that, but he couldn't control what his subconscious thought when he saw men in tights.

Steinar hadn't seen Diesen play often, as he'd been trying to stay away from football for ten years, but he'd been catching up recently with *Football Xtra*, live matches on TV and the Internet.

He'd watched through the highlights of Vålerenga's matches available on TV2's online player. They showed some detailed shots of Diesen. When he played on astroturf, Steinar noticed that he wore orange F50 indoor boots with white heels. Among other things, TV2 had also put together a skills guide video of an outside kick Diesen had performed with exquisite precision in an away match against Aalesund, zooming in on his boots. At the movies they would call this product placement.

Steinar picked up the Adidas catalogue he was given by Hjalmar Bakken. Bakken had drawn a circle around some of the boots, and had also added a couple of explanatory footnotes.

On astroturf, most players used either normal astroturf boots or fixed studs. Those who played with fixed studs, which were really intended for dry grass pitches, claimed that normal astroturf boots weren't good enough for key matches, they didn't have a clean enough touch to them. Astroturf boots were heavy and clumsy. Steinar had picked up on a terrible fuss when one well-known top division player described the newest model of boots from Umbro as being like pitta bread.

The risk of strain injuries increased the longer the studs were. If a footballer really wanted to enrage a physiotherapist, he would use the sharp rubber studs best suited to medium-wet grass pitches. These were the non-conformist choice. A very small number of players went the other way and wore indoor boots. All in all, the market was open for whatever shoe manufacturer took the trouble to make low football boots with trainer-style impact absorption and studs made for synthetic turf.

Ståle Jakobsen had been pretty clear on studs. On astroturf they were to wear fixed, medium-length studs, and screw-in studs on natural grass. Jakobsen wasn't that worried about strain injuries. He thought they were a new-fangled fad, but if you slipped and he saw that you were using the wrong footwear, he'd be furious. Steinar wouldn't say that he was afraid of Jakobsen, but it only took the slightest chance of rain for him to opt for screw-ins.

What would Jakobsen have said about indoor boots? They were flat but they also offered better contact with the playing surface, helping players to get a better feel for the ball. Was that why Diesen seemed to float across the pitch?

Steinar rubbed his eyes. It was still only early afternoon in Frogner, but the Shorunmo brothers had both nodded off and were snoring loudly. The door to number 48 opened. Out came an old lady with a walking stick. Steinar took a sip from his water bottle. He picked up the catalogue again. Shit! Steinar had been holding Diesen down on the ground when he'd provoked him at the training session, and he'd seen underneath Diesen's boots. Diesen was wearing normal fixed studs even though it was pouring with rain. If Diesen wore fixed studs when he knew there was a soaking wet pitch, and if he played astroturf matches in indoor boots, there was no chance he would've worn screw-in studs while training on a bone-dry pitch at Ullevaal on the warmest day of the year.

If the murderer had trodden on Golden's neck with long screw-in studs on his boots, there was no way it could be Diesen. Any kind of boot could break a person's neck if enough pressure was applied, but then the wounds would only have been superficial and not deep holes, like on the back of Golden's neck. Per Diesen didn't kill Arild Golden.

Where's the Lady?

'Shit!' shouted Steinar, starting the van. How could he have been so blind? He put his foot to the floor and the van leapt forward then the engine stalled.

The brothers sat up in the back. Clearing the car in front by just a few millimetres, Steinar turned the van round, with the help of the pavement on the other side, and raced up Niels Juels Gate. He called Benedikte's mobile and his home number. No answer. It was over an hour since he'd sent her the text, something was terribly wrong.

The brothers and Steinar's bike slammed hard against the side of the van as he rounded the sharp turn into Briskebyveien without slowing down. The brothers had no time to pick themselves back up again before they were thrown towards the other side as the van roared over Riddersvolds Plass. Then Steinar turned the wheel sharply and drove along Camilla Colletts Vei.

'What's going on?' asked Taribo.

Steinar drove on through the city, heading north, and onto the outer ring road. He kept trying Benedikte's mobile. Just after the bridge at Nydalen, they found themselves stuck in traffic. Two young lads were fumbling around in the open bonnet of an old Audi, with number plates that were home-made from cardboard. Only one lane was moving. They were crawling forwards at a snail's pace. He tried Benedikte's phone again.

The traffic eased off and Steinar turned left through a red light at the Storo junction. Crossing over the tram lines and the bumpy tarmac, the road was like a cattle grid. Steinar turned right at the bakery and didn't check for traffic when he darted over the crossroads next to the old Svetter'n cinema. He just managed to avoid crashing into the newsagent's as he went up Lofthusveien. He hit the brakes outside his house, ran out of the van and in through the door. He slid the last couple of feet on his knees, coming to a halt in front of a terrified Junior.

He held the boy by the shoulders, looking over every inch of him. Junior seemed to be unharmed. Steinar put his hands over his own face, breathing in and out with his eyes closed.

Where was Benedikte? She must have heard him coming in. Steinar took hold of Junior by the shoulders and asked him: 'Where's the lady?'

Junior looked at Steinar with a very serious expression and pointed at the door to the basement. Steinar opened it and turned on the light. He couldn't see anything at the bottom of the stairs. Junior kept pointing and said: 'Down there.'

Steinar heard the basement window being smashed. He ran down the stairs but he was too late. He heard footsteps making off over the lawn at the back of the house.

He looked around. Everything was like normal. The paint cans were where they always were, the architect's drawings were where they were supposed to be, and the makeshift goal he'd made for Junior out of cans and the brush handle was still there. Everything was as it should be except that door to the storage room was ajar. Steinar was certain that he'd closed it after he'd got out his football boots. He went over and opened it.

Benedikte was sitting with her back against the wall. Her head was hanging forward and her eyes closed. She didn't respond when Steinar lifted her up and carried her out of the cupboard. He put her down on the basement floor, checked for her pulse and listened for her breathing. Nothing. On the floor above, he could hear the Shorunmo brothers in the living room laughing at something with Junior.

Steinar shouted. 'Call an ambulance, quick! And don't let the boy down here!'

Steinar tilted Benedikte's head back, put a paint roller under her neck and started resuscitation. How did it go again? Was it breathe five times, then two heart compressions, or the other way round? Shit. He blew air twice into her lungs. Then he pressed down on her chest, keeping a fast rhythm. He probably had to keep that going a little longer. Ten times, twenty. He lost count and put his ear to her chest. Mouth-to-mouth again. Still nothing.

Steinar shouted and raised his fist, struck it against her chest. He breathed into her mouth again. He checked for breathing again. For her pulse. Still nothing.

He saw red bruises on her neck, hands had been pressing hard against her throat. Her airway must be blocked. How was he supposed to get her to breathe? Steinar saw an old first-aid box and acted on instinct. It was a mixture of madness, risk-taking, rage and memories from countless TV series. He grabbed an empty, sterilised syringe from the box. He only knew approximately where the needle was supposed to go in, but she would die if he didn't do something.

He felt his way down her neck, believing it was supposed to go in below the voice box, but what did that feel like? He found what he thought must be the bottom of her voice box, took one deep breath and thrust it in.

The needle went through skin, through tissue and something else, he wasn't sure what. He kept pushing until he no longer felt any resistance, as that would have to be the windpipe.

There! It felt as if he'd reached empty space. He pulled off the plastic plunger at the back of the syringe, put his mouth around the opening and blew as hard as he could. He blew until he almost fainted, then started heart compressions again. He blew in again, and then he felt it. A slight twitch in the lifeless body.

Slowly, Benedikte opened her mouth. It opened and closed again silently, like the mouth of a dying goldfish. It opened again. She pushed out a sound.

'Ma, Ma...'

'I know,' said Steinar, 'but hush now. The ambulance is on its way.'

She passed out, but Steinar saw her chest moving and felt a weak pulse against his hand just as the paramedics came running down the stairs.

Part 10

7 July 1991

While Arild Golden was waiting for his bag to arrive at Istanbul Airport, he thought through the coincidences that had led to this key first transfer. A transfer that he hoped would lead to a domino effect. A reputation as a dealmaking agent could attract better players and better clubs to take up his services.

The whole thing had started two weeks earlier in the terminal at Paris Charles de Gaulle Airport. Golden had landed there for a connecting flight on his way home from one of his many trips to Nigeria.

Sitting along from him was a man in his early fifties. He had greyish hair and a dark moustache and eyebrows. An expensive suit. Next to him was a sports bag that didn't quite fit in, with a logo that Golden didn't recognise but that made him curious. The man turned out to be the chairman of Turkish club Trabzonspor, and very liberal when it came to the Muslim rules on alcohol. His flight was delayed too.

An hour later, Golden had shown the chairman that beer and rum made a good combination, while also getting him to buy the captain of the Nigerian under-18 national team, most of whom were represented by Golden. They agreed to meet for formal talks in Istanbul the week after.

When the negotiations started, Golden realised why his fellow students and the lecturers at the BI Norwegian Business School had called him Goldfinger. He took over the negotiation room and instinctively saw how power was distributed in the club. Most importantly, he knew how much more time he'd have to spend with the chairman as opposed to the others who had less say.

He also noticed that the negotiations went even better when the player went to the toilet. Golden made his first business note: players should never be present at the negotiations themselves.

It was a lucrative deal for all parties, with the exception of the African club. *The contract was signed, and the chairman wrote the address of where the player should turn up on a small scrap of paper.*

Golden could feel that scrap of paper at the bottom of his trouser pocket. He'd gone through everything and was sure they hadn't forgotten anything. His bag appeared on the carousel, as did the player's two suitcases. Golden had decided to tag along with the player to his first training session, which was due to start in three hours. He would also join him to look for a flat and a car. His first transfer would be flawless.

They got in a taxi and Golden passed the handwritten note to the driver, who gave it a long, hard look before starting the meter and setting off. An infernal racket came pumping out of the stereo speakers.

'Excuse me, sir, are you sure this is the right direction?' asked Golden when they'd been driving for nearly an hour and seemed to be going further and further away from Istanbul.

'Hm?' said the driver.

'How far to the stadium?'

'I think maybe fourteen or fifteen.'

'Minutes?' said Golden, pointing at the minute hand on his watch. The driver shook his head and pointed at the shorter hand.

They stopped. The driver pulled out a map, but not a city map. It was a map of the whole of Turkey. Trabzonspor turned out to be a club from the city of Trabzon, 560 miles east of Istanbul.

They went back to Istanbul. Golden borrowed a phone at a hotel and got hold of the chairman at Trabzonspor, but it was too late. They wouldn't make it to the first training session, and it was a breach of trust. They were going to tear up the contract.

Golden pointed out that he still had his part of the contract, and that surely this mistake wasn't sufficient grounds for dismissal. There were rules in football too, after all. The chairman laughed out loud on the other end.

'Good luck with FIFA, then,' he said.

Beyond the Placebo Effect of Acupuncture

Steinar lifted up Junior and carried him out of the house and over to the white van. He ordered Yakubu and Taribo to get in the passenger seats, sat Junior on Taribo's lap and put the safety belt round them. He got in the driving seat.

The paramedics had taken Benedikte away at full speed. She was alive. There was nothing else Steinar could do for her now, other than avenge what had been done to her.

'Where are we going?' asked Taribo as they drove a slalom course past the apparently neverending roadworks just after Sinsen.

'To Vallhall,' said Steinar.

'Then it's probably quicker to drive down along Økernveien,' said Taribo, pointing.

'No, it's not,' said Steinar, carrying on along the outer ring road. Taribo nodded and put his hands round Junior like a protective airbag. Junior started laughing, turning his head to look at Taribo and pointing.

'Newspaper,' said Junior.

'Shit,' said Steinar, smacking the palm of his hand against the steering wheel. How was this going to affect Junior? Steinar had been impressed by the boy's memory many times before. Whatever they did, the boy remembered it. 'Been before,' was his standard phrase if they returned somewhere. It didn't even have to be a playground or something else that appealed to him, it could just as easily be a supermarket or a doctor's surgery.

Of course it didn't really matter that he recognised Taribo from the newspaper. Actually it was quite a nice thing, as Taribo was innocent anyway, but Steinar was worried about how much Junior would remember the assault on Benedikte. He didn't know much about how traumatic incidents like this might affect him later in life. A break-in, an assault, even an attempted murder. Steinar banged his hand against the wheel again.

Just before the new office building at Valle, Steinar bulldozed his own new exit from the ring road, driving over the grass, between some trees, over a cycle path and down towards the car park. He sped across it and slammed on the brakes outside the entrance to Vallhall, the indoor arena.

'You look after the boy while I'm in there,' said Steinar. The brothers nodded in agreement as Steinar went in.

'Steinar Brunsvik again,' said a thick voice, spluttering like a rusty old Evinrude outboard motor. 'Have you come to sign with us?'

Steinar turned his head and saw Hjalmar Bakken sitting on the deep sofa to the right of the entrance.

'Have the players gone?' asked Steinar.

'They went a while ago.'

'Do you know Ola Bugge?'

'What do you want with that pig?'

'I need to talk to him.'

'I think he's sitting in the cafeteria,' said Bakken.

Steinar started running and found Bugge sitting at a table. They'd never spoken, but Steinar had no time for courtesies, he slammed his hands on the table and leant over the football agent.

'Where's Marius Bjartmann?'

'I can't tell,' said Bugge.

'You don't know?'

'I do know, but I'm sworn to secrecy with my clients. I can't just tell anyone where they are and what they're doing.'

Steinar grabbed Bugge, lifted him up by his shirt collar and slammed him onto the cafeteria table.

'He's a killer. You're going to tell me where he is, and you're going to tell me now!'

'In that case you'll have to go to the police.'

Steinar slammed Bugge down on the table again. The girl behind the counter gave no sign of getting involved.

'Tell me where he is!'

'Go to the police!'

Steinar lifted Bugge from the table. He put his knee in his stomach, making him double over. Then he dragged him back to the entrance. His rage was back. It had been dormant all those years he hadn't been playing football, but now it was really back. If it had been a match, Steinar would have got one of his red cards, but there was no referee here. Just an executioner and executioners worked alone, executioners had no linesmen.

'Open up the dressing room,' said Steinar.

Bakken did as he said.

'Tape,' said Steinar, and Bakken fetched some rolls of sports tape. Steinar tore off Bugge's shirt and trousers and tied him to the massage table. He wound the sports tape several times round his chest, arms, hips and thighs. Bugge could barely move.

'Get me the physio's bag,' said Steinar. Bakken went to fetch it.

Steinar went on: 'Still sure you don't want to talk?'

'I protect my clients,' said Bugge.

Bakken came back with the physio's equipment. Steinar opened the bag.

'I had a physio when I played in the Netherlands who was a psychopath,' he said. 'He liked to cause others pain. A simple massage with him was a form of advanced torture, and his favourite thing was treating periostitis, inflammation of the membrane around the bones.' Steinar tapped Bugge's lower leg before he went on. 'The treatment involved him taking hold of the skin over the fibula and stretching it to increase the blood circulation and flush out the inflammation. The pain was colossal.' Steinar pressed his thumb hard down along Bugge's own leg. Bugge couldn't disguise how uncomfortable it was. Then Steinar took out two long needles from the physio's bag.

'These are acupuncture needles, the famous 21 centimetre ones. You use these on buttocks to get deep enough into the fat layer. They're used for treating sciatica, and I'm pretty sure they're not meant to be used on inflamed bones.' He leant over, aimed and pushed the needle slowly under the skin, down along Bugge's fibula.

Steinar took the other long needle, holding it like a knife this time.

'Last chance.'

Bugge shook his head.

Steinar used all his force to drive the needle down at an angle through the other calf and into the fibula. Then he took out the electrotheraphy device, attached the electrodes to the needles and pressed the button.

Bugge's legs started to vibrate.

Level two was already enough to make Bugge scream. Steinar turned the machine so that Bugge could see it went all the way up to ten.

'Where is he?'

'I can't tell you. I'm sworn to secrecy.'

'Where is he?' Steinar repeated, turning the current up to four.

At six, Bugge's screams could be heard throughout the building, but he still wouldn't talk. Steinar wouldn't have thought that feeble doughball would be able to hold anything back. He'd thought a slight gust of wind would be enough to make Bugge spill the beans on everything. His normal feelings no longer functioned, and torture didn't produce the desired effect. It seemed that there were only two things that could get a determined football agent like Bugge to talk. He'd either have to offer him money or intensify the torture.

Steinar tore off Bugge's last remaining item of clothing and moved the electrodes.

The Hunt

Bugge talked. He started babbling deliriously about Nigerians, people with scars, cowboys and Indians. He'd told them everything he knew, but Bugge didn't know everything.

Benedikte was in a life-threatening condition, and Steinar would forever blame himself if she didn't make it. He'd been too slow to realise what was going on. Of course the killer was a centre-back, only a destructive defender could think of doing something as idiotic as training on a dry grass pitch wearing screw-in studs. Since Vålerenga's other centre-back was that gifted Danish player, the killer had to be Marius Bjartmann.

'Did you find him?' Taribo asked Steinar when he got back in the van.

'He's gone. All I know is that he's using one of Golden's apartments. Bjartmann used it for his lover. Bugge thought he might have gone there, but he doesn't know where it is.'

'I did up one of Golden's apartments once, he owned several in the same block at Manglerud.'

'Do you remember where?'

'In Plogveien. I'll recognise the block when I see it.'

The wheels spun on the gravelly expanse in front of Vallhall. Steinar sped through the Vålerenga Tunnel, jumped when he saw the speed camera flash but didn't slow down. He turned off at Galgeberg, where the old gallows used to be, and swerved the van into the other lane to overtake a slow-moving Volvo up the twisting road along Ryenbergveien, which continued onto Enebakkveien. He turned off just before the car dealership at Ryen and past the modern white-brick building that didn't fit with the Rema 1000 supermarket occupying it. They raced towards the new block of flats at the bottom of the hill.

'Stop!' shouted Taribo. Steinar slammed on the brakes.

'Which one is it?' asked Steinar, pointing at all the blocks in Plogveien. He knew the road well. Mette had grown up here, just before the turn-off to Manglerudhallen sports centre. The name Plogveien meant 'plough road', and Steinar wished he were a plough, he wanted to pull out some weeds.

'Look over there!' said Taribo, pointing down Svartdalsveien.

Bjartmann was coming out of one of the low-rise blocks. Steinar put his foot to the floor, turning the wheel hard left at the same time. The sound of the van's engine put the whole neighbourhood on alert, including Bjartmann, but he couldn't get away from them now.

Bjartmann stood there like a rabbit in the headlights, then took off along the edge of the woods.

Steinar threw the van over the kerb where the downhill track turned to gravel. The woods opened up in front of them. Steinar caught a glimpse of houses in the distance, but he didn't have time to work out which way he was facing. He lost control of the van on the gravel, skidding and stopping with the van blocking the track. Bjartmann vanished into the trees.

Steinar got out, opened the back door and took out his mountain bike.

'One of you stay here with Junior, the other one follow me.'

The opening where the path began was quite narrow. Steinar had cycled along the trail once before, but found it too steep. He lowered his head and gripped the handlebars.

A curve of a street, Konows Gate, cut across the path. Steinar dashed straight into the road and spotted something approaching fast from the left. He squeezed on the brakes, twisting the handlebars at the same time hard to the right, and avoided the black Golf by a few inches.

Across the road Bjartmann headed for the second part of the trail, the bit that nobody uses, the steepest part.

Steinar pedalled as hard as he could to get the bike going again. Branches, nettles and weeds lashed at his face on the bends. The track was steep all the way, a small wooden bridge straight ahead of him.

When Steinar hit the bridge he saw that it led to a right-hand bend. A large birch tree just after the bridge. He jumped towards the tree, putting his shoulder to the trunk and letting himself ricochet off to the right. Miraculously, he landed back on the path. Then came a left turn. As he came out of it, he saw the path was blocked by a landslide further on.

Could he make it? Steinar caught a glimpse of Bjartmann the path below him and carried on towards the landslide. There was a narrow gap between the rocks and Steinar managed to manoeuvre the front wheel through it, the back wheel taking a couple of violent blows.

Steinar's relief at having got past the landslide was short-lived. Up ahead was another almost impossible right-hand turn. But there was a wire fence too, if he could get hold of it, he could use it to turn. He leant to the side, reached out his right hand and grabbed the wire, flexing his arm all he could. He knew it would hurt, but he wasn't going to let Bjartmann get away.

Time stood still for a moment as the bike left the ground, leaving him hanging in the air by his right arm. He came crashing to the ground, but leapt back onto his bike. A sign told him the path was closed.

He struggled through hazels and rowan, or whatever all those trees were called, until the path opened onto a grassy field with a couple of goalposts and some benches. He spotted Bjartmann at the other end of the field. Moments later Steinar reached the same spot and realised too late that he was heading down some small, slippery steps. He couldn't stop. He'd just have to try and stay on his bike, which was now going faster and faster, shaking terribly.

It was just a question of whether he'd survive this downhill stretch. His hands ached from the shaking of the bike, and the brakes smelt of burning rubber. He shot out through some bushes, bumping over stones and puddles and hitting a root that threw him and his bike into the air. He landed in the middle of the Alna River.

Both of Steinar's wheels were punctured and the handlebars were twisted out of position. The river was shallow but fast-flowing. Bjartmann was standing on a small wooden bridge over the river, pointing down at him.

'Stay away from me!'

'You stupid, spoilt brat. You're only 30 and make millions a year, why the hell would you kill somebody?'

'I'll tell you why. That dirty fucking cock jockey had started ignoring me. All he cared about was selling Per. You know how many games I've played in the top division? 250. It was my turn to be sold. I was the one who should be going to England to make some dough of my own. I've seen hundreds of players much worse than me turn into multi-millionaires. It was my fucking turn! And he told me as much. That fucking poof told me that such and such a team was interested. And, worst of all, I believed him. I was a fool. And you know what? They didn't have the fucking guts to tell me that they were an item. Somebody else told me. You know what they said when I confronted them? That they "loved each other". Fucking back-door bandits. So fucking sick. What do you think it would mean for me if it came out? You know how many nights we spend in the same twin room? Everyone would think that I was stabbing shit too with a stupid smile on my face.'

'How did you do it?' asked Steinar.

'I cleared a ball up into the stands, and I couldn't stand Hjalmar whinging about us losing balls all the time, so I climbed up to the VIP boxes. Through the window, I could see that Golden was in his office, so I climbed in to talk to him and explain how frustrated I was, but he was angry too. Angry that I didn't accept the relationship between him and Per. Then it all turned black. I hit him as hard as I could. He was lying there and I trod on him. I felt his neck snap.'

Bjartmann's eyes went up and down the river. He was weighing up different escape routes. He'd killed Golden and he'd also assaulted Benedikte right in front of Junior's eyes.

Steinar threw away his bike and ran the first few metres to the bridge at lightning speed. Bjartmann set off upriver, past some railings. An acidic remark by a journalist in *VG* had compared Bjartmann's turning speed to the Denmark ferry. Steinar had the muscles of a sprinter. He quickly gained ground.

About a hundred metres upriver he saw a narrow suspension bridge. It was several metres above a waterfall, the water foaming around sharp rocks. A fall there could be fatal. The bridge began to rock violently as they ran onto it. Bjartmann stopped half-way, grabbing onto the steel wires on both sides. Steinar threw himself at him, and they crashed together onto the wood. Bjartmann's mobile dropped out of his pocket, falling over the side and into the waterfall. Bjartmann instinctively tried to grab it, in vain.

The collision had also made Steinar lose his grip. Bjartmann jumped up and kicked. Steinar just managed to move his head to the right so that the kick just grazed his cheek. Bjartmann lost his balance, and Steinar was on top of him, holding his left arm against Bjartmann's collar bone and pushing him against the railing. Steinar raised his arm, made a fist and was ready to knock Bjartmann over the side and into the river. All Steinar's hatred built up in his fist as he pulled it back. It was like loading a crossbow.

This time, Bjartmann didn't miss. He kicked Steinar straight in the balls. Steinar curled up on all fours. Bjartmann set off another volley, this time aimed at Steinar's kidneys.

He lifted Steinar up. Now he was the one going to be thrown off the bridge. Steinar had thought he could beat him, but Bjartmann was younger and stronger.

'Why did it matter to you?' Bjartmann said.

'For my client's sake.'

'That fucking Nigerian?'

'That big fucking Nigerian,' said Taribo, who'd come up the last few steps towards Bjartmann from behind. He twisted his arm like a python round Bjartmann's neck, Taribo tightened his grip, biceps expanding and veins quivering. All colour left Bjartmann's face, his arms and legs slumped. Bjartmann wilted like a flower.

'Can I borrow this man?' asked Taribo. 'I thought he could stay in the forest for a couple of days with me and Yakubu.'

Steinar kept his eyes on Taribo for a moment.

Bjartmann had killed Golden and tried to kill Benedikte. Now that he'd been stopped, the worst of Steinar's rage subsided. Steinar remembered that he was a lawyer and a father. So was Taribo. Steinar knew what it might cost them if they took the law into their own hands. He felt his breathing going back to normal. He glanced at Bjartmann. He really wasn't worth it.

'Bring him back alive,' said Steinar.

Comeback

It was fascinating for Steinar to watch Junior sit down and do a jigsaw, read a book or, like now, draw. Small pockets of time came along now and then when the boy was able to be calm in his surroundings. And now that the Golden case was over, Steinar's appointments diary was free enough to enjoy it.

Junior was wearing a white T-shirt with a green crocodile on the front. For the boy, all crocodiles were known as 'Mr Croc' after a children's book that he liked. Steinar liked these small 'mistakes', like the fact that Junior called all tigers 'Tyger Tyger' after the poem. Steinar didn't want to correct him. That way, Junior wouldn't grow up quite as fast. But what was that? Steinar went over to him.

Snot was coming out of his nose. It wasn't yet another symptom, was it? Steinar took hold of Junior carefully by the neck with one hand, clearing up the snot with a cloth. Junior held his breath and didn't blink. He wasn't even really looking at Steinar, just on pause. Steinar let go, and Junior turned his full attention back to his drawing pad.

Steinar looked at the lines he was drawing, which filled the page. There were long lines drawn in black felt-tip, and he'd put some purple spots in between. Stop there, thought Steinar, it's a nice picture.

The phone rang.

It was Bjørnar Ramstad. 'Jakobsen's bed was empty,' he said.

'What does that mean?' asked Steinar, immediately regretting it. It could only mean one thing, that his old coach had died.

Steinar closed his eyes, put his hand to his forehead and felt a couple of wrinkles on the way towards his hair. His thoughts went back to hill running.

Jakobsen had forced him up Grefsenkollen. Run 100 metres, walk 50, run 200 metres, walk 50, run 50 metres, walk 50, run 200 metres.

'Steinar Brunsvik, you little devil, you weren't giving it your all. We're going back down 500 metres to do it again!' They'd carried on like that all the way up to the viewpoint, Steinar on foot, Jakobsen in his old Mazda 323, leaning halfway out the window and shouting orders at his player.

'I was sure that he'd died,' said Bjørnar.

'What?'

'He had just vanished, and when I asked the nurses, a wild panic broke out. It's quite unusual to misplace coma patients, after all.'

'Did you find him?'

'Guess where.'

Steinar didn't answer.

'In the canteen! Bent over a hamburger, with four empty sachets of Thousand Island dressing next to him. He was holding the burger in both hands, his mouth wide open.'

'Does that mean he's better?'

'Can't you hear what I'm saying? He's eating! I was sure that he wouldn't wake up again. According to the combined experience of the medical profession, he should've died long ago. One of the nurses used the word "miracle".'

'I'm on my way,' said Steinar, hanging up.

When they opened the door to Ståle Jakobsen's room on the second floor of the Cancer Centre, Junior stared wide-eyed at the man in the hospital bed.

Jakobsen patted his hand on the bed and Steinar lifted up his son so that he could sit on the edge. After a few seconds' silence, Steinar gave Jakobsen a bear hug.

'What's Daddy doing?' said Junior, who then became very interested in a blue machine with lots of buttons on a trolley. Steinar checked that it wasn't plugged in, then let his son play with it.

Bjørnar came into the room and took Steinar aside.

'I popped into Benedikte's room too. She's stable, but still unconscious.'

Steinar knew. It was four days since she'd been attacked and Steinar had been to see her every day. The short time that had passed since they first met had been filled with the Golden case, Junior's illness and the promise she'd given Steinar to sleep with him. In between all of that, he hadn't had the chance to get to know her properly. He hadn't

found out what Kringlebotn meant when he said she hadn't had it easy
as a child. But now that his days were following more of a routine and
he saw her lying there in bed, he realised just how much he wanted to
find out all about her.

'Do you know anything about her progress?' he asked.

'Too early to say, but she definitely would've died if it hadn't been for
you. How on earth did you get the idea of performing an improvised
tracheostomy?'

'I just did it. Didn't think about it.'

'Like when you were on the pitch?'

'Something like that. Listen, I'm worried about Junior. He was a
witness to the attack, do you know how that might affect him later on?'

'That's not my specialism, Steinar, but I can get you a child
psychiatrist.'

'Just tell me what you think, I'd value your opinion.'

'Well, they say that children's memories aren't really reliable until
they're four years old.'

'I don't believe that. Time and again Junior's shown that he's got an
almost photographic memory for people and places. I'm sure that he
remembers it. Do you think it'll affect him?'

'Honestly, I don't know.'

They went back to Jakobsen's bed. Bjørnar started telling Jakobsen
about his condition, but he was abruptly cut off.

'I don't give a shit about that. What I want to hear about is that
training session: eleven against eleven, the first team against the second,
and you scoring two goals to win 2–1.' Jakobsen looked at Steinar, who
didn't answer. 'Oh, for fuck's sake, you've been throwing your talent
away for long enough now. You were born to play football so tell me
now, yes or no, will you consider making a comeback?'

Steinar had loved every second of that training session, but could
he bring himself back to fitness enough to take that every day? Wasn't
it really too late? It was far too long since he'd played for Ajax, after all.
Or was it?

'Turn up the volume!' said Jakobsen. A blonde stand-in for Benedikte
appeared on the TV screen. The headline read: 'Marius Bjartmann
confesses.'

Bjartmann had been found tied to the blue turbine monument in
Svartdalsparken, by the river where they'd had their stand-off. A yellow
Post-it note with the message 'I killed Arild Golden' was stapled to his

forehead. His left knee was dislocated, and it was doubtful that he'd ever be able to play football again.

In the poll for footballer of the year, Bjartmann had received a huge number of votes over the past few hours, he was heading to the top. Meanwhile Vålerenga fans had set up a Facebook group calling for Bjartmann to be let out of prison for league matches. It was unlikely that any of the prosecutors had clicked on the 'Like' button.

When questioned by police, Bjartmann confirmed that he'd killed Golden, but he hadn't admitted anything in connection with Benedikte. She would have to wake up and identify him if he was to be convicted of assaulting her.

'Can you calm your boy down a little?' said Bjørnar, pointing at Junior, who was doing his best to push over the blood pressure and pulse monitor. Steinar lifted up his son and put him on his lap. A picture on the TV screen caught the boy's attention too. It was a close-up of Marius Bjartmann's face. Shit, thought Steinar, he should shield Junior's eyes from having to see the man who'd attacked Benedikte.

But Junior said: 'Daddy, who's that?'

Acknowledgements

Thank you to:

The father of the step over feint, Thorvald Steen, for his literary advice.

Football doctor Kjell Erik Strømskag for his advice on everything from tracheostomies to literature.

Psychologist-back Stål Bjørkly for his advice on psychology.

Heart surgeon Terje Aass for his advice on medicine.

Trainee lawyer Bernt Birkeland for his advice on legal matters.

Gunnar Stavrum, a tank of a striker as well as an editor, for his advice on financial crime.

Anchor Davy Wathne for his advice on television.

Skeid and Brumlebassen Nursery for all their comments.

Thank you to Kari Joynt and everybody else from the Norwegian publishers, Forlaget Oktober.

And thanks to Ole and Lisbet: we're alright!